Sleeping Together

Printed in the United States of America

ISBN: 9781732998414 (paperback)
ISBN: 9781732998407 (ebook)

Cover design by Scott Howard

Brass Anvil Books
Seattle, WA

Sleeping Together

Kitty Cook

BRASS ANVIL BOOKS

SEATTLE

THE BABY NIGHTMARE

At 120 miles per hour, Vanessa Brown achieved terminal velocity. The wind screamed around her flight-suited body as she sliced open a cloud. But Ness's breathing was steady in her helmet, and she sailed like an arrow toward a Cessna Skyhawk in a dusty clearing. Once she pulled her ripcord, she'd have only seconds to photograph Viper cartel members loading the plane with uncut cocaine before sailing away over the jungle faster than their machine guns could track. She'd land north of their base and rendezvous with the Blackhawk that would take her back to the capitol. With the evidence she was about to procure, she would finally prove President Dagwood was siphoning taxpayer money to bring drugs over the border. The coup to overthrow him would be bloody—and needed.

The trees below looked like broccoli florets and tripled in size by the second, but Ness maintained full control. The plane appeared below, and she grasped her chest for her ripcord pin. As her hand came away, she braced for the upward jerk of the chute—but she continued to plummet like a stone through water. In her hand was a baby's pacifier.

"What the shit?" Ness cursed in her helmet. She looked down and saw an infant strapped to her chest in a baby carrier—a girl, judging by the pink onesie, who had dark, wavy hair like hers. The trees were tree-size now and reaching for Ness with their wooden arms. She tore at the bundle at her back, trying to deploy the second chute. All she succeeded in doing was flinging wet wipes and bibs from

the diaper bag she could have sworn was tactical gear a second ago. The ground was coming for her huge and fast. The trees were waving goodbye. The baby opened its mouth to wail through droopy pink cheeks, and then—

My eyes flew open as I detonated from my pillow, dragging air into my lungs like a reanimated mummy. To my left was the open door to the unlit bathroom, with its coarse towels and the streaky pink mildew stains clinging to the tub. To the right, the light-polluted charcoal night of Seattle glowed through the window, punctuated by the twinkle of a faraway jet. The alarm clock on the bureau read 4:37 in yellow squared-off numbers. My room, like my life, was orderly, cozy, deliciously mundane. Everything was fine. Except I couldn't breathe.

"NESS!" My mensch of a husband, Pete, leapt heroically from his own dreams to kneel clumsily next to me in bed, as he had every night for the past three weeks. "IT'S A BAD DREAM, NESS!" He shouted as a thoughtless person would to someone deaf. I barely heard him over the blood galumphing through my brain, flooding it with adrenaline I would hoard and then discard, like Easter candy bought on sale and then unearthed from the pantry three Halloweens later.

"YOU'RE OK!" Pete yelled again, trying to lock me into an awkward embrace from behind that felt more like a high school wrestling hold. "HEAR ME? YOU ARE O! K!"

"Jesus, Pete, I know!" I snapped.

Pete is a grand man with many talents, but knowing when a gal needs more than five millimeters of personal space isn't one of them. I freed an arm from his grasp and pushed him down onto his pillow. He toppled over like a martial arts dummy, and for a fleeting moment I thought, *Serves him right.*

Then, just as immediately, I felt like a dick. "Sorry," I groaned, sitting in bed with my palms pressed to my eyes and my heart softening like butter left on the counter. "I shouldn't have done that."

"If you keep this up, I'll have to start wearing a cup to bed," he quipped, snapping his bedside lamp on. I looked up to see him settle against the headboard in our flannel (everything in the Pacific Northwest is flannel, especially in the winter) sheets, one arm behind his head, his blond sleep-tousled hair sticking out adorably. The other arm was spread across my pillow so I could curl up on his bare chest. And when I did, he arranged the blankets around us and cleared his throat. "Let me guess: another baby nightmare, eh?"

I nodded along his shoulder.

"You alright?"

I wasn't, but still I said, as musically as I could, "Oh, fine. Run-of-the-mill infant-related anxiety. I'm sure it's perfectly normal to wake up every night screaming at the prospect of procreation."

He pressed his lips to my forehead. "You're cute when you mask your terror with jokes."

We both knew that was my specialty.

Last month Pete had mentioned oh-so casually that he wanted to start thinking about—as he put it—"*our* having a family," which was code for *me* getting pregnant. I was willing to admit his wasn't an unreasonable request. After all, we were both in our early thirties, married over three years, and animals biologically programmed to pass on genetic material in a bid for immortality. Still I was surprised, because Pete had never until that moment expressed any particular need to nurture something other than me. Exhibit A: We are the only couple in this city that doesn't have a dog. Exhibit B: Pete does nothing to slow the sad, dry death of every potted herb I've ever brought home from the farmers market.

Because of this, I just assumed we'd be childless people who slept late and had brunch and traveled and read quietly and took care of ourselves, which was fine with me because for reasons I didn't like to remember, my brain wasn't exactly keen about a baby. My heart even less so. My uterus? Forget about it. But since the infant proposal, I was in a constant state of debate with my organs, negotiating with each of them in turn, trying to bring the whole caucus around to the idea of baby making. "Let's not talk about this now" was what I said the evening he brought it up, which he'd done in the most gentlemanly way. *Hey, Bug, can we talk about having kids? I want to know your thoughts.* But my thoughts, generally, were horrible, and I didn't want him to see.

That night I had the first bad dream, and my subconscious had been going gangbusters ever since.

I craned my head back so I could look into Pete's face. Growing up in the sunless Pacific Northwest had made him even paler than his Nordic background warranted, but it suited his bookish demeanor and his quick wit. He looked like a man who spent his free time in libraries thinking up puns, which wasn't too far from the truth. I ran my hand along the scrape of barely reddish stubble clinging to his cheek and said, "Remember that time we went out on Lake Union in someone's boat with all your work friends—and I drank too much and ended up hurling over the side?"

He smoothed a lock of hair out of my face. "How could I forget? A Duck Tour was going by and everyone on it started taking photos of you puking your heart out."

"It was all in my hair," I groaned.

"And you wouldn't calm down until I gave you a haircut in the boat with a filleting knife."

"Not even Vidal Sassoon himself could have gotten the barf out."

4

Pete fingered the edge of the bob I'd maintained since that day two summers ago. "You never grew it back."

"I don't deserve long hair," I said, pulling a hand up to my face so I could cover it in phantom shame. "God, that was embarrassing."

Pete cuddled me closer, rubbing his hand up and down my arm. "I'm sure you're not the first person to drink too much in the sun."

OK, so Pete didn't have a great concept of personal space— nor was he exactly savvy to my ambivalence about spawning. But he was loyal and loving at every turn. Even when I embarrassed him in front of his law firm colleagues, he chalked it up as one of my charms: my *ability* to upchuck at important functions. Through thick and thin, I had no doubt that man would forgive me for anything. Almost anything. After a beat, I took a deep breath, trying to sound nonchalant. "Do you think I'm mom material?"

"Because you threw up in Lake Union?" He pulled back to look at me, and when he saw I was serious, he broke into a smile and said, "Of course I think you're mom material. You're just scared about having kids. I bet every human our age shits their pants about the idea."

But what if my pants were happily shit-free on the no-kids side of this fence Pete thought I was on? And if he was on the yes-kids side, where would that leave us? What if I was wrong? What if my last egg went *poof* the minute I blew out my candles on my fortieth birthday just as I wished I could return to this moment when I could have said *yes?*

Here's the thing: I didn't necessarily want a baby, but I also didn't necessarily *not* want a baby. What I wanted was to be sure, because I never am—about anything. I am a jury the world is constantly tampering with. I think I want something, but then I talk myself into something else. I debate everything forever. You know

5

how they say if you're ever buried in an avalanche, you're supposed to spit and use gravity to determine which way to dig, otherwise you could go the wrong way and bury yourself even deeper? That's what my mind feels like sometimes: completely disoriented. I'm shivering, I don't know up from down, and I always seem to have a dry mouth.

Pete turned to face me, rubbing his knuckles gently along my cheek. "Do you want to talk about why you're so scared?"

The pain radiating from temple to jaw suggested I'd been grinding my teeth in my sleep, chewing on the words that threatened to spill from my mouth. *Just tell him*, a voice in my head said. *Tell him why you're nervous about a baby. Tell him everything.* It would have been such a relief to pry my cold, numb fingers off the secret I'd sheltered for more than a decade and hand it over, warm and beating, for Pete to coddle for a while. But that would mean having to look at it, and—

Nope. Just the thought of remembering was enough to set the prickle of panic at the edges of my heart. My diaphragm seized, and my lungs hung limp in my body like empty grocery bags. I inhaled a ragged breath to jump-start my circulatory system and said "I need to get up" through a plastered smile. In the Rembrandt half-light of the lamp on the nightstand, I sprang out of bed and yanked articles of clothing from my bureau without inspecting them, since I wore the same thing every day: black or gray top, black or blue jeans, ankle boots, also black.

"Where are you going?" Pete asked in alarm.

"Work."

"It's not even dawn."

"I know, but I can't sleep. Which means I'll just be tired later, so I might as well go into the office now so I can come home early." This sounded practical and responsible, two things I tried to hone in myself for fear that if I didn't, I'd fall apart completely.

"I'm worried about you," I heard Pete say as I ripped a brush through my hair. "Are you coming unglued?"

"No," I laughed to my cold feet as I pulled on socks. Alarming Pete by having a panic attack in front of him was not the way I wanted to spend my morning. Even after three years of marriage, I was still embarrassed when I farted in his general vicinity, so ugly-crying before the sun came up was completely out of the question. I turned and crawled up the bed to deposit a kiss on his lips. Clawing my way back down the quilt, I tossed "have a good one" over my shoulder, then sprinted for the living room.

"You too," he echoed. I crossed our apartment in five steps, trying to ignore how forlorn he sounded. I grabbed my backpack and boots and, still in my socks, barreled through the front door and closed it behind me. Crouching on the doormat, I rooted through my backpack in search of my Nikon, trying to think of anything besides *that night*. But the rum-and-cigarette smell of the recollection punched me in the nose. A memory of a hand clamped over a memory of my mouth, and I mimicked the act in real life so that I wouldn't scream.

Even in my panic, I was able to attach the lens to the camera methodically, like a marine assembling a rifle. *This is my camera. There are many like it, but this one is mine.* I forced my eyes open. I forced them to look through the viewfinder at the door of the unit across the hall. It was a basic door—aluminum, hollow, beautifully boring. I squatted there on the industrial carpet with the camera to my face like a sniper's rifle, willing myself to breathe.

It's this thing I do when I get overwhelmed: I take pictures. Sometimes I don't even actually take them, though it's more profitable when I do (more on that in a moment). What steadies me about photography is that it affords an excuse to study what's in front of me: not the work stress ghosting around the periphery of my nerves, or the darker memories of my past, but things that are real and present. I look at them. I listen with my eyes to that symphony of light and moment and detail and color and the way it can all come together to turn something boring into something lovely if you wait long enough—for the sun to move, for the stranger to turn, for the flower to bloom, for the perfect shot. I wait, and everything in my life becomes background noise, a car radio on a country road, blipping in and out of stations before settling into static.

Maybe this hobby of mine is a little weird. What's *definitely* weird is that Pete doesn't know about it: not my camera or my pictures or my stress. Sure, he knew I minored in photography in college, but he had no idea I still *needed* the camera. He also didn't know I'd made a tidy cottage industry out of my habit by selling pictures to Debby, a Pike Place souvenir monger who printed my moody photos of Seattle sights on T-shirts and hawked them to marketgoers. Her prices were strategically low, her stall cleverly placed at one of the entrances to the market within eyeshot of the bathroom. So when the Floridians and Californians showed up unseasonably dressed for downpours, they always grabbed one of her dry tops to change into.

I'd seen my photos riding the monorail, in line for a Seahawks game, and at Nordstrom. Once I even saw a whole family wearing my photos when Pete and I were at the Seattle Art Museum. I'd wanted to make a joke to him about my being on exhibit at the SAM, but I stopped myself before I could spill the beans. Secrets are Kegel exercises for the mind: they keep your brain sharp, your thoughts tight.

When I was a kid, I wallpapered my bedroom with pages torn from old *National Geographic* magazines collected from the library when they threw out the back issues. My dream to become a travel photographer is ironic considering I was born in Washington state and never left the country despite being three hours from Canada. Even now during my morning commute I sometimes imagined where I'd go if I got just one trip: Azerbaijan, Morocco, Mumbai. I'd picture the colors. The smoky smells of spice barrels. The bleating of camels. Sometimes when Pete worked late, I'd count the five thousand dollars I'd earned from Debby that I kept in a Doc Martens boot in the wayback of my closet and dreamed of how it would all taste through the lens of a camera.

Why didn't I tell him about any of this? Because it felt wrong to want something other than him. After all, Pete was borderline perfect in the husband department: he'd given me everything I'd ever asked for save a job at a famous travel magazine and oodles of money to blow gallivanting around the world. Seattle was expensive, my student loans were steep, and my salary wasn't exactly lavish. Expecting him to fund my wildest dreams didn't seem like a fair thing to ask, so I didn't bring it up at all.

When forced to think of a baby in my life, I only saw the pictures I would take of Pete: in his shirtsleeves, administering baths. On weekends at the aquarium. The meals he would cook! The books he would read! Pete would be a tremendous father, just as he was a consummate husband. (His job as a divorce lawyer allowed him to study imploding marriages the way astrophysicists contemplated dying stars.) His energy would compensate for my brokenness. I could birth a baby and literally never touch it again, and that child would grow up loved and treasured, cocooned completely in Pete's devotion, safe from the sharp corners of my heart. Even so, I couldn't bring myself to give Pete what he wanted, which was a baby and the truth.

The other secret my husband didn't know? I'd been pregnant once before.

I stared through my camera at the door across the hall like I could see through the fisheye peephole into my neighbor's apartment—laid out like mine, but decorated more stylishly. In the bedroom slept another Ness unperturbed by bad dreams and worse memories. That Ness wore silk pajamas and slept without blankets like people do in mattress commercials. That Ness still had long hair.

I pictured that Ness through the camera until my breath returned, until my heart resumed its normal ticktock and my palms stopped sweating. And when I felt myself come back, I pressed the shutter. *Click.* Reviewing the picture was unnecessary. Debby wouldn't buy it. Tourists didn't want pictures of doors, because they weren't beautiful, but not everything was.

And that's the thing I liked most about taking pictures: the reminder that ugly things are everywhere, and half the time no one cares.

SUNDAY, OCTOBER 7

Since our patients have to keep dream notes and shit, I figured I should too. So this is a notebook where I'll write down what happens when I take Morpheum. Maybe I'll make a discovery and get a raise? Fat chance, but hey, worth a shot.

(Side note: I'm sitting in a bar right now, and the bartender keeps flirting with me. She's all, "What are you writing about?" I keep telling her I'm a poet, because obviously I can't say, "I'm writing about how I steal drugs from my work." She digs the poetry line. Moleskine = kryptonite. The dude next to me playing Candy Crush on his phone is getting *no* love.)

So yeah. Morpheum. I'm tired—like, REALLY tired. I've been in the new apartment for two weeks, and I've probably gotten, oh, sixteen hours of sleep in that time. Instead of resting like a normal human I've been staying up all night, you know, questioning all my life decisions and my value as a human being. Went down to the pot shop last week to get some good weed to try and take the edge off, but that just made it worse. Started questioning my value as a human AND why my sneakers are so friendly. Bad vibes.

Anyway, I stole some pills on Friday—and by "stole" I mean, "didn't incinerate Stefanie T's leftovers when she completed the trial." (Whatever. Diana won't notice.) I took one for the first time last night and HOLY FUCKING SHIT. My patients have grossly undersold how great this drug is: It's the best thing I have ever ingested.

I dreamed I was a seagull, which sounds boring, until you factor in how much flying over the ocean you get to do. And I did a lot at a very high altitude, high enough to detect the curve of the Earth. There was an aura coming off the shape, like a vapor; it was beautiful. I didn't think about anything. I didn't feel anything. I just flapped my wings toward the sunset and then the sunrise (geographically impossible, but I didn't realize it at the time) and was completely blank and happy for a full eight hours.

When I woke up, I felt amazing, like I'd slept for weeks. And the best part is that I didn't think about June at all.

THE PILFERED PILL

WellCorp was headquartered outside of Seattle in one of the city's more pristine corporate hamlets. It was a low, sprawling campus with a kayaking pond, a hiking trail, and three different labs full of nervous rats and Bunsen burners. There was also a juice bar and a spectacular view of the Cascades from every conference room window. Ranked as one of the top five places to work in Seattle, it was a PNW yuppie wet dream. The on-site gym with complementary trainers. The free salad bar. The treadmill desks. Everything a pharmaceutical company needed to project WELLNESS in all caps.

I might have liked my job better if I worked at headquarters instead of its squalid downtown cousin, Urban Campus. The "campus" part killed me because the office, located in a Second Avenue high-rise within walking distance of Pike Place Market, was barely larger than my apartment. The nicer office suites of the building had views of the Olympics, but Urban Campus didn't have windows, mostly because there was no one to impress. It was here that WellCorp conducted its Phase 1 clinical drug trials, and the kind of people it sought out for these exercises were predictably down-on-your-luck types. They were people who, thanks to the increasing ludicrousness of the real estate market, now had to rent out their bodies to afford bus fare—which was why Urban Campus was a place you could get to on foot. The ceilings were low. The lighting was fluorescent. The vibe, in all caps, was HOPELESS.

Even the coffee in the break room was terrible: weak, sandy, concession-stand swill. How could WellCorp get coffee wrong in Seattle of all places—where public water fountains were practically plumbed with dry cappuccino? I shook my head as I made a pot in our office's kitchenette. Coffee Talk down the street wouldn't open until seven, and I needed something to tide me over.

I had a crush on one of the baristas there, and I inspected myself in the mirror above the sink so I'd know how mortified to be if he ended up taking my order. My brown eyes looked dull, each one boasting a purple smudge against my pale complexion like a footballer's greasepaint—the insomniac's calling card. Fortunately, my bob was doing that retro-looking thing I liked where it hangs in one undulating wave around my head like a sheet of lasagna. (Throwing up in that boat was the best decision I'd ever made, hairdo-wise.) And I hadn't *actually* cried, so facial puffiness was at a minimum. All in all, I didn't look bad, considering I'd slept just four hours and dressed in two minutes in the midst of a full-blown panic attack. I almost felt capable—until I tasted my unbrushed teeth.

The coffeepot went through a series of asthmatic death rattles as I surveyed the empty office in lieu of anything more entertaining to do. From the kitchenette, one could see the entire floor plan: on the left the small glass-walled lobby off the front entrance with its two molded plastic chairs, on the right the four-pod cube farm with waist-high walls, and beyond that Diana's office next to a large interview/conference room with windows overlooking the kitchenette. Everything was boring, clinical, cheap.

I wasn't in love with my job as a pharmaceutical trial assistant. Granted, it wasn't difficult to hand out pills to people and write down whether or not they got diarrhea when they came in to report their side effects—and I got to deal with a lot of interesting people for short periods of time, which suited my spritely attention span.

But what few perks there were to the job could be thwarted right out of the gate depending on what drug we were testing. The year I spent measuring forehead sprouts as WellCorp attempted (and failed) to cure male pattern baldness was one of the bleakest of my life, but recently our team had started conducting a trial for Morpheum, this little pink sleeping pill that guaranteed a full night's rest with the added benefit of fantastic dreams. The idea was to market it to people struggling with trauma that couldn't be escaped even in sleep: soldiers plagued by PTSD, shooting survivors, rape victims—maybe even Millennial women on the verge of motherhood. Pete had a full head of sandy hair, so I hadn't been terribly invested in the baldness cure. But as someone who hadn't slept in weeks, I was very interested in Morpheum's success.

The coffeepot hacked up the rest of the brew, and I took a cup of it to my desk to clean out my inbox—and scroll through Nat Geo Travel's Cambodia feature on Instagram, which turned into looking up flights to go see Angkor Wat. I'd barely done any work when my coworker, Altan, arrived, stumbling to his chair like he'd just climbed off a bull ride, wearing sunglasses despite the fact it was raining and we were indoors. He reached into his back pocket and removed his wallet, which he threw into his desk drawer as he collapsed backward into his chair. "Morning," I said without looking up.

Like me, Altan was a trial assistant for WellCorp in his early thirties. Unlike me, he was over six feet tall, born in Taiwan, raised in California, sloppy with his paperwork, and a habitual consumer of kombucha who would probably describe himself as "exceedingly chill, man." His desk faced mine from the other side of a low cube wall, allowing us to punctuate our workdays with chitchat. If I'm being honest, I didn't mind looking at him all day.

Another secret no one knew? I had a teeny, tiny crush on Altan Young. It was a harmless attraction, one I fostered to amuse myself for eight hours a day. I had no intention of declaring my love, leaving my husband, and riding off into some sunset wearing lingerie and lipstick for him: I was happy at home. But still I had this desire to make Altan laugh, to draw attention to myself with my wit. Maybe I needed the validation, or maybe I was bored—either way, my fondness was born and frozen in a kind of unrequited adolescent amber: in our every interaction, I idly wanted Altan to want me because I knew he never would.

Also, his hair was *amazing*. Thick, black, glossy, he kept it shorn on the sides, but the top was long and tussled and fell in his eyes with a casual messiness that deserved sonnets. He had cheekbones you could whet a knife against and golden skin that set off the depth of his brown eyes. He was built without waste, slim but not skinny, with a pleasingly tapered torso and long musician's fingers. He wore flannel shirts and weatherproof boots and dark-wash jeans cuffed to keep the hems from dragging in puddles. He'd grown a beard recently, a casual one—not the hirsute sculpture of the hipster, but a close-cropped shadow on his face that made him look more scruffy-stoner than manicured Viking. But I liked it. I liked it because it was so *not* Pete.

Altan lowered his glasses at me over the cube wall, *Risky Business* style, and smiled. "Jesus, you look like shit."

"Well, you look like ten shits," I fired back. The greatest thing I learned in middle school was the trick to earning the respect of boys, which was to be relentlessly clever and entirely bulletproof in conversation. Consequently, I'd spent the better part of my education perfecting the art of the swift return, the wide grin in the face of discomfort, the devastating one-up. "What the hell happened to you?"

He hung his head in faux shame, then raised his eyes mischievously. "Karaoke happened. Some friends and I went to that place where they deliver drinks to your room? Great idea until it was a terrible idea."

"You're a shit show," I said.

"I know." He sighed merrily. "What a nightmare. Speaking of which, how'd you sleep last night? I'm guessing by those bags under your eyes the answer is 'not good.'"

It would have been middle school suicide to flinch, so I buried my face in my coffee mug and pretended to sip from the empty cup. In honor of a slow Friday, Altan and I had left work early two weeks ago to bitch about work over IPAs. I don't often drink a lot in public, as a matter of principle, but for some reason that day I'd made an exception and had another. And that's when I blabbed to Altan about my nightmares. Predictably, he didn't seem to think too much of it—that's what's great about work friends: you can like them without having to *care*—and he cracked a joke about my getting pregnant that was so corny I blocked it from my memory like a trauma. But I returned the laughter like a tennis serve, and it was a relief to chuckle about the whole thing with someone who had no stake, like maybe the impending dissolution of my marriage and self-worth wasn't such a big deal after all.

I'd assumed this would have been the end of the conversation, except it wasn't. Every morning since then, Altan had been asking how I'd slept. That he remembered to ask was weirdly intimate: either he genuinely cared about my well-being or he was collecting fodder with which to shred me at a later date. It was probably the latter. It was definitely not both.

"I slept like crap, as usual," I reported sheepishly.

"What was the dream this time?"

An email alert drifted across my computer screen, and I clicked on it just to give myself something to do. "I was skydiving and the parachute wouldn't open. I had a baby strapped to the front of me in a— like a baby carrier. What do you call it?"

"A Bjork?"

"Yeah," I said. "One of those."

Altan looked at me for a moment, waiting for my reaction. "You're supposed to laugh," he clarified.

"At what?"

He shook his head in disgust. "The carrier is called a Baby*Bjorn*. Bjork is the singer. Are you sure you're not pregnant? You're getting your Scandinavians confused. Could be that baby brain kicking in."

Shit. I'd committed a cardinal sin of communing with boys. *I'd let a pop culture reference go unrecognized.* "I'm not pregnant," I said flatly, then lobbed the conversation back at him to spare myself more shame. "Do you ever have trouble sleeping?"

He trained his eyes on his computer screen and smiled with only one side of his mouth. "Not since the divorce."

Ah! Altan's mysterious divorce. I lived to hear him talk of it.

Altan and June had split a few months ago under hasty and mysterious circumstances. Because I had at one time mentioned that my husband was a divorce lawyer and Altan was too lazy to look for anyone else, he had hired Pete to represent him. And while attorney-client privilege prevented Pete from divulging all the details to me over brunch, I'd gleaned from the crumbs he *did* drop that the proceedings went with honey smoothness: Altan and June had no kids and—like most Millennials—no savings. To grease the uncoupling even further, Altan had ceded his share in their Ballard bungalow, which had almost doubled in value in the three years of their marriage. Pete had tried to talk him into selling it for his own good, but Altan maintained that he wanted the divorce quick and mercifully clean—like when Henry XIII imported Europe's best executioner from France to cut off Anne Boleyn's head.

OK. So it was unfair for me to assume Altan was the one who ended things, but that I didn't know exactly what happened made my imagination itch. Sometimes I found myself speculating about him—not obsessively, but definitely as an alternative to messing with spreadsheets. What did he *do* now that he was single? Where did he live? Was he happy? Did he have regrets?

And what was with that Moleskine notebook he now habitually carried in his back pocket, the impression in the fabric like the negative of a condom in a wallet? I sometimes caught him scribbling in it at his desk (pretentiously), and I could picture him posted up in some divey bar, drinking craft beer and crafting shitty *haiku*. The effect would be poetic, but I'd been work mates with Altan long enough to know he wasn't nearly as cool as he was trying to appear. What made him bearable was that he knew it, too.

Altan and I fell into silence behind our computers, until Diana's heels clicked into our suite and made a beeline for her locked office door. "Morning," she said.

Diana Wilson was a warm but no-nonsense woman who wore her hair in a short afro and kept her jewelry to a minimum. As the only person in our small office who had studied pharmacology, she officially presided over WellCorp Urban's medical trials, making Altan and me her glorified lemmings: we scheduled the interviews, handled the paperwork, and fielded the calls about whether or not WellCorp's drugs are compatible with recreational weed (they aren't), or if we drug tested for THC as part of the trial (we do), or if we'd kick participants out if they pissed hot on a THC test (we would). Dealing with the volume of humanity on the level we did was overwhelming, so WellCorp let Diana manipulate the chemicals while Altan and I handled the chemistry. She spent a lot of time locked up in her office, so I wasn't as chatty with her as I was with Altan. But I liked her because she was kooky and outspoken and never gloated that she was better educated than me and Altan combined.

"Ness, can you step in here when you have a sec?" I heard her call from her office. This was followed by the sound of her snapping on her many desk lamps (she abhorred fluorescents) and cooing to the fichus that lived on the closest bookshelf. Diana's half-dozen houseplants were all mostly dead in her windowless room, but she insisted on performing horticultural rounds every morning when she came in, complimenting each plant in an attempt to boost its morale.

I grabbed a pen and pad of paper from my desk and went to her office, where I found her inspecting a spill of English ivy, pinching one trail thoughtfully the way a doctor might check a wrist for a pulse. "Shut the door," she said. "I got an email from Jeff Simmons last night saying he wanted out of the trial."

I wrote this down. "He's Altan's patient, right?"

"Like the other five that dropped out to test Merck's newest beta-blocker." She clucked. "Who can blame them? They pay twice as much as we do. Still." She rounded on me so I could see the suspicion gleaming in her eyes. "It's weird that only *Altan's* patients are aware of this. Is he up to something?"

"Altan?" I said incredulously. Altan was about as crafty as Diana's wilted rubber plant. It was hard to imagine him cooking up a scheme, considering he was too lazy to pack a lunch. "In order for him to be plotting on the job, he'd have to care about it first."

"True," said Diana, her head cocked thoughtfully. "Still. Keep an eye on him for me, will you? I don't want him going Slugworth."

This term was Diana's own invention, one she'd stolen from *Willy Wonka and the Chocolate Factory* to refer to any kind of corporate espionage, her greatest professional fear.

"Of course," I said. "Did Simmons drop off his leftover medication yet or should I call a courier to get it from his house?"

The fear of Slugworthing made Diana strict about securing outstanding pills from our ex-participants.

"I already called the courier," Diana said. "He's on his way here with the meds. How many pills did Simmons have?"

"I'll have to check, but I imagine it was a few, since he was three months into the trial. I'll count them before I incinerate to make sure we have them all."

"Perfect," she said, patting the fuzzy leaves of an African violet, which I took as my sign to go—it was oddly touching to see her with her plants. I left her alone.

Altan was in the conference room with a patient when I got back to my desk, so I treated myself to a walk around the block in the cold drizzle just to wake myself up. This no-sleeping business was hell on my constitution: if I couldn't handle a few bad dreams, how was I supposed to cope with the marathon sleeplessness of having a kid? Not to mention the drain on my career and my already shoddy mental health and my dream of becoming a travel photographer—which, let's face it, was never going to happen. But having a baby would seal that deal in a way I couldn't ignore. Having a baby would be the death of hope, and that was hard to get over. Especially without rest.

I returned to the office half an hour later, my mood even more foul, to find a delivery receipt on my desk. "Was the courier here?" I asked Altan, who had finished with his patient and was applying Visine to his eyes.

"Yeah," he said, blinking. "Simmons's pills arrived. I put them in the incinerator for you."

"Thanks. How many were there?"

Altan stared back blankly, then his face crumpled as he slapped the top of his desk. "Shit, dude. Forgot to count."

"Dammit, Altan!" I rubbed my temples, trying to chase away what was rapidly becoming a migraine. Just because I sometimes had a crush on him didn't mean I was incapable of recognizing his worthlessness. "That's like the tenth time you've done that. You know we're supposed to catalog the pills to make sure none get stolen!"

"I know, but I'm half asleep. There were a lot, if that makes you feel better. Just put twenty-five in your log. Fudge it. Diana never checks."

"Of course she checks! You know how scared she is of Slugworths!"

Altan stood up and crossed into my cubicle so I could appreciate his full height. "Look, I'm sorry. Let me get you a peace offering. You need coffee? I'm running to Coffee Talk."

Damn him for knowing what a sucker I was for caffeine. "Fine. I'll take an Americano."

"Sure thing. Decaf?" He smirked so I could see his AC Slater-style dimples. "For the baby?"

"Seriously fuck yourself."

Altan laughed, reaching over the wall to grab his phone from his desk. "Believe me, I've tried. Back in a sec."

I blew out a breath and sat down to check my email. Five minutes later a text pinged my phone. *Forgot my wallet!* Altan had written. *The line is a monster. Can you bring it over?*

There was no end to his incompetence. *This is some favor you're doing me*, I texted back.

I'm the worst. Top drawer of my desk.

Altan's drawer contained only a billfold and a bottle of aspirin: not a pen or a paperclip or a pad of Post-Its in sight. The man half-assed his job so thoroughly he didn't even have office supplies. Pain throbbed annoyingly behind my eyes as I picked up the aspirin to inspect the label and wonder who under the age of seventy even took this stuff. How old was it? Young enough to work? Did I really care at this point?

I popped the top and turned the bottle over in my palm, expecting the chalky tablets I remembered seeing my grandfather take. But what tumbled into my hand were waxy, oblong, pink, unmarked capsules—identical to the ones Diana kept locked up in her office. I'd dispensed enough of them over the past few months to know: They were Morpheum.

Holy shit. Altan had a stolen himself a stash of closely guarded company property that had yet to be approved by the FDA. He'd gone full Slugworth.

I pocketed the bottle of "aspirin," along with Altan's wallet. *What an idiot.* Sure, Altan was a beautiful pain in my ass, as impertinent and impish as the little brother I never had. But I certainly didn't want him losing his job—especially so close to his divorce. There was something to be said about not kicking a man when he was down. Not to mention, he was the only person I had to talk to at work—and Pete's legal assistance didn't come cheap. Altan had yet to fully settle his bill.

WEDNESDAY, OCTOBER 10

Starting to suspect there's a correlation between what's going on in my life and what I dream about on Morpheum. Thought I'd compensate for taking dodgy medication by going on this whole vegan health kick thing for a bit. Now all I dream about is pizza: deep dish, Chicago style, with the sauce on top and cheese two inches thick. It tastes so good in the dream.

THE DREAM DARE

I jogged all three blocks to Coffee Talk so Altan wouldn't lose his place in line, and when I arrived he was stepping up to the counter. "Just in time! What do you want again?"

"I told you five minutes ago—Americano," I grumbled, handing him his wallet and double taking as I noticed Coffeeshop Crush behind the counter. He wore a peacoat and a full beard and a watchman's cap on his head, like he'd be leaving for the sea at any moment. I stammered in his direction, "Cool. Hi. How are you? Good?"

"Aye," he said, because he was *Irish* and straight out of a Joyce novel. I loved him. "Americano, then?" His teeth were crooked. It was adorable.

A tremendous goofy grin spread across my face. "Sure. Yeah. Cheers." Sexual attraction has this way of making me monosyllabic, and I prayed Altan wouldn't notice as he paid.

But he did, and he elbowed me in the ribs to prove it. "You like a little Irish Crème in your coffee?" he cackled as we shuffled down the counter to wait for our drinks.

"Can't blame a gal for looking," I replied with a lift of my shoulders. I shrugged a lot around Altan to prove I didn't care about what he said. Deciding that the whining of the milk steamer and the grumbling of the espresso grinder were enough to mask our conversation should anyone decide to eavesdrop, I took the aspirin bottle from my pocket and presented it palm-up, like I was asking for a tip. "I found this when I was looking for your wallet."

Altan looked down at the bottle in my hand, as impressed as if I'd been holding a dog turd. "Did you open it?"

"I did."

He didn't even bother looking squeamish. "Can you take aspirin when you're pregnant?"

"I told you: I'm not pregnant," I said through gritted teeth, leaning into him a little (I had to stand on my tiptoes) so he could hear me hiss, "And don't change the subject. You're stealing pills from work."

His eyes glinting mischief, Altan rocked back on his heels, hands in his pockets. "Guilty."

His offhandedness made me feel like a nag, like I was some uptight killjoy because I didn't want him losing his job and dying alone. I hated that feeling. "Are you selling them?" I asked.

For the first time in the past three minutes (hell, maybe even in his whole life), Altan looked genuinely scandalized. He snatched the bottle from my hand and trapped it in his fist. "Sell *Morpheum*? Are you *insane*? This stuff is priceless. I've never slept so well in my life."

I narrowed my eyes. "I thought you said you slept fine since the divorce."

Altan stared at me and licked his lips, hesitating, as if debating whether to come clean or continue hyping his superhuman ability to DGAF. Finally, he said, "I lied, OK? I sleep like shit."

His earnestness was unexpected, but he went on in all seriousness, looking around the coffee shop so he wouldn't have to meet my eyes: "The bed is too cold, or the night is too quiet, or the weight of the divorce is too heavy. I wake up a hundred times wondering where June is, and then I have to remember she's gone. My head was such a mess after the first few months, so I stole one of the pills—just to see if it worked—and *I finally slept.*" He dragged out the last few words as if savoring the feeling of the memory, of that moment he'd opened his eyes the morning after and realized he'd gotten a break. "I'd been falling apart for so long, and then I was steady for the briefest moment. It meant everything to me, just to feel normal. You know?"

He caught my gaze then, searching for something he didn't usually look to me for—a way of relating on a human level, a confirmation that I, too, knew pain, that he wasn't the only one existentially alone in a sea of people who possessed a satisfaction he could never attain. I nodded to ease his mind, to let him know that I also spent twitchy, tortured nights wondering what the hell it all meant.

"Americanos!" the barista called, placing two paper cups on the counter.

He took his cup and started for the door without waiting for me, forcing me to trail after feeling sorry for him. Altan played the fool so well that sometimes I forgot he had feelings. As work friends, we were not obligated to care about each other—but that didn't mean I shouldn't.

"I'm sorry," I said as we arrived on the sidewalk. "I didn't know you were taking the divorce that badly."

"Well, I am. *Aspirin* is the only thing that helps," he replied, leaning on what I already knew would become a code word, another little joke between us.

"And how long have you been taking it?"

"Since September."

"You shouldn't," I said as we walked back toward the office. "You could get . . ." Here I fumbled, trying to maintain the metaphor. "Reye syndrome."

"What the hell is Reye syndrome?"

"I don't know! I'm trying to talk in code. I'm saying these pills could be dangerous."

Altan took a sip of his coffee and shrugged, a complete return to his too-cool-for-school routine. "Nobody's died yet."

"How do you even steal them?" I asked, knowing Diana kept them locked in her office.

"I pocket what goes to the incinerator, then I fudge the log for Diana, who never checks. Anywhere else I couldn't get away with this, but WellCorp is so shady. There is zero accountability, and I haven't had a raise in two years." A jackhammer started up nearby, and Altan upgraded his voice to a low shout. "So I take advantage. Besides, I can't do my job if I don't sleep, so in actuality, stealing from the company helps me be a better employee."

"You're so full of shit," I grumbled into my cup, and then we both said in unison, "The fullest," because his comebacks were so predictable.

There was something admirable about Altan's ability to be this carefree, this self-serving—in such flagrant disregard for what you're supposed to do. Can't sleep? No problem. Steal sleeping pills from work. Blame the system for being flawed and stingy. Have flexible morals and sleep like a baby. *I* certainly wasn't the kind of person who got on board with this kind of disobedience, but I could see how a person, harried and driven to exhaustion, could get desperate enough to bend the rules in search of relief.

"Are the dreams really that good?" I asked.

"They're amazing," he said, as we walked. "I sleep instead of watching TV now, so I feel better in the mornings *and* I save on movie rentals."

"So, what happens if I tell on you?" I asked at the corner. We were across the street from our building, and Altan jabbed the crosswalk button while a half-dozen people sidled up next to us with their earbuds and bored expressions.

"You won't tell on me," he said.

"I won't if you give me one."

"What? An *aspirin*? Seriously?" Altan was genuinely surprised, which was annoying. I hated that I was so incapable of spontaneity that it stupefied people when I did something unscripted.

"Don't look so shocked. You're not the only person with problems," I said.

"Not at all. I just thought you wouldn't be into it: stealing from work, taking non-FDA-approved sleep medication. What with the baby
and all—"

"Would you shut the fuck up about the baby already?" I snapped, whirling on him as the light changed. Everyone around us started crossing, but I let Altan have it despite hating myself as I did, knowing I was committing another cardinal sin: never get hysterical. "I know mocking people is your thing, but I'm not kidding around with this baby situation, OK? I'm terrified, and I'm sorry I told you, and I'm sorry you think my fear is funny. But it's not to me, so shut up about it, OK? Just shut, the fuck, up."

The crosswalk was red again, and Altan was appropriately still. "OK," he said quietly.

"That's it? 'OK'? You're not going to crack some joke about how I must be hormonal to go off on you in the street?"

Altan set his coffee cup atop a newspaper box at the corner and pulled the aspirin bottle from his hip pocket. He removed the cap and motioned for my hand, turning it over so my palm made a cup, and tipped out one pink pill. "You sound like you could use some rest," he said gently, closing my fingers with his. "And you don't have to threaten me. You could have just asked if you wanted one."

His tone, for once, was genuine, and I realized it was nice to feel like someone cared about my feelings. Pete cared, of course, but since he had his pro-baby agenda, I couldn't trust him completely.

Wait, that was unfair. Of *course,* I trusted Pete. What I meant to say was that it was nice to have someone care *only* about me.

"Thanks," I mumbled, tucking the pill into the coin pocket of my jeans. "And look, I'm sorry I growled at you. It's just—"

"Don't apologize," interrupted Altan, picking up his coffee and motioning to the crosswalk, which was now green. "I needed to be told. I had no idea how freaked out you were about this."

"I'm not sure I want kids, but Pete does, and I don't know how to talk to him about it," I said. Without the frosting of my attempts to be witty, the truth was flat and ugly. But it tasted honest and comforting, like white bread. "I don't know what we're going to do."

Altan said casually, "I get it. I didn't want kids either, but June did."

"Is that why you got divorced?" I asked nervously, as he opened the door to our building.

"Not entirely."

Oh, I thought. Not exactly comforting.

SATURDAY, OCTOBER 20

Pete called yesterday to say my divorce was final.

I mean, it's what I wanted, but still . . . I can't help but wonder if I made the right decision. Ultimately, June is better off without me. She and I just didn't work in Seattle. I keep trying to tell myself that: that it was no one's fault, that things fall apart. Still. Sometimes I miss her. Nothing in the new place smells like her.

Last night I dreamed about Marrakesh—will I ever stop dreaming about goddamn Marrakesh?—except this time when we got to the hospital, June had the baby. She was wearing a white nightgown, and the baby was bundled up in a white blanket, asleep. We were both so happy, especially June. Her smile was electric, like it was when we went to Venice for the first time. In the dream we were crying, and when I woke up, my pillowcase was wet.

Dunno if this is supposed to mean anything. Was this my way of saying goodbye to her? Not sure. Would I have dreamed it without the Morpheum? Also not sure.

Do I care that this drug is altering my mind, when it feels so good?

Also not sure.

THE MERMAID

Pete was in the living room when I got home, still in his suit pants, his button-front shirt rolled to the elbows. (Being a lawyer meant he was one of ten guys who still had to wear suits in a town that otherwise embraced business casual; our dry-cleaning bills were enormous.) He was plotzed in his favorite armchair, the leather one I had bought him (cheap, because it was scratched on the side that faced the wall) for our first anniversary. "Hello, Bug!" he sang as I took off my boots, looking up briefly before returning to his book. He had his feet propped up on the matching ottoman, and I saw one of his toes was poking out of his sock.

"Gatsby again?" I asked as I passed on the way to the kitchen, grabbing his foot affectionately.

"Hmm?" Pete barely raised his head.

"You read that book every year."

He gave me his full attention then and beamed. "That's because every year I still don't understand you."

Nine years ago, I was a senior majoring in psychology with an overloaded course load and three degenerate roommates, the kind who made margaritas for breakfast. On a Tuesday. It was the time when UGGs were the height of collegiate fashion, and since I didn't want to spot mine in the rain by walking down to the student union, I did most of my late-night studying at this sleepy, nondescript sports bar near our apartment. I'd nurse a single beer during these sessions so I could justify sitting there all night. The usual bartender—some grad school bro who abused his position by pulling free beers for other grad school bros—took to rolling his eyes every time I came in with my laptop, so I'd developed something of an attitude I wore only to that place.

One evening, after depositing my textbooks at a sticky two-top, I marched to the bar to order whatever beer had the lowest ABV, only to find the bro had been replaced by a nerdish guy perched on a stool reading a book. He wore jeans and a solid gray T-shirt beneath a flannel—standard-issue college uniform—but his light hair was tidier than most people who frequented the joint: not exactly neat, but also not greasy. It stuck out at angles like he was a guy who rubbed his head absentmindedly when in deep thought. Sure enough, he reached up and fluffed the back of his head as he read. *Excuse me,* I called.

He didn't look up, so I said it louder—twice—and when he finally registered my presence, he hopped off his stool and slapped his book on the bar. *Sorry about that,* he said, politer than the normal bartender. *What'll it be?*

Beer. Whatever is the least likely to fuck me up.

He smiled and went to the taps to oblige. *You studying tonight?*

Yep, I said tersely.

So's my friend who usually works this shift. We have a law final tomorrow, so I agreed to cover for him.

Why aren't you studying? I asked as he passed the beer across the bar.

Because I already know everything. He grinned and patted his book affectionately. *So now I'm free to drink beer with Mr. Fitzgerald all night.*

I looked at the cover of the book and groaned.

"I still don't know how you hate *The Great Gatsby*," Pete said from his armchair as I dug through the fridge. "It's the great American novel!"

"Want a beer?"

"Sure. Whatever is the least likely to fuck me up."

Over the years we'd done this routine so many times to honor the moment we met, and I never got tired of reliving that crackle between us—that hit of stranger danger I felt when talking to a handsome bookworm separated only by a yard of oaken bar.

It demonizes women, I'd told Pete that night. My textbooks sat abandoned next to Gatsby, and the place was empty before finals, so Pete was bored and free to chat. In the background, a Pearl Jam CD played quietly through the speakers as it was contractually obligated to do in every college bar in Seattle through the year 2045. I continued to rage: *Daisy Buchanan is arguably one of the worst-portrayed women in American literature. She's painted as a self-obsessed, airheaded flirt who ignores her kids and refuses to blow up her marriage to Tom for her sappy ex-boyfriend who shows up out of the blue because he's forlorn and horny.*

Aw, don't say that about Jay, Pete said with mock offense. *I always thought of him as being this quintessential romantic. There he is: staring out over water at Daisy's green light, wistful and tortured, waiting for his one true love—*

I rolled my eyes. *Meanwhile, Daisy is busy. She's married; she's got kids. She's completely forgotten about this clown. And then he shows up expecting her to drop everything and fawn over his shirts, which is disgusting. When do we see him ask her for consent? Does she even want her whole life wrecked? Maybe she was doing OK without him.*

I'm pretty sure she wasn't, argued Pete, leaning on his elbows across the bar. *Tom Buchanan isn't exactly a prince.*

Well, neither is Gatsby. In fact, he's worse. At least Tom knows he's a bastard. Gatsby doesn't. He's probably the kind of guy who orders for you in a restaurant—who makes all your decisions for you and just expects you to roll with it.

But Daisy does roll with it, Pete said. *Maybe because she loves him?*

My Pete had always been a hopeless romantic. How ironic that he'd grow up to be a divorce lawyer.

My laugh then was high, breathy, incredulous. *She doesn't love him! She's married to a wife beater and lacks the money or job opportunities to leave. So she rolls with Gatsby first because he might be a ticket out and second because women are trained to roll. Since birth. It's our worst curse and greatest skill.*

You make it sound so unromantic when you put it that way, replied Pete.

"And do you remember what I said back?" I asked, handing him a bottle of IPA in our current-day living room.

Pete dog-eared the pages of his books, a habit that would disgust most bibliophiles. But I enjoyed that about him, the way he worshipped things through use. He folded the corner of his page and tossed the book on the coffee table so he could make room for me to curl up with him in his chair. "You said, 'There's nothing romantic about being a woman.'"

"And there still isn't. Your whole life you're stuck making everything easier for other people—like that's what you'd choose from a menu. And this is why I feel sorry for Daisy Buchanan: no man cared enough to ask what she really wanted."

"You *also* said that when we met," Pete recalled faithfully, taking a pull from the bottle. "And do you remember what came next?"

I remembered: Pete had leaned even farther across the bar—practically supine on it, stretching his lean soccer player's body toward me and drawled, *So, what do you really want, Vanessa?*

I blinked a few times, stunned, trying (unsuccessfully) to remember a time someone had asked me that before. So many answers floated through my mind then like a chorus of ghosts: my dream of working for *National Geographic*, the way my high school teacher had called my photos mediocre. I remembered the size of my student loans. I thought about that party I went to sophomore year and wished I'd stayed home. There had to be something sexy to say to this bartender, but I couldn't bring myself to flirt with such an important question. Instead I said, *I want people to take me seriously. Automatically. Without question. I want to walk into a room and have people think,* Now there's someone I don't want to fuck with.

Pete had nodded as he absorbed this, working his hand through the back of his hair. *Well, I hate to disappoint you,* he said, flicking his eyes toward mine; I heard the *click* of a lighter as he did it. *Because I very much would like to fuck with you.* And then he blushed and dropped his gaze to the cover of his book, as if he couldn't keep the Lothario act going a second longer. *With your consent, of course.*

"It was a bold move, counselor," I said, clinking my bottle to his.

He chuckled at the memory of his own audacity. "Well, I'm known for my bold moves."

Then modern-day Pete leaned over to kiss me, and I remembered how I'd given him my number so he could call after finals and invite me out for pizza and more debate. Four dates later, and after he had gallantly asked permission, we slept together in his Capitol Hill apartment, where I moved after graduation and then never left. Pete finished law school and got a job at a firm that specialized in uncoupling tech-based fortunes. After a handful of retail jobs, I fell into the WellCorp gig and started secretly taking pictures, and now here we were: stable, and somewhat moneyed if you could forget about the student debt. Still in love.

He pulled back from our kiss and took another sip of beer. "So do you want to talk about having kids?"

I shook my head, strategizing the perfect distraction as I set my bottle on the coffee table and moved my hand down his chest to rub the crotch of his pants. "I thought we could practice making them."

"In a minute," he said, all serious. Removing my hand from his groin, he watched it as he interlocked our fingers, not meeting my eyes, like he was a child asking for something he knew he wasn't going to get. "What if we never finish this baby conversation, and then our chance passes us by and it's just the two of us forever?"

My heart wasn't wearing a seat belt: it slammed into my ribcage. The two of us forever sounded like the greatest thing I could ever think of. So why did he look so sad? I put my hand to Pete's cheek and nudged his face upward so it was close to mine. "Would that be so terrible?"

"No," said Pete with a watery smile, brushing his lips over my knuckles. "But you know what they say about more and merrier."

"Not always true," I purred, resuming my rubbing. "Sometimes it's nice, just the two of us." I felt the victory of his going hard beneath my hand, like I'd actually convinced him to abandon his dreams of fatherhood with a single erection. "See?" I whispered. "Isn't this nice?"

"You're distracting me. I know what you're trying to do here."

"No you don't," I said as I peeled off my top.

I tried not to think about all the things my husband didn't know as he kissed me hard, working his hand through the waistband of my jeans. Then all the things my husband didn't know melted away as I felt it then, the nerves beginning to fire, the pleasure centers of my brain whirring to life like giant machinery. My whole body tightened as I focused on Pete's hand, how he slipped it beneath my underwear to brush me, softly, *there*.

It was the exact sensation that had woken me at a house party my sophomore year at WSU. I'd had too much to drink and had gone in search of a bedroom to lie down in, believing stupidly in my human right to sleep without being violated in a heinous way. It was dark when I came to, and someone who smelled like foamy beer and Camel Lights already had his fingers inside me.

There was the foggy, inescapable feeling of a bad dream when I tried to protest: my tongue was lead, my mouth felt like it had been stuffed with cotton and sewn shut. All I could do was moan crankily like Frankenstein's monster, at which Beer and Cigarettes had his friend, Axe Body Spray (who was stationed at my head), clamp a hand over my mouth. And then he had the gall to laugh as he undid his belt, "Listen to her. The bitch likes it."

More was not always merrier.

Pete didn't know about that night. The time for revealing this was probably around date five—the Moroccan restaurant with the floor pillows It was certainly too late to paint my sexual assault as a "fun fact" about myself. One does not simply say to someone over brunch after almost a decade of being together, "Oh, by the way, I was raped in college." Or maybe one did, but *I* didn't know how.

So I squashed the memory as best I could, but every now and then it got parole and paraded around—most often during sex, which was unfair. Pete nibbled my ear, another throwback, and I went rigid beneath him, a reaction he historically mistook for pleasure. I squeezed my eyes shut and threw my head back to distance myself from the memory, from the act, from my husband who now felt like an enemy—at least in my mind. "Oh god!" I cried, which was Pete's cue to retire me to the sofa.

I didn't stop him, because I didn't actually want him to stop— not really. What I wanted was to *want* him to keep going, to *not* want him to get it over with. I wanted to wish it would last forever. But my mind was elsewhere, powerless, mute.

"I'm close!" Pete groaned. I dug my nails obligingly into his back.

"Me too!" I lied. And when he buried his face into my collarbone and shuddered, I felt nothing but relief.

He lay on me, rubbery, spent, the way I'd felt after the party when I walked home alone in the gray light of morning. The way I'd felt a month later, after the drugstore test, at the clinic, with the doctor as he asked, not judgmentally, "Do you know who the father is?"

I knew the candidates only by their smells: Beer and Cigarettes, Axe Body Spray, and finally Vodka/Irish Spring, who had stumbled in on the scene and decided—why not?—to join in. If there were such a thing as an olfactory lineup, I would have reported the incident in a heartbeat. But it had been dark, and I'd been drunk. And I didn't want to go through what that implied to certain people: I just wanted to chalk the whole thing up as being a life lesson about communing with boys and put it behind me.

But that backfired when I got pregnant. Ironically, had I reported everything, I could have gotten a pill immediately, and then I wouldn't have been at the clinic in a paper dress on a paper runner, telling the doctor that I didn't know who the father was. But no: I just *had* to curl into bed for three days after it happened, crying and missing all my classes, instead of hauling my bruised body down to the Bartell's to ask for a Plan B in public like I should have. I'd seen enough *Law & Order* to know what a gal was supposed to do.

So there I was, armed with a woman's right to choose, having to make a choice about the consequence to a thing I had not chosen—like that was a fun decision, like electing to have an abortion was as frivolous as selecting sundae toppings. Maybe it was for some women, but even though I was then and am still now pro-choice, it was like voting to eat vomit over shit.

Pete lifted his face from my neck to kiss me on the forehead. "I love you," he grinned.

"I love you too," I echoed, because it was true. I loved him, and Pete loved what he knew of me. He didn't know that I'd been pregnant once—and then after a doctor's visit, I wasn't. And while there were many ways to weather what had happened, I'd chosen the hardest one, which was to throw the book at myself in lieu of anyone else to incriminate. I'd been browbeating myself for years like a medieval Monty Python monk to trick my heart into thinking justice had been served. It was the least I could do.

That I refused to forgive myself for a thing that hadn't entirely been my fault was probably the reason I couldn't trust myself to make decisions. When reality is something you regularly warp like Silly Putty, it's hard to tell what's solid and right from what you've forced yourself to make sense of for various reasons. Anyway, because of all this, and regardless of whether I truly believed it, the idea of putting another baby in my body felt abhorrent, on par with eating Chernobyl-grown tomatoes.

After we had sex, I sat on the sofa wrapped in a blanket while Pete changed into sweatpants and called for a pizza. While we waited for it to arrive, he emptied the dishwasher and prattled on about his day while I blankly drank another beer, making appropriate "No way!" and "Get out!" noises when he paused. It felt like I was watching the whole evening play through the wrong end of a telescope, everything tiny and far away.

When the pizza arrived, we ate it while watching *Jeopardy!* on the sofa, Pete smugly crowing all the right answers through a mouth full of pepperoni. But I couldn't hear anything. I used to feel things when I thought of that night—anger, shame, sadness. But sometimes now I felt zilch, which was horrifying, like waking up blind. When I looked at that night, it sometimes deafened me to everything else. It rang in my ears like tinnitus.

After dinner, I took my backpack to bed. It was calm in the sleepy half-light of the bedside lamp. I brushed my teeth, slathered Gold Bond on my hands, and donned one of Pete's old flannel button-fronts that he kept so I could steal them to sleep in. Sitting up in bed against the pillows, I fidgeted with my camera, peering through the lens half-heartedly at our bureaus, the alarm clock, my bathrobe hanging on a peg near the closet, waiting for that moment when I would know if something was beautiful. It didn't come.

I swept the room, finally setting the sight on my jeans, which were draped over the back of a chair I kept in the room expressly for the purpose of draping jeans over. There was Morpheum in my pocket. I could hear it singing. I quietly put my camera away and padded to the bathroom for a glass of water.

A few minutes later, I was in a warm and briny sea shallow enough to register the sunlight filtering through the surface, illuminating a tremendous coral metropolis below. I dove for it, noticing how little effort the motion took. I looked back and saw that my legs had been replaced with a starfish-orange mermaid's tail, streaked with crusty purple barnacles sparkling like rock candy against my large scalloped scales. My primal mind briefly registered that I was dreaming, a fact I promptly forgot as I turned and surged toward the reef. OK, so I was naked from the waist up, but the ocean was my shirt, my waist-length hair trailing like a superhero's cape as I swam. My hands also floated behind me, unneeded. I turned a few somersaults in the water for good measure, twirling my arms at my sides like I used to in the neighborhood swimming pools of my youth. Laughter popped out of my mouth in muffled bubbles as I corkscrewed down.

The fish were dressed like tarts—Busby Berkeley showgirls in sequins and pastels, their fins undulating burlesque fans. A neon yellow moray eel smiled cheekily at me from his cave while ornamented pufferfish the size of basketballs floated by like Parisian hot-air balloons. There wasn't much to listen to; the silence of being underwater pressed in on my ears so I heard only the gurgling of swimming things, slow and rare bubbles of sound. I looked down at my hands, and from deep beneath the dream my real brain blinked a warning like a hotel room smoke detector. *Hang on,* it said. *This is usually the part when a baby scares the shit out of you.* But in my arms I cradled only a mermaid's version of my Nikon in iridescent purple, like it had been dipped in a slick of oyster nacre.

A lime green shark sailed through a field of jellyfish made of burgundy bullion fringe. Corals glowed semi-translucent in Jolly Rancher hues, and to their glassy branches clung tiny brittle seahorses origami-ed out of tinfoil. Everything was designed to be the most visibly interesting experience I'd ever had, and as I put my camera to my face, I couldn't help but be dazzled both by what I saw and how I felt: alone. Completely alone. And *free!* I was all by myself in this frenzied buffet of beauty, able to eat as much as I wanted for as long as I liked.

Propelled by my tail, I snapped photo after photo without ever stopping to check if they were turning out right. Because I knew they were right. They, like all things around me, were fucking *fantastic.*

THURSDAY, NOVEMBER 1

Patient Molly Q. came in today with a black eye. When I asked her how she got it, she said she "fell down the stairs"—used finger quotes and everything, like she knew how full of shit that excuse was. Jesus. I hate to see that.

Get this: says last night she dreamed she was a seagull who flew across the Atlantic (!!!!) Is this common? Does Morpheum just have ten thousand preset scenarios that play at random like a dream jukebox? I thought it was supposed to be customized.

Anyway, I hope she'll be OK.

I dreamed about Marrakesh again last night, only this time, no happy ending. In fact, it felt just like a replay of when it really happened. First bad dream I've had on Morpheum. Maybe Halloween gave off bad juju.

THE LEERING
BOSS

The day I married Pete I vowed to spend the rest of my life cataloging each of his distinctive smiles. There was the electrified grin he put on whenever a waiter arrived with food. The absent-minded Mona Lisa crescent he made when he was lost in a book. The faux-shocked "O" that morphed into a wide smirk when he got my goat in a joke. And then there was my favorite, the loose and dopey beam he made when he was completely in love with me. He made it as I surfaced from my ocean dream the next morning, his slightly crooked bottom teeth contrasting boyishly with the crow's feet taking root in the crinkle of his blue eyes. "Morning, Bug," he said as I buried my face in my pillow and wiggled my toes to make sure they weren't actually fins. "*You* slept well."

When I poked my head back up, my smile was huge. "I did," I said, reveling in an insomniac's relief that comes with a full night's sleep. I briefly thought of Altan, how happy he'd been just remembering this feeling.

"No nightmares," said Pete, matching my face. "I take it you're feeling better?"

"It's a start."

I flopped onto my back and stretched my arms overhead, completely vulnerable to Pete as he steamrolled on top of me to plant a kiss on my forehead. "I'm glad," he said, rolling off the bed just to make me laugh. Clambering to his feet, he added, "You better get up. We're late."

"But the alarm just went off."

"For the sixth time. I couldn't bear the thought of waking you up."

The line between romance and sociopathy was so fine. "So you've just been watching me sleep for thirty minutes?"

"I did some reading when I got too bored," Pete said as he sauntered into the bathroom, where I could perv on him from the bed as he brushed his teeth. He had a casual handsomeness that I didn't always take enough time to enjoy: the bird's nest of his hair, the curves of his shoulder blades, the constellation of freckles scattered across his back.

When he was done with his toilette, I switched places with him in the bathroom and watched as he ceremoniously applied the pieces of his charcoal suit, like armor. "This is the worst striptease I've ever seen," I said around my toothbrush.

He straightened his tie behind me in the mirror. "I'll show you a better one tonight." He winked at my reflection. (There was a subtlety to winking that, adorably, Pete had never mastered: when he did it, it looked like a flinch.) He spun me and dipped me in a goofy dramatic kiss, wiping the toothpaste that had transferred from my mouth to his on the back of his hand.

"See ya later, Bug," he said, righting me before hustling out of the bedroom. I heard him whistling—whistling!—as he put on his oxfords, and then the door shut and I was alone.

Waking up from Morpheum sleep felt like coming back from vacation in that it was *clarifying*. I suddenly remembered all the things

I was supposed to be doing that I'd forgotten were important, like appreciating my husband and watching sunsets and other forms of self-care. I decided to treat myself to a good flossing and then a leisurely walk to work.

The world outside was glorious. OK, so it was drizzling, but the rain felt cool and fresh on my face as I walked down Cap Hill among dozens of Patagonia-clad urbanites with their hiking backpacks and purebred dogs. As I neared my office, I turned automatically to go to Coffee Talk before realizing I wasn't even tired enough to warrant an Americano. Course correcting in the middle of the sidewalk, I nearly tripped on a golden retriever as I skipped into my building, bounding up the stairs to flit like a hummingbird through the front door of the office. I'd never felt so alive and raw to the world, like I was mainlining solar flares. Listen closely, and you could hear this buzzing sound coming off of me, like a bug zapper. Or a downed power line.

"You're late," Altan accused when I twirled to my desk.

"Am not."

"Are so. I have never in two years beaten you to the office. Ever."

I dropped my backpack and stuck my nose up snobbishly. "I decided to sleep in."

"Did you?" asked Altan, equally airily. "And tell me, how were your dreams?"

Diana was in her office; I could hear her talking through the open door. Whether she was on the phone or conversing with her plants was hard to say, but I thought it best to answer Altan's question discretely. I crossed into his cube and took a knee near his chair, pretending to tie a shoelace I didn't have on my Chelsea boot. "You didn't tell me it would feel like *this*."

Altan reached for his back pocket and pulled out his Moleskin notebook, flipping it open to a blank page. "What did you dream about?" he whispered, uncapping a pen.

"I was a mermaid," I told him. "But it wasn't like I dreamed I was a mermaid: I turned into an *actual* mermaid. I could taste the ocean and feel the warmth of the water. I woke up and I swear my fingers were pruned." Here I spread my hands out in front of me to double-check as I continued to babble. "I had a camera, and I was all by myself taking pictures of fish—"

"Are you a photographer in real life?" Altan interrupted.

Whoops. The only person who knew I was a photographer in real life was Debby, and it felt vulnerable to fess up to it—especially to Altan. I didn't like the idea of his knowing something Pete didn't, but it seemed equally silly to lie because it wasn't a big deal. "Not professionally or anything," I muttered. "But I like to take pictures in my spare time."

"Do you wish you could do more of that?"

There was heat on my face, despite the fact WellCorp kept the thermostat at a miserly 65. "Kind of. Why are you writing this down?"

He stowed the notebook and murmured, shooting a glance to Diana's office to make sure she wasn't close enough to eavesdrop, "I have this theory that Morpheum amplifies the Freudian aspects of dreams. It detects what you're looking for, like a nocturnal mood ring. I've been writing down my dreams every night to discern patterns."

"Really?" I crinkled my nose. It was difficult to imagine Altan taking such an extracurricular interest in anything, much less his job. "So what do your dreams say you want?"

"Depends on the day. Sometimes when I'm feeling stressed, I'll dream I'm binging Netflix, except the shows aren't real. My mind makes them up. I'll watch a whole season of something like *The Wire* but not *The Wire*—all while wearing dream sweatpants."

"Huh," I whispered, dropping the shoe-tying act and taking a seat on the floor. "So what do you think my dream means?"

Altan bent forward. I was close enough to detect the zest of him, the mint of his toothpaste, his aftershave, the detergent of his shirt and how it failed to mask the wet leather of the jacket he'd been wearing moments before. Something about him smelled familiar, though there was no reason it should. "Well, why do you like taking pictures?"

Again, I felt my stomach twist. No one had ever asked me this before, and suddenly I didn't know how to put the answer into words. "I feel really present when I take pictures," I said lamely. "Some people meditate, but my mind wanders. When I have something to look at, it doesn't. I really see things with a camera. I focus."

"Fair enough," Altan said without a hint of dismissal. "So why would you be doing it underwater, without any people around?"

"Maybe the Morpheum is telling me I want some space. To think things through."

"There you go." He leaned back in his chair, clasping his hands behind his head. "Last night I dreamed I was a grizzly bear in a river catching salmon as they jumped upstream, grabbing the fish out of the air with my jaws. It didn't feel violent, though. I was just a bear doing bear things. It was very chill," he mused.

"What does it mean?"

"That I was trying to catch little pink bullets in my mouth? Probably that I need to steal more Morpheum."

I sniggered. "Or maybe you really just like salmon."

He smiled at me then, and I noticed suddenly just how straight his teeth were. Of all the times I'd seen him flash a grin after a joke, how had I not noticed until now?

"So," I said, trying to sound casual. "Do you have any more, ah, *aspirin?*"

"I had a feeling you'd ask." Altan checked Diana's office one last time and then reached into his backpack, retrieving a Bayer bottle from the front pocket. "There's one left in here."

"Cool. Thanks." I tried not to sound as shifty as I felt. "And is that all you have?"

Just then Diana burst through her office door, grabbing the lintel on either side of her for support. "Has anyone seen my lab coat?" she cried.

I sprang to my feet and pocketed the bottle in the smooth, guilt-free way of the morally upright. When *had* I last seen Diana's lab coat? "You wore it for the Christmas photo," I said. "Why do you ask?"

But the second the words left my mouth, I knew. Altan said, "Oh, shit."

He leapt out of his chair and scrambled past me to help Diana root through the kitchenette cabinets. I fled to the rarely used coat closet in the lobby, calling out behind me, "How much time do we have until he gets here?"

"He said he was parking in the garage," called Diana.

From Altan, another more urgent "*Shit!*"

He was Malcolm Jacobs, the pretty-boy son of Dean Jacobs, WellCorp's founder and CEO. He had been stationed as the Urban Campus's "office manager" for the past two years, which meant he'd show up occasionally at lunchtime, coffee in hand, his shoes dry from parking his BMW in the garage downstairs, complaining about traffic that was a fraction of what it was when the rest of us commuted. Workwise he was good for nothing except needlessly complicating days that ran fine without his input. Take the time he decided to implement a "paradigm shift" that forced everyone to wear lab coats at the office. "We want to inspire trust in our patients," he'd said, which in corporate doublespeak meant: "We want to pass the whole staff off as doctors so our clients don't ask questions about the experimental pills we feed them."

Everyone hated this idea, especially Diana: her distaste for Slugworthian subterfuge went both ways. So the white coats were only worn when Malcolm actually came to work, which occurred so rarely that we didn't bother storing them within easy reach. "Found them!" I shouted from Diana's office, where I'd located the three garments hanging on the back of her door like hungover ghosts. I rushed out to the lobby with an armload of polyester, and everyone shrugged on their uniforms just as we heard the elevator doors open.

"Morning, all," said Malcolm, striding through the lobby to find us lined up like the downstairs help. In a movie, Malcolm would be played with the inflated charm of Christian Bale in *American Psycho* and the inflated body of Christian Bale in *Batman Begins*. His muscles strained against custom suits that he probably had tailored to match his handshake, which was like a blood pressure cuff. He had dark, close-cropped hair, electric blue eyes, and sugar-white teeth that sparkled against his perpetually tanned face. "How are we all today?"

"Malcolm," Diana said with absolutely zero enthusiasm. She crossed her arms in front of her chest. "What a surprise. It's been forever."

Malcolm represented everything people wanted in a white-man's world but didn't automatically get: stupid amounts of money, power, privilege, *plus* the ability to be on boats during working hours. Diana, especially, loathed him with an unmitigated disdain. After all, *she* was the medical professional who made all the decisions about our patients and acted as Altan's and my de facto manager for the 360 days a year Malcolm was "working from home." She was doing the job of two people and making half of what Malcolm spent on spray tans in a year. We all hated him in our own ways, for myriad reasons, but could all agree that he was a black-belt wanker.

"I've been meaning to check in sooner, but things have been crazy," Malcolm said, not at all apologetically. He was carrying an actual briefcase—not a backpack or a satchel but a tiny pigskin suitcase, like it was a prop in a play.

"Oh? Have you been spending a lot of time at HQ?" Diana was needling him, because we all knew Malcolm had no professional value. His dad had probably given him the job for tax reasons.

"I've been sailing the Mediterranean," he replied, his voice like lard. "So beautiful this time of year. You should really go."

Diana laughed at his little jab at her bank account. "How am I supposed to go to Europe when I haven't had a raise in three years?"

Malcolm laughed along with her—such jokes!—then turned toward Altan. And then kept turning to me. "Hello, Nessie," he said, using a nickname only my mother had permission to employ. He swept his eyes down my lab coat and up again, then came in for a hug—odd, since he hadn't done so much as give Diana a handshake or Altan the middle finger. He held me tight to him, his palms smashed into the spot between my shoulder blades. *Ugh.* I swear I heard him inhale. "You look great. Have you been working out?" he said, still pressing against my breasts.

Malcolm had this way of being a little too personable with me, which I hated. But since we saw him so rarely, his behavior was easy to laugh off for eight hours at time. And laugh I did, because the shit that came out of his mouth was so unnerving it had the unintended effect of turning me into a one-woman sitcom audience. "Working

51

out?" I shrieked like a coked-out kookaburra over his shoulder. "No, I've just been working. Working hard! For the money!"

"Yeah, well, I heard everybody's working for the weekend," he murmured in my ear, and I laughed again, helpless as a ragdoll in his embrace.

Malcolm finally released me, standing back to appraise me again, still holding one of my hands like we were about to waltz together. I hated that he felt entitled to touch me, like his money empowered him to possess anything in the world. "Still, you're practically skin and bones! You should let me take you out to lunch."

How kind of him to address my physical appearance! The idea of being alone with Malcolm while he talked about sailing or polo or scrimshaw or whatever else rich people think is interesting was enough to put me off food. *Forever.* "I really can't."

"Aw, come on. You can't be *that* busy." I tried to not take offense to that as he took a step forward to close the gap between us.

I took a step back. "I have an appointment at lunch. But I'm free this morning if you'd like to schedule some time in the office." At my side, I saw Diana nodding encouragingly.

"Booked up," said Malcolm. In slow motion I saw him reach a hand out to hold me by the back of my elbow. It was a tender gesture—one I did not want. "I have to discuss the Morpheum trial performance with Diana all day. How about dinner? Come *on*, you have to eat."

The worst part about Malcolm's "attention" was that it wasn't insidious enough to lodge a formal complaint, so all I could reasonably do was grit my teeth and act like it wasn't happening. The shame associated with this—with pretending I was OK with, or (even worse) too stupid to notice, the liberties Malcolm took with me—was almost as uncomfortable as his touch. "I really can't," I said through a wide, dipshit grin.

The smile must have been big enough, because Malcolm raised his hands in surrender. "OK, I give up. But if you pass out from starvation, don't expect me to give you mouth to mouth."

Mentioning mouth-on-mouth action was a weird thing for a boss to say, so weird that my usual nervous tittering ratcheted up to a full-blown moony cackle. I could tell it pleased him as he led Diana to the conference room, and I hated that he was aroused by my discomfort, that I had to worry about this kind of bullshit in a job that was already rife with it. I couldn't wait for Malcolm to sail off again so we could avoid him for another two months.

"Oh, Nessie!" called Malcolm from the conference room door. He crossed back to me to stand with his hands in his suit pants pockets in what I assumed was supposed to be some kind of "casual boss pose" he'd learned while getting his MBA. "I hear we've had some patients drop out lately. There's someone I want you to sign up for the Morpheum trial—Sam Stevens. Can you schedule him for an intake appointment this week? He's already in our system."

"Sure?" It was odd that Malcolm had taken such an interest in our patient roster. I was surprised he even knew what drug we were testing.

"Super," he said, clapping his hand on my shoulder again, and squeezing. I stood there and waited for him to go to the conference room before I sat at my desk and shuddered like a wet dog trying to dry off.

Once the door was closed, Altan whispered across the wall from his pen, "Is it just me or does Malcolm seem especially interested in you today?"

That he'd noticed was comforting, because sometimes I wondered if I was being sensitive with my attitudes toward touching.

And then I wondered why that mattered, because a preference was a preference regardless of provenance, and I did not need a reason to dislike my boss's lingering over me like a meal. But still I confirmed, "So you saw it too?"

Altan frowned and shot a side-eyed glance toward the conference room door. "*Nessie*," he said mockingly, "they could see it from *space*."

TUESDAY, NOVEMBER 13

Been working on a theory that Morpheum has wish-fulfillment capabilities—like, it can detect what you want most in your life and give it to you in your sleep. Case in point: the night before last, I dreamed I was camping with some lady who was ostensibly my new girlfriend. It was cold but the campfire was amazing, and we were just sitting under a blanket and chatting. The stars were extra clear.

And when I woke up, I realized that's what I wanted: to be in love with someone who doesn't mind not having roots. It feels really cheesy to say it, but hey—not like anyone is going to read this.

So that was my wish-fulfillment theory. And then last night I dreamed that June and I hosted Thanksgiving dinner for all the living presidents of the United States. Then halfway through dessert, Hillary Clinton stood up and shot everyone point-blank, like in a Tarantino movie. I mean, I guess I wouldn't *mind* that, but could it be considered a thing I actually *want?*

THE COLE
PORTERHOUSE
ARGUMENT

True to his word, Malcolm did spend most of the day in the conference room with Diana, leaving me free to enjoy my Morpheum energy as I sailed through a surprisingly productive Tuesday. Five o'clock found me with a clean inbox and a desktop so free of unfiled paperwork that I was able to scrub the coffee rings off the laminate. I even booked Sam Stevens for an intake appointment, just like Malcolm had asked, before I said goodnight to Altan and buzzed up to Cap Hill in the rain. On the way home, I decided to cook Pete dinner for probably the first time since our first anniversary, swinging into the market near my building to buy ingredients. With my backpack full of steaks, potatoes, two bottles of red wine, and brie for hors d'oeuvres, I skittered home, resisting the urge to splash in the puddles for kicks.

I was searing steaks to the soundtrack of *Anything Goes* when Pete's keys jangled in the lock. "What's all this, Bug?" he asked, kicking his off his shoes and loosening his tie, a perfect portrait of a Normal Rockwell husband. His suit jacket slipped from his shoulders and landed on the ottoman. "Cooking!" he gasped, crossing into to kitchen to grab me around the waist. "Who are you? What have you done with my wife?"

I giggled appreciatively. "It's Cole *Porterhouse* night."

"Cooking *and* punning?" He kissed me grandly as I stood helplessly clutching a spatula. "I've never loved you more!"

"Let me go!" I squealed. "I'll burn the steaks."

He stood back to admire me, ruffling his hair thoughtlessly, his signature goofy grin on his face as I took the pan off the stove and stuck it in the broiler. "Well, I was going to change. But a dinner this nice warrants more formal attire," he said, retightening the knot of his tie.

"Don't be ridiculous! Go get your leisurewear on."

He slapped a wedge of brie on a cracker and popped it in his mouth, chewing as he settled on a barstool at the kitchen island that doubled as our table. "Absolutely not!" He sprayed crumbs. "I would never insult dining this fine with leisurewear."

"Then what happens when you eat too much?"

"I'll undo my belt under the table. I did promise you a striptease, after all."

"A New York strip tease?" I said, forking the potatoes out of the oven.

Pete barked a single laugh: *Ha!* "Who knew there were so many steak puns in the world?"

A few minutes later I joined him at the island with our good plates and even a pair of candlesticks I'd unearthed from the back of the cupboard above the fridge, where I stored the relics from our rarely used wedding trousseau. The whole scene felt very civilized. *Tres* adult. "So how was your day?" Pete asked, slathering butter on his potatoes.

I let my fork and knife clatter on the counter for dramatic effect. "Malcolm actually came into the office today."

"No!" gasped Pete. "Did he make you wear the white coats?"

"Of course," I resumed eating. "I think he's trying to sleep with me."

"Because he's forcing you to wear more clothing? I'm not sure it works like that."

"Not because of the coat. He keeps offering to take me out to dinner."

"What's wrong with that?"

I shrugged. "Normally, I'd say nothing—you know, if he did it for everyone. But he just does it for me, and it's awkward. Even Altan noticed."

Pete shrugged. "Altan's probably jealous."

I almost choked on my steak. "*Jealous?*"

"He probably has a crush on you," Pete said. "I see it all the time with divorced guys. It's like they don't know how to be alone so they glom onto whatever female is nearest, asking them for fashion advice or decorating help. Like a surrogate wife."

"Altan has never asked me for fashion advice. And we have, like, *zero* chemistry," I said—which wasn't untrue. Despite my petite crush on him, we were just friends, which was exactly how I wanted it. "He's lazy and judgmental and all he does is tease me. The last time *that* was sexy was in middle school."

"I was all about that game in middle school," Pete mused.

"I bet you were. Were you a bra snapper?"

Pete clutched the knot of his tie in horror. "Heavens, no. When I meet St. Peter, there'll be a lot of sins on my record. But bra snapping will not be among them."

"I always knew you were a quality man," I said, raising my glass in a tiny toast. "Bra snappers are the worst."

The rest of the meal was spent reminiscing about our respective awkward middle school years, a topic broad enough to extend into dessert. It wasn't terribly difficult to picture a boyish, too-skinny Pete reading books at recess, trying to impress girls with his knowledge of the Hardy Boys—but it was still endearing to consider nonetheless. It was nice to see Pete—really *see* him, over a sit-down meal with the TV off. It was so easy when we were tired to just look at each other in passing while foraging for leftovers, but after my Morpheum sleep I had the energy to be the wife he deserved. And when the second bottle of wine had been emptied and after Pete had sappily and sloppily slow-danced me around our tiny kitchen to "I Get a Kick Out of You," he folded me into his arms and said, "So how shall I thank you for this delicious meal?"

I looked at him through hooded Bette Davis eyes. "You could do the dishes."

He laughed at this. "Gladly. But is there anything else you want?"

"That depends. What do you feel like giving me?" I flirted back. We were both a little tipsy, and sexually speaking I was ready for a palate cleanser. Maybe it was because I'd hated remembering the sophomore incident during the previous night's coitus. Or maybe it was because Malcolm had this way of making me feel like Marilyn Monroe on that windy sewer grate—and not in a good way. Regardless, I was happy to be warm and buzzed and draped in the arms of my beautiful husband, who was trying to dirty talk me.

"I was thinking that first we'd go into the bedroom," he said.

"Ooh, that sounds inventive," I giggled, leaning into him. He smelled like dry cleaner's starch. "And then what would happen?"

Pete dipped his head toward my throat so he could trail kisses up to my earlobe. "Well, I'd lay you down on the bed and undress you slowly, and then I'd lick every inch of your body."

"Like a cat?" I said dreamily, and Pete chuckled.

"Yes, like a cat. A very *sexy* cat." His voice was hypnotic and honey smooth. "And after I take off *my* clothes, we could do that thing two people do when they love each other very much."

"Oh yeah?" I ran my fingers through his hair. "What's that?"

"We could make a baby."

My laugh was immediate, like a gunshot—the loose, wild braying of drunk people. "Why the hell would we do that?"

Pete pulled back so I could see his face. He looked confused, which was confusing. "Because—" he stammered. "Because you decided you want to have a baby, right?"

I reclaimed my arms from around his neck and stepped backward so I could fold them across my chest. "What gave you that idea?"

"You didn't have a nightmare last night, and you cooked me dinner with candles," said Pete, blinking. "I thought you were trying to tell me you were ready."

"Jesus! I was ready to eat steak!" I said, bewildered as to why it seemed like everything I did—had a nightmare, confused my Scandinavians, ate red meat—transmitted hidden baby messaging to the world.

Pete was embarrassed, and this turned itself into anger. "Well, I don't know what to think! You're not exactly into talking about this and so I'm just trying to read your cues—"

"There are no cues!" I cried. "I have no agenda. There is no evidence. I—" I stopped. The flash came to me lightning quick, the cool light of the ocean, how it shimmered off my scales—how sure I'd felt alone in the deep. And then I said, "I'm not sure I want kids." The words had a sturdy, round shape to them as they left my mouth, only instead of bubbling up to the surface, I watched them sink between Pete and me like stones.

In addition to Pete's smiles, I had come to learn his frowns. I studied his face now for the Pouty Furrowed Grimace (when he couldn't find his keys), or the Flared Nostrils of Frustration (when I was late to meet him)—but I looked at him and all I saw were his normal warmth and humor, like I'd said something cute. "Aw, Bug," he said. "Everybody says that."

"But I mean it!"

"No, you don't," he cooed, pulling me toward him and rubbing his hands up and down my back, speaking softly, like my mind was a skittish horse that could be coaxed and calmed, instead of its own steadfast thing.

And sure enough, I already felt myself backpedaling as I looked at my feet, felt myself rationalizing my opinions, as if I needed to. "I just feel like I haven't done anything extraordinary with my life, you know? I went to school, got a ton of debt, got a crappy job to pay it off."

To his credit, Pete didn't try to debate me. I continued, staring at the tiles, pressing the top of my head gently into Pete's sternum. "Remember when I wanted to be a photographer?"

Pete snorted. It sounded like a bomb. "You haven't taken a picture in years!"

This wasn't true, but he didn't know. "That doesn't mean I haven't missed it!" I countered, raising my voice. I was pissed. At Pete, for knowing so little about me, and at myself, for not showing him—then at Pete again, for not insisting he learn, and for not trusting me when I said things. I was pissed at myself for not wanting a baby, and pissed at those boys for taking that desire from me all those years ago. I was so, *so* pissed I thought my heart would explode hot tar and turpentine. Had I always been this angry? Since college, yes. The rage had been simmering in my stomach for years, and it took all my attention and energy to keep it from boiling over. I consciously unclenched my fists and lowered my voice as I asked, civilly, "Maybe we could take a trip? So I could take some photos?"

"Sure, Bug," he said, smoothing my hair. "If you think it'll help. Where do you want to go?"

I turned to address the counter, brushing cracker crumbs into my hand with a nearby dish towel. How many times had I asked myself this question on the bus? Morocco, Mumbai, Melbourne—they all seemed impossibly exotic. And expensive. Instead I chose a base model, with training wheels: a starter trip. "How about Paris?"

Pete's reply was immediate and flat. "We can't afford Paris."

I'd known he'd say that, and I had my answer ready. "Well, if we don't have money to travel, how the hell can we afford a child? Do you know what day care costs?"

"Day care?" Pete looked truly taken aback. "I just assumed you'd stay home with the baby."

Oh. It was *on*. I threw the towel on the ground. "Why would you even *think* that?"

"Well, you hate your job, for starters!" Pete was waving his arms like an orchestra conductor. "You're always saying how much you can't stand measuring hair plugs."

"They weren't plugs; they were sprouts!" I railed back. And sure, I *did* hate WellCorp—"But that doesn't mean I want to stay home all day with a baby I don't even want!"

Pete dropped his hands and blew out a deep breath. "Look, I'm sorry for assuming." His voice was more annoyed than aggressive, like he was frustrated with the fact we were fighting more than he was with the cause. "But all I can do is guess since you refuse to talk."

But I wasn't done. "Because *you* don't listen: *I don't want this baby!*"

"We should have this conversation another time," Pete said coolly. "You've been drinking."

My mouth fell open but nothing came out, even though there were so many things I wanted to say, chief among them that he had *also* been drinking, and no one was calling *him* hysterical. There was the anger, sure, but worse was the betrayal that Pete could think that after a few glasses of wine I wasn't capable of making up my own goddamn mind, of saying no.

"I'm going to bed," I managed, crossing to the bedroom and slamming the door behind me.

Pete stormed in behind me to get his pillow. "I'll be on the sofa, if you need me."

"Fat chance," I returned at the door as it closed.

SATURDAY, NOVEMBER 24

Molly Q. dropped out of the trial yesterday. She had her arm in a sling—"fell down some more stairs," she said, but she couldn't make the finger quotes this time—and the Morpheum interferes with her pain medication. So she's gone. I pocketed her leftovers and gave her my number in case she needs anything. It felt like a weird thing to do, but I hated the thought of her having nowhere else to go.

Dreaming a lot about the June years, back when we traveled. Last night Egypt, and the night before Java. June is not in them, but all my old friends are. I guess I miss having people to hang out with. All the friends we made in Seattle took June's side in the divorce, and it's not like WellCorp is a good place to develop a social circle. Ness is pretty cool, but not sure we've reached Friday-night hangout status. Palling around with my workmate and her husband, who is also my divorce attorney, would feel too much like a pity party.

Maybe the dreams are trying to tell me I need more people in my life. That I spend a lot of time talking to myself in a notebook is also probably a good indicator.

Need to work on my Tinder profile. Ugh. Should have never gotten divorced.

THE JEROBOAM

Alone in our bathroom, I brushed all the enamel off my teeth, threw on my customary flannel button-down, and got into bed, sitting up against the pillows so I could cross my arms over my chest again and fume. Replaying the fight in my mind, I kept focusing on one particular exchange: *I mean it. No, you don't.*

How dare he? Pete had asked me what I wanted when we first met and believed me then—so why didn't he believe me now? Why did *I* have to justify my position on the baby question when *Pete* didn't? Couldn't I just want something without reason? I flipped over and punched a pillow that was already perfectly fluffed. I punched it again to make sure.

It was then that I remembered the bottle of "aspirin" in my jeans pocket, and I decided to make a night of it. Off went the shirt. On went the silky, lace-trimmed, blush-pink nightgown with the thigh-high slit I had worn on our honeymoon and a handful of times since. In the mirror on the back of the bedroom door, I looked like one of those Russian émigrés from the '20s who moved to Paris after the Revolution and adopted the local look. I looked *good*, I thought through the wine—dangerous and sexy. I dry-swallowed the Morpheum and got into bed, leaving Pete's bedside lamp on so he'd have ample light to see by when he came to bed and found me, beautiful in repose and not at all worried about our fight. (I knew he'd come back: he hated that sofa.) With the cuff of the sheet expertly folded over the edge of the duvet, I settled into bed and waited triumphantly for sleep.

I found myself in Paris. Not the modern one of denim and selfies, but a roaring twenties Paris full of champagne saucers and cigarette smoke and feathers and fringe that matched perfectly with my nightgown-*cum*-evening dress. In kitten heels, I negotiated the cobblestones outside sidewalk brasseries, past café tables bearing bread baskets and wobbly curlicue chairs placed side-by-side so people could drink wine while facing the street. Huge Gatsby-era Duesenbergs roared past, their horns howling, *ah-oo-gah*. Somewhere someone was playing an accordion, squeezing an Edith Piaf tune out into the warm night.

A waiter with a pencil mustache gestured for me to sit as I ambled past his café, and I realized with a double take that he was Coffeeshop Crush with his beard shaved off. He brought me a glass of champagne, which I drank by myself while (suddenly able to understand French) eavesdropping on nearby conversations—alone with the contentment that comes from being by yourself and happy. When the waiter returned, I found him transformed into Altan in a tie and arm garters. My real brain somewhere laughed at this cameo, but dream me only blushed.

"*Bon soir, madame*," Altan said, taking my hand and helping me to my feet. "That is *quite* the dress."

"Merci," I said, twirling beneath his arm as if we were dancing. "Do you like it?"

When I finished the spin, Waiter Altan tugged my arm so that I fell into his chest, my hands pinned between us so I could feel his heart beating. "I'd like it better on the ground," he said huskily, running his fingers down the satin of my body and gathering the fabric at my hips in his fists. He jerked downward cleanly so that the spaghetti straps ripped as easily as dandelion stems.

I stood there naked in the middle of Paris while Altan stepped backward to admire me in the flesh. I let him, taking a moment to appreciate him back in a way I was too embarrassed to do at work: the width of his shoulders, the tumble of his hair, the tight smoothness of his skin, how cleanly his shirt traveled over his taut belly to tuck into the front of his pants. His eyes traveled over my breasts and arms, down the curve of one hip before crossing to the other. He revered me, wide-eyed and smirking, and then he took one step forward and crushed my mouth in a kiss.

A small bubble of protest floated up my throat—the tiniest "oh!" of surprise—before popping and dissipating into the night. My conscious, crocodile brain knew it was ridiculous to be kissing my coworker while time traveling through France, but dream me *loved* it, and I threw my arms around his neck and arched my back to reach him better, my fingers creeping up the nape of his neck to tug a fistful of his thick, dark hair.

Altan pulled away to cradle my face in his hands. "What are we doing? Is this OK?"

Music continued to throb in the background, but this time a woman was singing. For all I knew, Edith Piaf had been resurrected and was standing in the doorway of the café now, belting out "Non, Je Ne Regrette Rien" for the whole neighborhood. But I only had eyes for Altan. I tilted my head backward so that the gaslight caught my face a la Vivien Leigh in *Gone with the Wind*. "Monsieur," I announced, cupping my hand to his cheek. "I regret nothing."

He kissed me again, slow and deep. His use of tongue was completely appropriate considering the locale, I thought, as he walked me backwards into the sea of café tables until I felt one hit the backs of my thighs. I pushed Altan away and turned, so he could see my bare ass as I bent and swept the wineglasses and china plates off with both arms (god, I've always wanted to do that!), laughing as they broke on the sidewalk around us. And then, facing Altan again,

I hopped backward onto the naked table and spread myself like a lunch, my head hanging luxuriously off the edge.

Suddenly he was hefting a jeroboam of champagne the size of a small cannon. He yanked the cork out with his teeth (improbable, but who cared?) and poured it all over me, into my open mouth, over my torso, down my breasts, further south, lower now and everywhere, the bubbles fizzing like tiny parades, fireworks going off in my darkest places, lighting me up. The real me would have panicked about the mess or rolled my eyes at the sheer ridiculousness of this seduction, but dream me took over and I felt nothing but the gleeful lust of the completely un-self-conscious. When Altan spent the massive bottle, I lifted myself onto my elbow and swatted it out of his hands so it shattered all over the sidewalk. I grabbed his necktie like a leash and yanked down so that he had no choice but to kneel where I wanted him, in the bread crusts and cigarette butts and broken glass, his face planted just above the champagne between my legs. "Here," I demanded, trailing a talon down his cheek to hook him under the chin. "Drink."

His smile was wicked. And then he did.

I came so hard I sat up in bed.

"NESS! NESS!" Pete was shouting. Having found his way back to our room (I *knew* it!), he was trying to gather me in his arms—which was sweet but disorienting, as usual. He crumpled me into his chest to quiet my shaking, running his hand over my damp hair, our fight temporarily forgotten. "Oh, Bug," he moaned, heartbroken. "What are we going to do about these nightmares?"

"It wasn't a nightmare," I gurgled into his collarbone.

He let go immediately. "It wasn't?"

Yawning, I shook my head and rolled back over onto my side. Almost instantly, the Morpheum tugged me back to Paris, where I found Altan still on his knees in the street.

SATURDAY, DECEMBER 1

Molly Q. called. She said she left her boyfriend and wanted to know if I wanted to go out with her. I said I couldn't without getting fired—something about violating corporate ethics—and she understood. Which was good, because she's not exactly my type.

Still, I'm glad she's getting herself out of a bad situation. She mentioned Morpheum had helped her realize how miserable she was in real life, and it's nice to finally be working on a drug that could have some positive effects on people. Not like the baldness cure. That was the worst.

What's funny is that I dreamed about her last night. I dreamed she was marrying a Buddhist monk, which was weird, because I'm not sure they can even take wives? But whatever. He was kind, and he said on multiple occasions that he was a pacifist. I guess I want that for her, for her to have a peaceful life. I guess I want it for myself too.

THE TELL-TALE
MOLESKINE

If Morpheum had a flaw, it was that it made getting out of bed in the morning a complete nightmare. Sure, when I pried my eyes open Wednesday after hitting SNOOZE at least eight times, my body felt better rested than it had in years. But that didn't mean my mind was ready to embrace daylight with all its domestic squabbles and pivot tables after frolicking through French freak-fest all night. I looked over at Pete's side of the bed to find he'd left without apologizing or saying goodbye. *Coward.* Reluctantly, I got up.

By the time I got downtown, the line at Coffee Talk was too long for any reasonable person to wait in, so I went directly to the office to put the free shitty coffee on (force of habit outweighed my caffeine need), reflecting, as I did, on how balls-out bonkers my dream had been. I'd never had a sex dream (or actual sex, come to think of it) quite like I had last night. It was completely devoid of artifice—real and open and alive. What the hell did it mean?

If Altan's theory about Morpheum wish fulfillment was true, maybe my subconscious wanted me to be less inhibited, more adventurous—plausible considering the temperature of my life was about as tepid as a mug of tea made in a microwave. I hadn't chased my dreams. I hadn't broadened my horizons. I hadn't been any of the places I'd dreamed about over the *National Geographic* back issues of my youth. And while it was easy to blame Pete or my finances or my circumstances on the state of my affairs, frankly a lot of it could be chalked up to that party in college. If a routine night out could be twisted into something miserable and dangerous, what incentive did I have to go in search of actual peril?

Either the dream was trying to tell me in its weird, convoluted way that I needed to come to terms with this and be braver—or it meant I needed a pounding from Altan. Because that's what I'd gotten after I'd fallen back asleep: first on the railing of *La tour Eiffel*, and then, improbably, in what looked like Louis XIV's bedroom at Versailles, and *then*—

"So you gonna get some coffee or what?" a quiet voice said behind me.

Speak of the devil. "Oh! Hi, Altan!" I squealed, sounding embarrassingly girlish. I cleared my throat and lowered my voice to its normal octave. "Yeah, hey, how are you? What's happening?" This also sounded stupid. Altan noticed.

"Just trying to wake up," he said, lifting his empty mug to show me like I was simple. "Um, what's happening with you?"

"Same," I said. "Same, same, same."

Altan narrowed his gaze suspiciously. "You OK? You didn't have that baby nightmare—"

"No, nothing like that." I watched him pour a cup of coffee. The act was incredibly sensual, though I couldn't explain why. Maybe it was the length of his fingers or the spread of his palm or the way the backs of his hands rippled when he gripped things, like a mug. Or my ankles.

"Earth to Ness!" Altan teased.

My eyes snapped to his, and I realized I was breathing like I'd just run up stairs. "Huh?"

"You were saying?"

More panting. "I was?"

He smirked as put the mug to his mouth and took a sip, all the while regarding me over the lip. When it became clear that I'd been struck completely mute, he said, "OK, well, I'll be at my desk, *not* being weird." Turning to go to his cube, I heard him humming under his breath.

The tune was familiar. It took me a second to place it.

And when I did, my heart seized, turning itself inside out. The smooth and dependable rhythm of my life twitched tweaker-like, gasping and forgotten in the bathroom of a shady club.

"What song is that?" I asked.

"Huh?" said Altan, turning back.

"That song. What is it?"

"Oh!" He flashed a guilty smile, embarrassed to have been caught doing something mindless. Altan was rarely awkward: his belief in his own coolness was usually so sturdy and sure. "Some French song that's been stuck in my head all morning. I think it's from *Inception*, the song they used to wake people up."

He turned to go again, but I grabbed him by the arm and pulled him around so violently that coffee sloshed all over his hand. "Hey!" he protested, but I was on him, close.

"'Non, Je Ne Regrette Rien'?"

"What?"

"The name of the song. Is that it?"

"I don't know!" he said, shaking coffee from his fingers.

"When did you hear it?"

"Beats me. I must have dreamed about it."

My mind was a dryer on high as it tumbled down the side of Everest. "How?"

"How what?" asked Altan.

"How did we—" I stopped, because I couldn't say it. I did not have the words. I couldn't form the thoughts. I didn't even want to suggest the hypothesis until I had confirmed it. "Did you write your dream down in your notebook yet?"

Altan froze. And then he blushed. My god, Mr. Give-No-Shits actually *blushed*.

"Give it to me," I demanded. Altan's eyes ballooned out of his head, and his hand flew to his rear pocket to protect the evidence, in a gesture that would have been hilarious if I wasn't on the verge of a panic attack. "Give me. Your notebook," I said, advancing. Altan turned tail, banging his mug on the counter and flying to his desk to dive ass-first into his chair. I launched myself after him, clawing at his jeans.

"Jesus Christ, Ness!" Altan hissed. "Leave me alone or I'll call HR!"

"You don't understand. I *need* that notebook."

"What the hell is this?" asked Diana as she emerged from the conference room. Both Altan and I stopped mid-scuffle as we realized she had her white coat on, which meant Malcolm was in residence. He didn't usually come to the office twice a quarter much less twice in one week, but sure enough—*shit!*—he followed her out like a fart.

I broke away, stood up straight, and opened my mouth so these words could tumble out: "Altan stole my Moleskine."

Altan snapped his head to the side to look at me and audibly gasped, like he couldn't believe I'd stoop so low. "Bullshit!" he cried. "This is *my* notebook—"

But I went on: "He stole it out of my desk. It has all my patient notes."

Diana's voice brimmed with crisp, motherly authority. "Altan, give it back."

"No way! It's mine, and—"

"Look, I get enough of this nonsense at home with my kids. I certainly don't need it here. So, Altan, either give Ness her notebook back or give it to me. Your choice." Diana held out her hand like she meant it, like she was King Solomon whetting a knife over a squirming infant.

Altan's jaw clenched; I saw the bulge at his temple and knew I'd won. "Here," he grumbled, fishing the journal out of his back pocket and slapping it into my palm.

"There. Was that so hard?" Diana turned to Malcolm as if to shoot him a commiserating eye roll. But then she remembered she hated him and shuffled off to her office, probably to complain about all of us to her plants.

Notebook in my hands, I hurtled to my desk and tore through its pages until I found the latest entry. Altan's handwriting could best be described as "drunken cursive," but I could still make the words out. *Wet dream about Ness in old-timey Paris*, he'd noted. *Not bad.*

My mind started melting down. I could feel the gray matter getting droopy and oozing along the sides of my skull like one of those floppy Dali clocks. There were childhood memories in there too, and movie quotes and some Nirvana lyrics. It was all leaking through my ribs and pooling in my stomach, coagulating in a gelatinous mess that made me want to vomit.

I didn't hear Malcolm as he perched on the edge of my desk in his navy blue suit. "Hey there, Nessie. What's your day looking like? I'd love to take you out."

"No," I said, shaking my head side to side. What was I even disagreeing with? All of it. Everything going on in that moment was abhorrent.

"Aw, come on. I know this great bar down the street," said Malcolm. "Delicious mussels. We could split a bottle of wine?"

I stared at the notebook, wishing he would leave. *Wet dream. About Ness. In Paris.*

He tried again, his voice heavier than usual, like he was trying to throw it over me like a net. "Now that we're deep in the trials, I'm going to be spending a lot of time here getting to know the patients so I can give progress reports to my father. We're going to be working together closely, so why shouldn't we be close?"

I saw Altan's eyes flick up to witness this scene from his side of the cube wall just as Malcolm put his hand on my shoulder, and something in me snapped then. Whatever fear or professional respect or willingness to play along I had for Malcolm, I felt it stretch and break and bounce through my body. I slammed the door on the Paris dream situation for a brief moment as I focused my full indignation on my boss. "I don't want to have lunch with you, Malcolm."

He pulled back, shocked, like he couldn't believe a woman would choose not to plied by lunchtime wine and his sticky company. "You don't?"

"No. Your attention feels inappropriate."

His eyes grew wider, but in fact neither of us could believe what I was saying. "Nessie! Are you accusing me of—?" He stumbled off, unable to finish the sentence. Possibly because he'd never heard the phrase "sexual harassment" before.

"I'm not accusing you of anything." *Out loud.* "But I've told you repeatedly I don't want to have lunch. I've tried to make meetings with you in the office, but you seem hell-bent on seeing me socially, which I do not want. Please stop asking."

I could have flicked a Junior Mint into Malcolm's open mouth.

"And please stop touching me," I added—because why not? Might as well make a full list of demands as I was sitting here digging my professional grave. "Hugs, back claps: I'm not a terribly touchy person, so a handshake will do if you insist on something. Thanks."

I got up from my chair before he accused me of being melodramatic, before I apologized for overreacting, and, pocketing the Moleskine, I said to Altan, "Come on. Let's go to Coffee Talk." Without waiting for him to follow I turned and walked away. In my mind, I flicked a cigarette, and the whole office exploded in my wake.

Altan caught up to me as I was waiting for the elevator. "Holy shit," he whispered. "That was awesome."

"Was it?" My voice, my legs, my heart were trembling. "Don't get me wrong: it felt awesome. It also felt suicidal. I don't know why I did that."

The elevator arrived and opened with a *ding*. "Because he had it coming?"

"Well, sure," I murmured as we got in. I punched the Lobby button. The doors closed. I was babbling from nerves. "But maybe the Morpheum made me do it. Ever since I had that mermaid dream, I can't get that freedom out of my mind. I want it all the time, you know?"

Paris blipped through my remembering, how hard Altan had taken me on the café table. How much I had loved it.

"I do know," he said, leaning against the elevator wall, twisting the fingers of his left hand with his right. His Adam's apple twitched as he cleared his throat. "Which brings me to what I wrote in the notebook."

"I had it, too," I said, my stomach lurching into my throat as the elevator descended. "The Paris dream. I had it."

TUESDAY, DECEMBER 18

On my way home from work yesterday I bumped into June on Capitol Hill. She looked amazing—she always does, but she was especially done up. Said she was on her way to "meet someone." It was nice of her to not rub the fact that she's dating in my face. It would have been better if she had, because then I'd be mad at her instead of wondering if she still makes that little moan when she's kissed.

Last night I dreamed I had a threesome with Mila Kunis and Natalie Portman from *Black Swan*. No secret as to what that means: I need to get laid.

THE ACCIDENTAL INFIDELITY

Said Altan: "What do you mean, you 'had' it?"

The elevator paused to let some people in, and Altan and I shifted into one corner and watched them talk about meetings they were going to, deadlines they were going to miss, TV shows that had aired the night before—normal things people talk about when they haven't just stumbled upon what could be an earth-shattering neurological breakthrough. In the lobby, we let them go in front of us, and then on the sidewalk I said, "We had the same dream. You were a waiter." I was barreling up the street as if trying to escape what I was about to say, spitting words like machine gun rounds. "You were wearing arm garters. And I was there too, and I was wearing—well, I wasn't wearing much."

"You didn't start that way," said Altan defensively. There was panic in his voice. "I'm not a complete scoundrel. There had been a nightgown at one point."

"Until there wasn't. But I was there. We were in a café, and then we were in Versailles—"

"Wait." Altan stopped short. I doubled back to look up at him as he stood stock still in the middle of the sidewalk. His eyes changed, the irises contracting, his pupils deepening like peepholes as if to show me the part of his brain that *realized*. He whispered, "Are you saying we had some kind of sex dream mind meld?"

My head bobbed up and down.

A long, awful moment passed as all the implications—mental, medical, ethical—came slamming to the forefront of my mind to wave at Altan's cerebral cortex. "Oh my god," he whispered. "I did that thing with the croissant."

"Shut up!" I hissed. "Don't say anything until we have coffee. We need to think, and we need coffee to think, so let's go to Coffee Talk. OK?"

Altan wasn't paying attention. He was staring at me in abject horror. Hours seeped past without his moving. I snapped my fingers under his nose. "OK, Altan, time for coffee. *Altan!*"

I was about to slap him across the face and shout, "Get ahold of yourself!" like they do in the old movies. But he finally came to and lurched toward Coffee Talk, me trotting behind. When we arrived glassy-eyed at the counter, we stood there mouth-breathing like stoners while Coffeeshop Crush asked what we'd like.

Too stunned to flirt, I turned to Altan. "Quick. What am I going to order?"

He furrowed his brow and put two fingers to his temples like Professor X. "White mocha?"

Both the barista and I skewered him with a glare for different reasons. "Americano, please," I ordered. "And a . . ." I turned to Altan again so he could speak. His eyes flicked toward mine, asking, *You can't tell?*

I shook my head imperceptibly and Altan said, "Another Americano."

In silence, we paid and shuffled to wait by the espresso machine, moving gently, slowly, like survivors of an earthquake afraid a false step might cause an aftershock. Collecting our coffees, we picked our way to a table in the window. Altan mumbled as we sat, "So I guess I can only get in your mind when we're asleep."

"Huh?"

"When we ordered." He said this like he couldn't believe he was saying it, as if every word that fell from his mouth was an exhausting surprise, like a rope of knotted scarves that just wouldn't end. "I couldn't read your mind."

"Try it again," I demanded. "What am I thinking right now?"

He replied without hesitation. "You're freaking out. You're freaking out because we maybe fucked each other in some parallel dream universe, which may also be a medical discovery."

I waited. "*And?*"

"And . . ." Altan put two fingers to his temple again, squeezed his eyes shut. "I got nothing."

"Oh, well that's a relief." I took a shaky sip of coffee. "For the record, I was thinking how annoyed I am that you think I'd drink a *white mocha.*"

He laughed, breathy and frail, "You're seriously making a joke?" And then he rocketed forward in his chair. "*What the hell is going on?*"

I gaped at him, wishing I could think of something clever to say. But I had nothing. There *was* nothing. Altan and I were experiencing a thing for the first time in history, like Adam and Eve wiping fruit juice from their chins. It was an occasion momentous enough to warrant a "What hath God wrought?" or "I am become Death" or "One small step for man." But I looked at my workmate/accidental lover and said, "I have no fucking clue."

He slumped backward in his chair, running a hand through his hair and then down his face where it stopped to clamp over his mouth. One of us needed to be practical, and it wasn't going to be him, so I removed his notebook from my back pocket and slid it across the table. I leaned forward, bracing my elbows on my knees, dipping my head in a hybrid of the pose you're supposed to do when you're hyperventilating and the pose you're supposed to do when a plane is going down. My voice was hard and authoritative when I said, "Altan: focus. What do we know?"

I heard him slap the notebook and drag it toward him across the tabletop. He ripped it open to a new page, clicked his pen. "We both took the pills. And then we shared a dream."

"Have any of your patients reported this before?"

"No. Yours?"

My brain in my upside-down skull felt like the clapper of a bell as I wobbled my head back and forth. "So what makes you and me different?"

"Maybe it's because we're coworkers," Altan said. I imagined him ticking possibilities off his fingers with his pen. "Or we've had coffee together. We both hate Malcolm. We both love jokes. Maybe we're soul mates."

I snapped my head up so fast I nearly gave myself a neck injury. Altan had his palms near his ears like he was surrendering. "Ness, calm down. I don't know what I'm saying. *None* of this makes sense." His face lit up suddenly, like he'd been touched with divine inspiration. "Do you think that French song from *Inception* was on purpose? Like, our brains were trying to tell us something about the dreams, like that they were fabricated—"

"I never saw *Inception*."

Altan was crestfallen, and then: "Wait: *you never saw* Inception? That movie is amazing!"

I swallowed more coffee with a *gulp*. "I swore off Nolan after *The Prestige*. Nothing will top it. I refuse to even entertain the notion that it's possible."

"Holy shit," admired Altan. "Maybe we *are* soul mates."

I laughed weakly. Our minds were gone, but our senses of humor were still intact.

He went on. "So, the song might have been random. *Or*, maybe my subconscious was playing it because I was controlling the dream."

"Or maybe *my* subconscious was playing it because I've always wanted to go to Paris."

"You've never been to Paris?"

"No," I said. "I've never been anywhere." A memory of last night's fight with Pete wafted in and out of my mind like a feather; I didn't even try to snatch it. "Focus."

"Look at me. I'm making a list," Altan said, addressing his notebook. "So we can develop a testing plan for next time."

For next time was the scariest thing I'd heard since *white mocha*. "*What* next time? We can't do this again. *Ever.*" For some reason I looked around in case someone was obviously listening to our conversation. No one was. "We have to tell Diana."

"Tell her what? That we've been illegally stealing experimental medication from work and that we'd like to get fired? Do you know how hard it is to get a job in this town if you're not a 20-year-old MBA holder who likes to work for free?"

"Shit," I whispered under my breath. "We could stop? Pretend it never happened?"

"I can't unsee this," said Altan. "I can't unsee you. Every time I look at you now I get—"

"Shut up," I squeaked for what felt like the fiftieth time that day. "We can't talk like this."

He leveled a glare at me. "I was going to say 'inspired.' Ness: we could change the *world*."

Altan let that sink in while he sipped his coffee, and then he said, "Consider the medical implications of this: what if we could interact with people in their sleep? What about coma victims? What about dream therapy? What about saying goodbye to unconscious loved ones?"

"What about mind control? Dream torture? Mental spying?"

"All breakthroughs have risks. Think about penicillin. The Internet!"

"Skynet," I said. "Jurassic Park."

He clucked his tongue, disgusted by my pessimism, and I leaned forward with my hands on the table. "Altan Young, don't pretend you're not completely full of shit. You don't care about helping people. You care about getting high."

"Why are these mutually exclusive? Can't we get high *while* helping people?"

"We shouldn't," I said. And then the memory of the fight I had with Pete blew back through my mind, and this time I closed a fist around the thought, around all the things I *should* be doing: having babies, telling the truth, being a whole and enlightened person, thrilled with the blessings I had. But how does a woman cope with the yawning disconnect between what she wants and what she's chosen? There had to be a way to eat cake and have it too, to make an eternally regenerating zero-calorie dessert. Maybe Morpheum was it.

Altan felt my hesitation, and he pounced. "Look, you know how good Morpheum feels. Rest, clarity, direction: it's all there in one little pink pill. Who doesn't need this? We have a duty to the world to explore what this drug could do."

I narrowed my eyes at his little inspirational speech. "Or we need to find out if we need to sabotage the trial and bury this pill so far down it never sees the light of day."

"That, too!" he said brightly. "Either way, we have to keep taking it. I can't do it on my own. I took that pill for months, and I never experienced what we had."

He looked at me and raised an eyebrow playfully, and I remembered it all again: his hands on my ass, his bottom lip between my teeth, the sweat and noise and color of our dream. My breath caught, my belly clenched with desire that rapidly gave way to guilt. Now that I knew side effects of Morpheum could include dry mouth, rash, and mild infidelity, where did this extracurricular drug consumption fall on the spectrum of cheating? Probably somewhere between thinking about the cast of *300* when masturbating and texting nudes to strangers, but I wasn't exactly certain—and I sure as hell wasn't going to ask Pete.

Altan looked at me from across the table, and I remembered the intensity of his eyes when we came together, how they seemed to look right into my brain. He fished a Post-It note out of his pocket; it had been folded on itself to create a little pouch, and when he pressed it in my palm, I felt the cylinder of a pill in there. "I need you, Ness," he said. "I need this. I need to feel like I'm doing something extraordinary with my life."

Hadn't I told Pete the same thing last night? "Are you in my brain right now?"

He squinted. "I don't think so. I'm not sure."

I thought about what he did after work and decided it probably wasn't all hanging out in dive bars writing poetry and picking up girls. June had likely taken all the comforts; Altan had compostable flatware and loads of debt and the same crappy job as I did that offered little opportunity to feel useful. We could probably both stand to take a vacation from reality.

"I'm in on one condition," I said, pocketing the pill. "We can't have sex again."

"Aw, man!" said Altan in mock protest, and when I glared at him he held up three fingers. "Fine. Scout's honor. No sex. But you can't blame me for trying." He dropped his voice. "That was the best dream I ever had. Every time I think of it I get—"

"Inspired?" I said.

He looked down and blushed, again! And it was—dare I say it?—sexy to see him flustered. Altan, king of cool, was as hot and bothered as I was about our REM-time rendezvous. A thrill tingled up my spine as I realized I had that power over him. He cleared his throat and looked back up at me, his face breaking into the same grin I'd seen last night in my sleep.

"Something like that," he said.

THURSDAY, JANUARY 3

Finally got my ass on Tinder and went on a starter date with this nondescript girl. I knew I wouldn't like her even when we were chatting online: she isn't remotely funny, and then at dinner she said she'd never seen the original *Star Wars*—but she saw the prequels. Complete deal breaker.

Last night I dreamed of fucking Princess Leia. Possibly related? Then again, who *hasn't* had this dream?

Significant to note that Leia was wearing the green poncho from Endor, not the Jabba the Hut bikini. Because I'm a classy guy.

THE SASQUATCH

Pete texted me just as I was unlocking the door to our apartment. *Working late*, he wrote. *Representatives from some bald billionaire showed up this morning asking what would happen if he divorced his wife. They want ten hypothetical scenarios.*

So I guessed we were pretending we hadn't fought. I threw my keys in the bowl by the door and kicked off my boots as I texted back: *Which bald billionaire? This town has at least five.*

Wouldn't you like to know? He added a smiley face, and I snorted a little. It was so un-lawyerly to use emoji. *Anyway, don't wait up.*

With medication like Morpheum, I wasn't planning on it, but still I said, *OK. Good luck.*

My phone pinged one last time as I set it on the counter to make myself dinner. *I love you,* it read, which was Pete for "I'm sorry we fought, and we'll get it all sorted out soon enough."

And while my anger for him was still coal-hot, I felt the same way. I sent him a kissy-face, and he replied with a thumbs-up. For all their banality, emoji had their uses, like smoothing over a fight that had yet to be reconciled.

In the dream that night I was dressed for hiking: boots, jeans, this flannel jacket I'd had when I was nine years old that I wore *everywhere* because Kurt Cobain had just died and Seattle was taking it hard. I was a full-sized adult as I stood in the dream in a cool, misty forest, but I felt small. Maybe the smell was throwing me back: damp earth, decaying wood, the dark green of chlorophyll mixed with the rain-pregnant ozone of a gray sky. It smelled like Saturdays hiking Deception Pass and my parents' attempts to instill in me an outdoorsiness that didn't stick. I hadn't smelled it in ages.

One of the benefits of having your own dream forest was that there weren't any spiderwebs to walk through. I hiked up a neat trail, enjoying a solitude that I'd never felt anywhere else, mostly because there are few things more private than the human mind: there was no chance of being surprised or interrupted or threatened or contradicted. Before Morpheum, even before the baby nightmares, I'd had this habit of waking up at 3 a.m. sometimes, and rather than go back to sleep I'd stay up all night thinking: about work, life, photography, memories. Sometimes I'd conduct these grand orchestras of fantasy where I was famous or rich. Pete would snore next to me, and I'd lay in bed, imagining. The dream felt like that, the deep peace of dark night when your bed is warm and everyone else is asleep.

I thought of this as I hiked. Massive oak and maple trees towered overhead, reaching toward each other across the path like relatives at a wedding. Their roots snaked thick upon the ground but never in my way. Birds chattered, unseen, and my mind wandered to memories of those weekend hikes with my parents, how my father would always tease me about Sasquatches. How my mother, who had an almost comical fascination with birdcalls, would teach me the names of the specimens we saw. What were they? *California scrub jay*, I thought as a blue bird landed on the branch above me. *Townsend's warbler*, I remembered, and then a small flash of yellow and brown darted across the path. It took me a moment to realize the birds were appearing only after I remembered their names, and

I had this moment, a frightening, wonderful moment, where I suspected I was calling them into existence.

"Bald eagle," I said out loud, and just like that, a huge brown and white bird soared toward me up the trail, right at eye level. "Holy shit," I breathed in disbelief as it came closer—and didn't stop. The joy of discovering magic quickly morphed into terror as I turned to run and plowed smack into a tall, slim figure loping out of the forest.

"Sasquatch!" I screamed, as we both went down into a patch of prehistorically massive ferns, memories of my father's Bigfoot stories fresh in my mind.

"Where?" cried Altan, who had landed on top of me. I'd been so infatuated with my hike that I'd forgotten he'd be here. He pushed himself up on his elbows to scan the surrounding forest—an action that dug his hips poignantly into mine. *Zap.*

"Um, false alarm," I said weakly, and he snapped his head down to commandeer my gaze with his, his face close enough to mine that a lock of his hair swept against my forehead. Thankfully there wasn't an actual Sasquatch to grapple with, because we were powerless to move. Altan's eyes glazed over like a doughnut.

God, I loved his cheekbones. *Think about his cheekbones,* I commanded as he shifted his weight so that the front of his jeans rubbed against mine. But I could only remember Paris, and I wanted to go back there. With him. *No.* "Please get off," I whispered.

I felt the words as much as I heard them: that's how close we were. "I wish you'd let me."

It took me a moment to recognize the double entendre in his voice, which was completely devoid of joking. Altan was dead serious as his gaze roved my face, asking me with his brown eyes if I wanted an encore of last night. And I did. Oh god, I did. I wanted an encore and then three curtain calls to boot. He tilted his head so that his mouth hovered above mine, and I swore I could taste him, a memory of a flavor. "Will you?" he asked, his lips brushing my own so slightly, not quite accidentally. "Let me?"

It took every ounce of strength I had to shake my head.

"Bummer," Altan whispered, letting his eyes drop to my lips one last time. And then in one swift movement he leapt to his feet and stood over me, offering a hand to help me up.

I didn't take it, electing instead to roll awkwardly through the underbrush until I was on all fours, and then I pushed myself up. *Smooth.* "So," I said, dusting off my hands.

Altan had his fists so deep in his jeans pockets that his elbows were locked. "Yup."

The tension between us was still vibrating like a bass guitar string. Every move he made plucked it. I looked at him and took a breath. "This is harder than I thought it would be."

His eyes lit up, and I realized my mistake. *"That's what she said!"* he crowed, pumping his fist in the air at his own cleverness.

And even though I was secretly glad we were back to ribbing each other (instead of rubbing each other, *gulp*), I rolled my eyes because it's what I would have done in the office. "Must you always make a joke?"

"Yes," he said genially but without any hint of mischief. He rocked casually back and forth on his heels, his hands re-mashed into his pockets. The bald eagle swooped in a circle above us, and we watched as it landed on a low branch. "I make jokes because I'm insecure."

I blinked at him like an owl. The wind had changed, the air different. "Was *that* a joke?"

"No. I joke so people like me." He turned and glanced at the sky overhead like he was checking the clouds for rain. "When you're the Asian kid, everyone assumes you're a nerd, so I grew up being funny just to be something else."

His earnestness was dumbfounding. "That's like the realest thing you've ever said."

"Right?" He laughed, sounding briefly like thirty percent of his old self. "I don't know why I'm telling you this. I've never had a conversation in a Morpheum dream. It's pretty surreal—like I can say anything I want and it won't feel weird. Want to try?"

I paused to take stock of the mood. The atmosphere felt honest—clean—and I had this desire to blab, like I'd had one too many drinks at a party and was making new friends. "You know how I told you I take pictures?" I found myself saying as we started walking up the trail. It was edged in small, even rocks and carpeted in a layer of springy moss. "Well, I sell them for money in the market. Pete doesn't know." I said this like it wasn't a big deal, and amazingly it didn't feel like one. There was a wetness to the air that made it feel heavy, like it was made of memory foam. The weight of it trembled slightly when I spoke.

Altan cocked his head to one side. "He doesn't know about the money?"

"He doesn't know about any of it. The money. The camera. What I do with my free time."

"Huh," said Altan as he digested this. "Why do you do it?"

In real life I would have had to think about this, but the answer leapt from my lips: "I like keeping secrets. Makes me feel like I'm in control."

"Why do you need to feel that way?"

"Because I never am."

It was crazy, the way we were talking, like we weren't even capable of shame. "Anyway," I said. "Photography is kind of a pretentious hobby. I don't like anyone knowing I have artistic tendencies. I'm surprised I'm even telling you."

"I'm glad you are. I like to know things about you." He took his hands out of his pockets and shook them out a bit, like his fingers were cold. "Sorry, I know I'm acting weird. Everything feels extra real here—even my feelings. It's so gross."

Something about his last sentence vibrated the air. It was subtle, like throwing a lentil into a pond. The sky rippled ever so slightly. "Do you feel that?"

"Yeah," said Altan. "Strange." He craned his head upward to study the branches crisscrossing over our heads again. "I can't believe this is all fake."

"Well, not all of it is fake. This memory is real. I used to go hiking here with my parents."

He walked around the trail, admiring the trees as if I had painted them on a canvas. "So this is your brain . . ." he said, placing his hand on a trunk. "I like it."

No one had ever complimented my mind so plainly before, and I was filled with an almost sexual satisfaction. "Thank you."

"If this is your head, can you control what goes down?"

That's what she said. "What do you mean?"

"Can you make something happen?"

Attempting to comply despite being completely overwhelmed with possibility, I closed my eyes—which was strange because they were already closed in real life—and remembered this time my parents and I saw a bear cub when we were hiking in the Cascades. He was about the size of a beagle, and we only spotted him from a distance, but still Mom and Dad were desperate to hustle me out of there in case the mother showed up. Naturally, I was a complete pain in the ass and refused to leave. I sat down on the ground and wrapped my arms and legs around a sapling because the scene was so damn magical I couldn't bear to leave.

As a compromise, Mom offered me the camera around her neck and allowed me to take a picture of the cub so I could remember that moment forever. For the longest time I had that photo tacked up to my bedroom mirror. It was crappy—I had no sense of framing back then—but it was my first, and I was proud. And I realized standing on the trail, feeling the cool, moist air and hearing Altan breathe beside me, that I'd always been a photographer, even before I knew how to work a camera. Something in me had always craved a way to capture those moments of beauty.

When I opened my eyes, the cub was bounding out from the underbrush. It plopped its front paws on Altan's thighs.

"Aw, *cute!*" gushed Altan as he knelt on the dirt of the trail to dig at the magic spot behind the bear's ears. His was the same reaction I'd had when I was nine, and it was funny to see a grown man be equally smitten with such an adorable, plucky thing. "Did you do that?" he asked me. "Did you make the bear?"

"I think so," I said. It was pretty ballsy to admit out loud that you're capable of magic; I didn't want to be the first to say it. "Maybe I did." The air rippled. Was it because I was lying? "I thought about him, and here he is."

The air was still.

The cub licked Altan's hand and rolled over onto its back so he could scratch its tummy with both hands. "Who's a good boy?" Altan cooed goofily. I knelt next to him and added my hand to the fur, momentarily charmed by his tenderness.

"I never knew you were capable of anything besides sarcasm," I said, knocking my shoulder into his.

"Well," Altan said as he dipped his face to *rub noses* with the bear. "I'm not nearly as heartless as you think I am. I mean, I'm pretty heartless." He looked wistfully up the trail as he said this, as if remembering something that made him sad. I felt a ripple again, and then he smiled half-heartedly. "But not entirely."

And just as I was about to ask him what that meant, a tremendous roar shattered the silence of the forest like an atom bomb. Altan scooped the cub into his arms as we both popped up to standing, his eyes as wide as dinner plates. My mouth went completely dry. "What the hell was that?" Altan said.

The roar exploded again, and we turned to see a blur of fur race toward us through the woods—upright on two legs, though its arms were almost long enough to brush its knees. I gasped, grabbing Altan's arm as we backed up the trail. "Are you doing this?" he stammered.

"No." My heart banged against my ribs like a xylophone.

The blur slowed as it stepped onto the trail. It was ten feet tall and covered in shaggy orangutan fur matted and tangled with leaves. It had a primate's disturbingly human hands: fleshy pads on the palms, and fingernails. Its teeth were pure grizzly, but the facial expression was human—and I'd seen it before. It could best be described as Al Pacino's in *Scarface* right before everyone says hello to his little friend.

There was a brief moment when the whole scene ground to a halt so I could comprehend what was happening. Jesus Christ. It was a Sasquatch. Welcome to the Pacific Northwest.

And then time kicked back in. "Shit, shit, shit!" shouted Altan, turning to break into a run. His sneakers slipped on the leaves, and he went down on one knee, still holding the cub to his heart like a football. I pulled him up by his free hand and we sprinted over the sticks and moss of the trail. The leaves were dry, so we could hear the stomp and crunch of the monster as it pursued, but only when it wasn't roaring, which was never. "Make it stop!" screamed Altan.

"I can't! I don't know how!"

"You're the one who likes to be in control—so control!"

The Sasquatch jerked me up by the scruff of my flannel jacket and held me like a sack of trash, my arms and legs flailing uselessly. Altan glanced over his shoulder, saw I'd been caught, and, still clutching the cub, picked up a fallen pine tree with his free hand, anchoring it into his hip like a jousting lance. It was a gesture so impressive that it occurred to me to admire it even as I was seconds from being torn apart.

"HEY, ASSHOLE!" he shouted. "PUT HER DOWN!"

The Sasquatch rounded on him, dropping me to my feet in the process, and I sprinted for Altan. He hitched his chin to tell me to get behind him, but—*duh*—I was already planning on doing that so I could brace him beneath the weight of his weapon. And maybe also use him as a human shield. Anything was possible in dreams! Did WellCorp know its pill was prone to this level of fucked-uppery?

The Sasquatch snarled, shifting its weight from leg to leg, stymied by Altan's weapon and his little furry hostage. From behind him I got up on my tiptoes so I could hiss into his ear: "Have you heard that urban legend about how if you die in a dream you die in real life?"

"Yes," he said without looking back.

"Do you think it's true?"

"I hope not. Can you remember a dream where you died?"

"I always woke up before."

"Me too," he said grimly. "So fingers crossed."

The cub was struggling to get free, so Altan transferred it to me so he could hold the tree trunk with both hands. As I scooped the bear to my chest, the cub reached his front paws baby-like toward the beast. Understanding landed on me with a *thump*, like a trained hawk. "I think they're friends," I said to Altan.

"Who?" he asked, because he couldn't see.

"The bear and the Bigfoot."

"Shit, really?" He turned to see the cub crying in my arms, and immediately his posture shifted from death-doling to differential. "Hey, sorry, man!" he called to the Sasquatch in his friendliest California-cool way. He let go of the tree with one hand and held it up in a shrug. "We didn't know he was a pal of yours."

The Sasquatch shrieked in response, but Altan remained calm. "How about this: I let the bear go and you let my friend go, and we'll call it even, OK?"

The answer was a deep growl, a Doberman's warning. "How do we know if he agrees?" I asked Altan over his shoulder, cheek-to-cheek with him in the least romantic way possible.

"He's not killing us, so let's take that as a sign." He turned his face slightly toward me, his beard bristly against my cheek. "Now back up fifty feet and let the bear go."

I shook my head side-to-side so he could feel my *No* against his shoulder. "Don't worry," he said. He took a step backward, pushing against me so that I had no choice but to do the same. "You go first. And then I'll follow."

The air was rippling again, this time in warning, and I knew he was lying. "How? When I put this bear down, we'll have no leverage."

"It'll be OK."

"How will that be OK?" I shouted. The Sasquatch roared again, and instinctively I snaked my arm around Altan's waist, wondering if you could fear-crap your pants in a dream.

"Go," said Altan, pushing against me. "He's not waiting much longer."

His stomach was taught beneath his shirt, but as I stared at the Sasquatch over his shoulder, I could only think of how soft and vulnerable the human body was. I turned my head and pressed a kiss into the side of Altan's neck—I wasn't sure why I, and he didn't ask. Maybe it was for luck, maybe as thanks, maybe it was because I cared about him and I didn't want him to die in his own subconscious at the hands of a mythical creature with steak knives for teeth.

I took the cub and backed up the trail slowly, appraising Altan's broad flannel-clad back, the way his feet were planted, how his body meant business. I couldn't see his face, and what was crazy was that I couldn't imagine it either. The Altan I thought I knew was irreverent and mischievous and laid-back to the point of being comatose. And for all I'd speculated about him, it never occurred to me to see him as someone as complex as this. Beneath his affable class-clown façade was someone brave and strong and selfless, someone with insecurities and coping mechanisms—someone human. "Keep going!" he called after about twenty feet; he must have been counting how many times my boots crunched the fallen leaves. "Make sure you're clear!"

"Since when do you care about my well-being?" I asked, my voice shaking with nerves.

"Since always," he said plainly, and I felt the truth of it in the air like an oncoming rain. I didn't know what to do with this—besides hope that when I woke up I'd get the chance to find out.

"OK!" I said. "Putting the cub down now!"

The bear's paws hit the trail, and he scampered merrily toward the Sasquatch like a dog returning to its owner. Briefly I dared to believe we'd all be softened by the sight of his roly-poly butt disappearing into the underbrush. Maybe the Sasquatch would let us live happily ever after and we could all go out for granola? Altan must have hoped so too, because he lowered the tree slowly to the ground in surrender.

"There," he cooed to the Sasquatch, holding his hands up to show he had no weapons. "Your friend is safe. My friend is safe. We cool?"

From my position on the higher ground, I saw the Sasquatch narrow his eyes, as if thinking about whether or not he wanted to forgive us. And then, like a flash, he lunged.

WEDNESDAY, JANUARY 23

Another day, another date—this time with Sarah, a paralegal at Pete's office. He set us up, which was cool of him (he's my lawyer, not a matchmaker) but still she was *meh*. Her nails were suspiciously long, and she had a very complicated manicure. I know that's supposed to be sexy, but I couldn't stop looking at her hands, and not in a good way. How much money does that cost? And who has that kind of time?

And how does she wipe herself?

I thought of June, that week in Australia we thought we were tough enough to shear sheep. Jesus, it was hot. We were filthy. She was picking shit out from under her nails with the tip of her pocketknife before dinner. Now THAT's a woman.

Last night I dreamed I was a veterinarian in charge of declawing the tigers for Siegfried and Roy's newest Las Vegas show. It either means I'm avoiding long-nailed women or I might be considering the gay lifestyle. Honestly, I'd probably have better luck in this neighborhood if I did. On my walk home after the date some guy called me a snack. I guess I'm flattered? Sure. Why not?

THE UBER-DRIVING PROFESSOR

The movement was all at once: the way my eyes flew open, the way my arm flung out, the way I speed-dialed Altan as I sprinted to the door in Pete's flannel shirt, forgetting that I wasn't wearing pants and had no idea where Altan lived. I also didn't know how to resuscitate someone who'd been mentally eviscerated by a Bigfoot, but still I felt this heart-pounding need to do *something* fast. "Hey," Altan answered as I was tugging a boot over a bare foot. "What's up?"

Collapsing forehead first into the door, I let out a long shaky breath. "Oh my god, you're alive. I thought you were dead, are you OK?"

"Yeah." He chuckled. "Why?"

Why? "Because you just got attacked— And I thought that maybe— You said you weren't sure— *Did you know you wouldn't die?*"

"No. I mean, I was, like, ninety percent sure I would be OK, but not a hundred. No." His laugh was tinged with the can't-believe-my-luck giddiness of someone who had been too busy texting to notice the bus before it breezed through the crosswalk just inches from his nose.

I sank down on the arm of Pete's chair. "You— You saved me."

"I did," said Altan. He was quiet for a moment, as if he were trying to pick out the appropriate words from a pile at his feet. "It seems my subconscious is . . . fond of you."

My chemicals were changing: I could feel them bubbling, my heart rearranging itself like a Rubik's cube to accommodate a deeper caring for Altan that I had not known before. "My subconscious is fond of you, too," I confessed. My crush had been innocent, born out of boredom, but now it felt more solid than the gumminess of before.

"Huh." Altan sounded thoughtful.

I pictured him lounging rumpled in the sheets of his bed, which were white because he was too lazy to choose a color. And then I added, lest we started gushing any more than was necessary, "But my regular consciousness still thinks you're a dumbass."

His laugh was low and sexy. "Fair enough," he said. "So I'll see you at work?"

"Yeah. 'Kay. Bye!" I hung up and tipped myself backward into the chair so I wouldn't have to see the grimace/blush combo waiting for me in the mirror above the sofa. Coffeehouse Crush was going to be jealous when he realized I'd gone monosyllabic for another man.

So would Pete, for that matter, assuming we were still married. His shoes were gone from their spot at the door, denoting he'd probably left for work without speaking to me for the second day in a row. I texted him just to prove I was the bigger person. *Hey. You alive?*

I was walking into my building an hour later when he replied. *Barely. Work sucks. Miss you.*

Now that I knew he wasn't intentionally avoiding me, I felt a little softer toward him. *I miss you, too. You going to be home tonight?*

Hopefully! Wanna have dinner? I'll make reservations. Bastille at 7:00?

Sounds good, I typed as I pulled up at the elevator, glancing up to notice Malcolm standing next to me, also messing with his phone. The light from the glass-front lobby was hitting him perfectly, glinting off his fat watch and the sheen of his indigo suit. *Shit.* Malcolm had picked the most inconvenient time to develop a work ethic, now that Altan and I were stealing company property. I pocketed my phone without hitting SEND. "Good morning!" I chirped, hoping he wasn't still sore about my blowing off his lunch invitation yesterday, accusing him of behaving inappropriately, and then storming out like a child/badass—depending whose side you were on.

Malcolm glanced at me and nodded before returning to his phone. He wasn't on my side.

When the elevator arrived, we got in, and I pushed the button for our floor, trying again to be pleasant. "So how's it going?"

"Fine," he said without looking up. The doors slid closed like a trap.

Three floors went by without elaboration. "Is everything OK?"

Malcolm didn't just roll his eyes: he lassoed them around his head like a cartoon cowboy. "You've made it very clear you have no interest in socializing, and you even implied my attempts to make conversation were some kind of seduction, which is not even remotely the case. I'm trying to leave you alone as you asked. So why are you even talking to me?"

"Because I thought we could still be pleasant to each other, even if I don't want your hands on me," I snapped, automatically. "Is that not the case?"

Both his and my eyes grew wild and wide, his in anger and mine in fear. What the hell had just come out of my mouth? The elevator doors opened with a crisp *ding*.

A gray-haired African-American gentleman was standing in our lobby. "You must be Sam Stevens!" I shrieked, thrilled to have a distraction to take the edge off of Malcolm's anger. "Malcolm! This is the gentleman you wanted me to sign up for the trial. Today's his intake interview!"

Sam was whippet thin in the way of people who are taller than they could ever be fat, and he had a slight stoop that suggested he'd spent a lot of his life bending down to talk to people. An angular jaw paired well with brown slacks, a white dress shirt beneath a black V-neck sweater, and a tweed blazer. "I take it you're Vanessa from the email?" he asked, completely unfazed by the fact that I sounded like a cosmetics-counter lady on uppers.

"I sure am!" I took him by the elbow despite his being at least nine inches taller than me and paraded him past the cube farm (Altan wasn't in yet) and Diana's office, where I saw her through the door as she Windexed her rubber plant. I deposited Sam in the conference room and went to the kitchenette to make us each a cup of coffee, thinking Malcolm couldn't confront me if I never sat still. I would keep moving forever, fixing drinks, going to the bathroom, and refilling my pens from the supply closet. I'd do all my work on my phone, in motion. He'd never catch me.

"Make me a coffee, won't you, Nessie?" Malcolm said as he breezed past from out of nowhere. "I'll be in the conference room when you're ready."

"Ready for what?" I asked dumbly.

"Routine performance evaluation." I swear I could see the fog of his voice: that's how cold it suddenly felt. "Just want to make sure you're doing things the WellCorp way."

"Of course," I said, as I thought, *Oh shit*. Malcolm was mad at me for speaking my mind.

"You'll have to forgive how I look," Sam was saying to Malcolm when I arrived with three coffees, having lost the courage to spit in Malcolm's. "My wife did all the laundry. She ironed everything, even my underwear. But she died last year, and now I look like an unmade bed."

Malcolm had a vein in his temple that was threatening to burst. He sat cross-legged across from Sam with his hand cupping his mouth, every muscle tensed, like he was wishing his father had installed windows in our dinky little office so he'd have something to jump out of. Clearly, Sam had been talking his ear off since I'd been gone.

"Now, the last time I wore this jacket was probably when I was still teaching," Sam went on, accepting the cup from me with a gracious smile. "I used to be a professor at the University of Washington. Twentieth-century American lit. See the elbow patches?" He put the coffee on the table and rotated his arms inward. "Mary sewed these on so I'd look the part even though we'd bought the jacket new." His laugh was a lipstick of a laugh, the kind designed to fool you into thinking here was someone more beautiful, more confident than he really was.

Usually our patients weren't so forthcoming with personal details, but Sam's chattiness in conjunction with his thinness suggested he was starved for both food and company now that he was a bachelor again. I wanted him to eat. "What was your favorite book to teach?" I asked by way of inserting myself into the monologue. I'd stopped by my desk to get my lab coat so Malcolm wouldn't have anything else to ding me for, and the polyester made a swishing sound as I took a seat.

"*Fahrenheit 451*. Great book. Social commentary, killer robot dog. What's not to love?"

I smiled. "And your least?"

Sam pulled a face. "*The Great Gatsby*. All those rich white men? No thanks." He tilted his head ever-so slightly toward Malcolm, who had dribbled coffee on his silk tie and was trying to wipe it off with a Kleenex.

I buried my smile in my notebook. "I hate that book, too. The writing is beautiful, but it's terrible to women."

"It goes for people as well as books: Beauty does not forgive ignorance," Sam pronounced.

"Who said that?"

"I did. Just now." He took a calm sip of his coffee, and I realized then that I liked Sam, with his tweed jacket and his quick wit. Sure, he talked too much, but what else was I going to do with my day?

"I quit teaching when Mary got sick a few years ago," he went on, as if I'd never interrupted. "She had breast cancer, and she needed a lot of care. Eventually it got her."

At this, he pulled a woman's necklace over his head from beneath his shirt and handed it to me across the table. It was an old-fashioned oval locket with scrollwork on the cover, and inside was a woman's wedding-day portrait. "That's her," he said proudly. "That's my Mary in 1972. She always wore this locket when she was alive, only she had my photo in it, of course. When she died, I considered burying her with it, but in the end I couldn't. It was probably selfish to keep it, but I'm sure she'll forgive me when I see her again. She knows I'm a fool."

"It's beautiful," I said appreciatively. Malcolm sighed in boredom as I handed it back.

"We have a daughter, Maria, probably around your age, just as brilliant as her mother. She works for Microsoft. My whole life is full of smart women!" He laughed again, shaking his head as if remembering a host of charming things now gone, and then he grew serious. "Or it was. Sometimes I forget Mary's not here anymore, you know? I have to remind myself."

Sam looked at his hands and fumbled with his wedding ring a beat longer than a happy person would have. "Anyway, they'd already replaced me at the university by the time she passed, so I started driving an Uber. It's a great job for someone of my fashion sense since people only see me from the back. One of my passengers told me about the drug trials, and here I am."

Malcolm's annoyance as on the verge of overflowing. "How would you say you sleep?" I asked, trying to get the conversation on track for the purposes of my performance evaluation. It was a clunky transition over to the WellCorp intake script, but it served its purpose.

"I don't," Sam said without real complaint. "It's hard to sleep alone. The weight of the bed is off. Sometimes I get all the laundry and pile it up next to me under the covers to try and fool myself into thinking someone's there. But it doesn't do the trick, and it's probably why all my clothes are wrinkled." The man had a never-ending supply of laughter that made you want to cry.

Funny: Altan had said the same thing about when he and June broke up. I thought of Pete, how I hadn't seen him in two nights. I'd forgotten to miss him, with all the excitement of the Morpheum, and it caught up to me as I flipped through the paperwork Sam had sent in. "I see you don't take any medications. Do you drink or do recreational drugs?"

"Can't afford it—mentally or financially."

"Would you say you're in general good health?"

"Despite my broken heart? Fit as a fiddle."

I gave him a half-smile to acknowledge both his joke and his pain. "Well, judging by your medical history I think you're a good candidate, but give me a second to check one last thing."

"Be my guest," said Sam returning to his coffee.

Since Diana was doing nothing but polishing her plants, I thought it would be good to get her opinion on Sam in case there was any concern about his being so lonely. But as I left the conference room for her office, I heard Malcolm hiss as he followed me out, closing the door behind him, "What the hell are you doing?"

His tone was sterner than a casual inquiry required, and I turned warily. "I'm not sure we should sign Sam up. He has insomnia and difficulty doing everyday tasks; you heard what he said about the laundry. He might have some underlying depression that could get us in trouble."

Malcolm shook his head. "If he hasn't been diagnosed, I don't see why we wouldn't take him. It's hard to find someone his age who doesn't take a shit-ton of blood pressure meds."

"Even so, I'm not convinced he's completely healthy. What if he becomes addicted?"

"None of the chemicals in Morpheum are habit-forming," he huffed. I was pretty sure he pulled that exact line from the intake script.

"That doesn't mean the drug isn't addictive. If he started dreaming about his wife—"

Malcolm narrowed his eyes. "Why would you assume that?"

Suddenly I was aware that Altan had come in and was watching from his desk. His earbuds were in, but I couldn't hear the tinny bleed of secondhand music. But I could feel the touch of his gaze on my face, and it made me nervous. "I'm not saying he *would* dream about his wife, but I am saying he *could*, and that could wreak havoc on someone already having emotional troubles. Has WellCorp considered this kind of use case?"

Malcolm pulled himself up into full corporate mode. "It's not your job to ask these questions. Your job is to sign people up and pass out pills. It doesn't require a lot of thought."

My mouth opened and closed wordlessly, like a hand puppet. There's a fine line between cocky and dicky, and Malcolm was definitely overstepping it. But hadn't he always? When was the last time I'd been valued for anything I brought to the table professionally? Now that I'd established myself as someone unwilling to fawn over him, I held zero value.

Malcolm stepped toward me in his suede oxfords. They were the shoes of a man who went between cars and garages, who never set foot in the rain. "WellCorp doesn't need people who have to ask permission to do things. WellCorp needs people who can make decisions on the spot—who don't get distracted by *what if* and can focus on *what is*. And *what is* is this guy is fine to sign. So, Ness, make a decision: is he in or out?"

The moment had a whiff of the Always Be Closing scene from *Glengarry Glen Ross*, with Malcolm playing Alec Baldwin's role in his nice suit and expensive haircut and big stupid watch and his casual cruelty. I half expected him to throw the office coffeepot away, claiming it was for closers only, and I felt the panic of someone cornered. "Why are you trying to push this guy through? You're never here. You don't know the pill like the rest of us do."

Malcolm ignored this. "If you can't make a decision, I need to find someone who can."

A lot was wrong with this situation, and I would have been completely within my rights to walk away. But I didn't. Maybe I was wrong about Morpheum. Maybe I *was* too focused on the hypothetical. Maybe Sam wouldn't dream of his wife and fall into a depression so deep he'd kill himself. Or at least that's what I told myself as I dropped my eyes to the floor. I said, "In."

Malcolm patted my shoulder, and I tried not to flinch at his touch. "Good girl," he said. "Now finish up the paperwork, fix Sam his meds, and get him out of here. If I have to hear about his dead wife for one more second, I'll lose my mind."

"Right away," I said, as Malcolm let himself into Diana's office. I went behind him to fetch the Morpheum starter kit from one of her cabinets. It contained four pills and a color brochure featuring stock photos of strategically lit women sleeping with their hands beneath one cheek, pressed together as if in prayer. I petted the fuzzy leaves of her African violet as I hurried back to the conference room.

It only took another ten minutes to fill out the paperwork and schedule Sam's next interview, at which I'd give him more pills, but he chatted for another thirty after that. I didn't rush him for a second.

TUESDAY, FEBRUARY 12

John J. dropped out of the trial today after two months. He's practically the only born-again Christian in Seattle, and he came in this morning livid that he'd been having nothing but sex dreams for the past week. Said we were putting them in his head on purpose because we did "the devil's work."

I was going to pocket his pills until I realized I'd accidentally switched him to placebos at his last interview; must have reached for the wrong bottle when he came in for his refill. So joke's on him.

Fucking pervert.

THE DIVORCE STORY

After work, Altan and I trudged up Pine to his apartment, so he could dispense three weeks' worth of pilfered Morpheum to me for our cockamamie extracurricular experiment. His building catered to grad students and the recently divorced with microunit holding pens barely larger than parking spots. The building was surprisingly close to mine. "You didn't know?" Altan asked, punching the code on the keypad of his building's front door. "Pete and I used to meet nearby for beers to discuss my case. He always picked up the tab. He's a good lawyer."

"I had no idea," I said, following him in, trying to picture my actual husband and my work husband engaging in any kind of meaningful social way. It was too mind-bending. "Pete's pretty good at that lawyer-client confidentiality thing."

"There's a lot you two don't tell each other." Altan didn't say this judgmentally, but more as an observation. I chewed on it as we climbed two flights of stairs and navigated a straight hall with carpet the exact gray color of the walls.

"Do you think that's a bad thing?" I asked.

"I am not the person to ask about relationships," he replied, unlocking his apartment and throwing open the door. "If I were good at marriage, I wouldn't be living here."

Altan's third-floor "efficiency" studio betrayed just how much he'd sacrificed in the divorce. All the furniture was IKEA—and not even acceptably plush upholstered IKEA, but the hard stuff. In the living room was one POÄNG armchair and a square MALM end table bearing a battered Mac laptop that presumably doubled as a television. There was a small bathroom along the wall opposite the front door, and beside it a ladder that led to a crawl space where I was afraid to imagine Altan sleeping because it was slightly pathetic.

But beneath the shabby bachelor feel of Altan's apartment was the musk of his dudeness. There were no throw pillows or lap blankets or scented soaps by the kitchen sink; no art deco posters hung in oversize frames. He had some photos duct-taped to what I guessed would be his living room wall, but other than that everything was unadorned, utilitarian—exactly how he liked it. I was charmed. Sure, I'd seen the inside of Altan's mind, but the inside of his apartment was equally intriguing in that it brooked zero bullshit.

The breakfast bar bore evidence of a last-minute morning: a red Solo cup and a crumb-strewn compostable paper plate that Altan hastened to dispose of as he swept into the kitchen. "Want a beer?" he asked, as he threw his keys on the gray Formica countertop and crossed to the waist-high refrigerator.

"Nice digs," I said sarcastically, grimacing at a pair of boxer briefs that had taken up residence beneath one of the barstools at the breakfast bar.

Altan shrugged, handing me an IPA. "I wasn't planning on staying long, but it'll do. And the ladies *love* it. Who doesn't appreciate a grown man in a modern-day dorm room? If having to climb a ladder to have sex doesn't turn them on, the half-size fridge certainly gets them going."

"I'm surprised you have room for beer."

"That's all I have room for," he said, smiling. "Now spin around so you don't see where I hide my Morpheum stash."

I rolled my eyes as I pulled from the beer and turned my back to the counter. "How many places could you keep it, in this closet?"

"You of all people should appreciate the joy of having a secret," I heard him say.

I wandered over to where Altan had taped up his photographs—landscapes mostly, with a few recognizable landmarks thrown in. There was Altan, holding up the Leaning Tower of Pisa in perspective. Here he was in a selfie, backpacking through a jungle. A gondola in Venice. Angkor Wat, recognizable to me only from magazines. "Did you take these?" I asked, barely raising my voice to call over my shoulder.

He was banging around the kitchen—presumably to distract me. "Most of them. You're the photographer. Are they any good?"

"Not really," I said, taking another gulp of beer. "The locations are nice, but your composition is crap."

Predictably, he was unflappable in the face of insult. "Well, you'll have to give me some pointers before my next trip."

One of the photos at the top had been taped facing the wall. "Why is this one backwards?" I asked, lifting it like a flap so I could see Altan grinning with a woman on a deserted beach. "Is that June?"

I heard Altan say, "Mmm."

"And so you, what, only look at this one when you're feeling masochistic?"

"Something like that," he admitted without shame.

I studied the photo and tried not to notice how good Altan looked shirtless. He wasn't grotesquely muscular, which I didn't mind: men big enough to kill me just weren't my type. But he was lean in the way of surfers, with well-defined biceps and a tight set of abs. Sure, I'd seen his body in the dream, but I was shocked to see it matched real life. Equally intriguing was the look in his eyes as he mugged for the camera alongside June. He looked like a man in love, having the time of his life. I'd never seen him look like that.

"We met in Thailand," Altan said over the sound of his opening and shutting more cabinets. "I was bumming around as a surf instructor after college, and she was teaching English. We hit it off right away. She's so brave and funny—up for anything. And we just kind of stuck together."

I heard the plinking of pills hitting something metal, like rain on a tin roof, and he went on: "We went everywhere: lots of Asia, Morocco for a bit—doing odd jobs, dodging visas, living in shitty apartments. Sometimes we just camped. It didn't matter. She just felt like home, you know?"

I did know. It was the way I'd felt about Pete when we first met: that solidness, that assurance of only needing one particular beating heart to make my day. "We got married in Italy, this nowhere town," said Altan. He'd stopped moving, presumably lost in his own thoughts. I continued to face the wall, picturing the warm cobblestones of his wedding day, the ochre of the old buildings. "Neither of us is Catholic, and I'm pretty sure the priest was drunk. We used to joke it didn't count, but when we went to get divorced, we found out the hard way: it counted."

I didn't dare turn around. "So what happened?"

Altan's voice strained to sound casual. "She turned thirty and decided she wanted 2.6 babies, the white picket fence, the whole domestic life. So we came back to the States. She got a job at

Amazon for the maternity leave, and I got the gig at WellCorp. We bought this tiny—I mean *tiny*—house in Ballard just as the property boom was warming up, and there we were: with a mortgage and matching nine-to-fives, eating takeout from countries we'd been to in real life. It all felt . . . like a photocopy. Or something."

He trailed off again. "*And?*" I goaded.

Altan sighed. "I got bored."

"You got *bored?*" I repeated flatly to the wall. "What are you, thirty-five?"

"Thirty-four, thank you very much. And yes, I got bored. It's hard to explain. WellCorp kills me, and I hate staying in one spot. I get itchy."

I snorted to myself, but Altan didn't hear me. Granted, I also wanted to travel and not have kids, but it was revolutionary when a woman had wanderlust. When a man did, it was typical. "So I left her in Ballard. Gave her the house and promised never to set foot over the bridge."

This explanation felt a little too simplistic, since it didn't account for why Altan had taken the divorce hard enough to warrant sleeping pills, but everyone needed their secrets, so I didn't push. "If you're so itchy then why are you still in Seattle?" I asked.

"I have to pay her alimony until she gets remarried, which won't be long, because she's brilliant and she wants kids. And when she does, I'm going to burn this furniture, pack up my backpack, and get gone. You can turn around now."

The idea of facing a workday without Altan to smirk at suddenly hit me with a pang of grief. I tried not to think about that as I returned to the kitchen in three steps. There were two Altoid tins placed on the counter—one peppermint, one wintergreen. Altan held out his hands palms-up as he intoned ceremoniously, "Do you choose the red or the blue?"

Oh, Jesus. More pop culture references. "It's been forever since I've seen *The Matrix,*" I confessed. "Which one am I supposed to pick?"

Altan returned to his normal voice. "I mean, they both have thirty Morpheum in there, so it really doesn't matter. But for the record, the red pill is supposed to tell you the truth and the blue pill will show you comforting lies."

"I can't handle the truth," I said, selecting the blue wintergreen tin as I congratulated myself on a successful movie quote.

Droned Altan: "You chose . . . wisely."

Indiana Jones and the Last Crusade. "How many film references can you make in one conversation?"

He looked up and to one side the way he did when he was calculating the cleverest comeback. "Forty-two."

"*The Hitchhiker's Guide to the Galaxy* is a book."

"That they *turned into* a movie," he said triumphantly. "So it counts!"

There was something attractive about this game Altan and I played, a friskiness in trying to one-up the other in every conversation. I changed the subject since I couldn't seem to win this round. "So what's the plan for tonight?"

He pulled the Moleskine notebook out of his back pocket, opening it to a page splashed with his chicken scratch. "Well, I think we've made a few important discoveries. First, we know that someone dictates the setting of the dream, but we don't know how. We've also established that the dream won't kill you in real life, which is good! What else do we need to know?"

"Oh, golly," I said sarcastically, spreading my fingers on one hand to count off. "How does the pill work chemically? How do you establish a connection with a person? Then how do you break it? Are there deeper mind-control possibilities? Is this the end of privacy as we know it? Can I magic things out of thin air like I'm at Hogwarts?"

"Slow down!" complained Altan, hunched over his notebook. He had the tip of his tongue sandwiched between his front teeth as he wrote, repeating out loud, "How. Does. It. Work."

"Is that seriously all you got?"

"No." He looked up to grin. "I got most of it."

Sometimes Altan's playfulness was attractive, and sometimes it got on my nerves. This was one of the latter times. "Hey, if we're going to do this together, I need you to take this seriously," I said. "We're risking a lot here: our jobs, our health." *My marriage.*

"It sounds so un-fun when you put it that way," he mock pouted, and then he fanned the pages of his Moleskine so I could see that three-quarters of it was filled with notes. "But rest assured, I take this seriously."

And I knew he did. I looked around and saw just how much he needed this experiment, what with his broken heart and his cheap furniture, the present he was dying to dodge until his life got better. I lifted my nose a bit to peer into the notebook. "Are you sure you didn't just write 'All work and no drugs make Altan a dull boy'?"

He cracked a smile. "A book *and* a movie reference! Ten points for Ravenclaw!"

We spent the rest of the afternoon hunched over Altan's counter solidifying the experiment, developing a list of questions we could attempt to answer, ignoring the sheer terror we'd experienced the night before in the hope that we might have better, Sasquatch-free luck in future endeavors. I was hoping that once we'd figured out how the drug worked, we could force the reaction in one of our patients and spill the beans to HQ without incriminating ourselves. That was *if* the experiment proved that the dream-share capabilities of Morpheum were harmless. If it turned out Morpheum could be used for evil . . . "What would we do then?" I asked. "Tell the FDA? Call the *New York Times*?"

Altan held up a finger to silence me. "What's that noise?"

I held still and heard the faint buzzing of my phone, lodged deep in my backpack, simultaneously registering that Altan's microwave clock read 7:14. "Shit," I hissed, plunking down my third beer and scampering to my bag to fish my phone out. "Hello? Pete?"

"Hi, Bug! I'm at Bastille and they're about to let our table go. Are you close?"

I blinked at Altan across the kitchen. The lie was as smooth as yogurt. "I'm home," I said.

"What? Why?" asked Pete's tinny voice. In the background were the sounds of couples on date night: ice tinkling in glasses, low murmurs. "Didn't you get my text?"

"What text?" Why was I lying? Was it because I didn't want to admit that I'd forgotten my husband as I stood drinking in another man's kitchen?

"I texted you this morning. I made reservations for us at Bastille."

"You did? Oh my god! I didn't see it. I'm so sorry!" I put my hand over my mouth in faux shock to sell the lie, even though Pete couldn't see. "Well, shit! Should I come there, or—"

"I think it's too late. The hostess is giving me dagger eyes."

Speaking of dagger eyes, Altan was narrowing his gaze at me from across the breakfast bar. He pulled from his beer suspiciously while I said, "Oh, drat." The hokiness of the swear didn't sound convincing.

"We could go somewhere else?" Pete suggested.

I should have said yes, but I was tired after dealing with the discoveries of the week—ironic, considering I'd been sleeping great. Still, the thought of dealing with crowds and noise was unappealing, not to mention having to make up with Pete (we still hadn't properly reconciled from the baby fight), which would require more emotion and drama. Frankly, I just wanted to take my Morpheum and get into bed and dream about some other reality, even if it might contain a Bigfoot. "Actually, I feel like I'm coming down with something—some kind of cold. I'm just going to go to bed. Is that OK?"

"Sure," said Pete, though he didn't sound totally convinced. "I'm pretty hungry, though, so I might grab something out here and meet you home."

Turning away from Altan, I covered the receiver with my hand, like that would prevent him from hearing me as I spoke five feet from where he was sitting. "OK, Worm. I'm really sorry."

"It's fine. I'll see you soon."

Altan pounced the moment I hung up. "*Worm?*" he said, his voice laced with mockery.

"He's Bookworm," I said tersely, pretending I wasn't embarrassed. "I'm Shutterbug."

"Aww," cooed Altan. "That's adorable. So why did you lie to Worm? Would he not approve of you being in another man's house un-chaperoned?" He followed this with a deep pull from his beer.

"Not if he knew what you could do with a croissant."

Altan spat beer in a fine mist, his eyes huge and brilliant. Our repartee had always been the slightest bit flirtatious, but now it felt to me as if the banter was replacing the sex we couldn't have, and there was triumph in making him conversationally . . . come, as it were—with a pun, with a thought, with something he hadn't expected that left him blushing and panting and speechless. His laughter, once he'd stopped choking on his beer, was thunderous, and I thrilled to have made him feel so good.

"Anyway, thanks for these," I said once he'd calmed down, shaking the mint tin full of pills as I grabbed my backpack and headed for the door. I wanted to quit while I was ahead, to breeze out of there and leave Altan with my taste in his mouth.

He wiped his chin on the hem of his T-shirt as he followed me to the door, still chuckling at my joke. "I'll see if I can get my hands on some more—in case we need to keep going. Good thing I told my patient Nina today that the Merck trial pays so much more."

I gawked at him in his doorway. "Have *you* been tipping off our patients about Merck so they turn in their medication?"

Altan lifted one shoulder coyly.

"You may have screwed our entire trial," I said, not unimpressed.

"Well, maybe it needs to be screwed. We'll find out in the next three weeks how safe this drug really is. And in the meantime?" He opened his tin, put a pink pill on his pink tongue, and washed it down with a swig of beer. "I'll see you soon."

I shook my head as I left, completely in awe of how Altan got away with being so cool. When I got home, my apartment was empty and quiet. I brushed my teeth, crawled into bed, dry swallowed a Morpheum, and switched out the light just as Pete opened the front door. "Bug?" he called quietly into our darkened bedroom. "Are you asleep?"

But before I could answer, I was.

WEDNESDAY, FEBRUARY 20

Been thinking about Molly Q.—not in any kind of sexy way but just wondering how she's doing, if her arm healed up OK. Sent her a text just to say hi, and she said she was doing well. Thought about asking her out for coffee but don't want to complicate her life. She just left an abusive boyfriend. Last thing she needs is me giving her a complex.

So I called up Sarah from Pete's office—the one with the nails. We went out for tacos and took a walk around the Hill. She's fine. I mean, she's better than sitting at home alone all night.

We bumped into Pete. He was out with some lawyer friends, and he seemed good. Mentioned he and Ness were thinking of starting a family soon. Strange—she hasn't mentioned that at work. Not that we're very close or anything, but we do chat a lot.

I felt jealous of Pete as I was walking Sarah home: he had that steadiness that people have when their lives are certain. I used to have that. Now I have nothing but these weird Tinder women and this hutch I call an apartment. Meanwhile, Pete has most of my money and a future with a woman he loves. And Ness *is* pretty cool: she's funny as hell. June used to laugh. We both did. Things were better then.

Dreamed about the day I got married and woke up feeling hungover, but that's probably not the pill's fault. That's just my life.

THE KASBAH

"Altan?" I coughed through a midday haze of dust. The air was dry and beige, and it was like breathing bread crumbs as I pattered around a narrow dirt street guttered on either side by market stalls, barrels of dates and pistachios, and storefront windows choked with gold bracelets. Woven rugs hung everywhere like bunting. "ALTAN!" I shouted, as a nearby mosque started up its call to prayer, revving into action like a World War II-era siren. "Where are you?"

"Here," he said, materializing out of the dust in his customary jeans and flannel, both fitted to his lean frame. He was eating a handful of dates, spitting the pits into the dirt like he didn't give a shit who cleaned them up, because it was a dream and no one would need to.

"Where are we?" I said, craning my face to shout above the noise.

"Marrakesh." He finished the last of the fruit and took my hand, but something about him was off-balance. He looked grim. The street was clotted with bodies, people shouting and haggling and gossiping in Arabic or Berber. "This must be my memory. June and I came here the year we got married."

Recalling the story of their impossibly romantic whirlwind courtship, I said, "Let me guess: you made love on that orange cart by moonlight after you saved her from getting mugged by a carpet salesman."

Altan helped himself to an orange as we passed, and when he spoke his voice was flat. "You're going to feel like an asshole when I tell you. She had a miscarriage on that trip. The hospital we went to is up the block. I recognize the street."

I stopped short in the road, pulling his arm so he could face me. Another motorbike slowed next to us, idling loudly so its owner could admire some persimmons. I shouted over the sputtering, "Altan, I'm sorry. I shouldn't have—"

"It's OK," he said, a little more somber than his usual self. "We'd just found out—"

He waved his hand and the roar of the scene dialed down as easily as if he'd punched the volume button. "We'd just found out she was pregnant the night before," he said as he started to peel the orange, dropping bits of rind in the dirt. "It was a shock, to say the least, but we were excited. Even though the baby meant the end of our traveling, I was OK with it. It felt like parenting would be its own adventure of sorts." He smiled at the orange, at the memory. Not at me. "We spent all night picking out names, which was stupid. We shouldn't have done that."

His face fell, and suddenly Altan was focused solely on removing the stringy white strands from the outside of the fruit like he was grooming it, monkey-style. "She wasn't very far along, and shit happens."

"But it's still hard," I said, because I knew. And suddenly it all came rushing back to me: the doctor's office, the coldness of the stainless steel—the nurse who'd held my hand as I cried for so many reasons.

"It was, especially for June," He was looking down still, and he sniffed. "She blamed Marrakesh—maybe the water here was contaminated, or she ate some bad lamb. Maybe she blamed herself. She didn't blame me, even though it was my idea to come here. But I always thought that if we'd gone somewhere else, maybe it would've . . . and then we'd still be . . ."

He was squeezing the fruit so hard that juice was dripping down his wrist into the dust. I took the orange from him and tore it open; he helped himself to a piece, and another, chewing slowly, buying time. When he spoke again, his voice had steadied. "Either way, she wanted to move back to the States after it happened. We tried everything to get pregnant again: pills, shots, IVF, meditation. Nothing stuck, which was crazy because we knew it was possible. But the stress of it all took a toll on her," he said without meeting my eye. "And on me. In the end I couldn't hack it. After two years of trying, I didn't want to try anymore. But she did, so I left."

I felt it then: his conflict and guilt and regret. The emotions rolled off of him and onto me in waves, and I felt what I imagined was exactly how he did when he thought about June. It was awful. "Why didn't you tell me at your apartment?" I asked.

He pulled a section from the orange and offered it to me. "It's too hard to think about, much less articulate, when I'm awake. But in here? The dream takes the edge off the memory slightly—the way you fall out of love with your wife for wanting something more than you. How powerless you feel when you can't give it to her. How much you resent her for being unhappy for so long. It's easier to pretend I'm some wanderlusting travel bug than to fess up to what an asshole I am."

"You're not an asshole," I said. The air refused to wobble as proof.

"Are you sure?"

"The air. It wiggles when you lie. Haven't you noticed?"

"I noticed, but I didn't know why."

I turned to face the street and shouted, "ALTAN YOUNG IS AN ASSHOLE!" at the top of my lungs. No one turned, but the air shivered all around us. "See? Not true."

He tried to look like he wasn't convinced, but I thought I saw the corners of his mouth turn up as he started to amble up the street, reaching back to take my hand when I followed. I tried to tell myself this wasn't romantic: after all, the Moroccan men we passed in the market were doing the same thing, per Arabic custom (I'd read that in *National Geographic* once). It was cozy, the idea that friends should hold hands. Why not? But still, when we touched, there was heat between our palms, our fingers interlacing like lovers' legs. It felt more intimate than friendship, maybe even marriage: we were journeying into a heart of starkness, each of us visiting the planet of the other's most unfiltered mind. Not even twins were this close.

We walked along in easy silence, observing the street scene on half mute: the clothing salesmen, the clay tagines, the soup ladles and CDs and other bric-a-brac strewn across bed sheets beneath patio umbrellas. "I was pregnant once," I confessed in that dreamy truth-serum state. Usually panic came to crush me any time I thought about The Baby That Never Was, but this time it was milder than usual—still there, but also on half mute.

"Oh yeah?" asked Altan. "What happened?"

I nudged him with my shoulder as we walked, embarrassed all of a sudden to have brought it up. "I don't want to talk about it."

"Maybe you do. Why else would you have mentioned it?"

He had a point, but still I closed my mouth, refusing to take the bait. Altan pulled my hand toward a sidewalk café, where we helped ourselves to a table. (There were always cafés waiting for you in Morpheum dreams: it was great.) Instantly, a waiter appeared bearing two demitasse cups of coffee on a silver tray, and I wondered if Altan had manifested all of this for my comfort or if it had just happened naturally, coffee being the one thing I always needed. "Fine, don't talk about the baby," he said. "I'll ask questions, and you just nod or shake your head. Alright?"

The sun was bright and warm, and I squinted up at him, wondering if he'd be able to guess what happened, wondering how it would feel to reveal the most agonizing month of my life without having to say anything at all. My head twitched up and down.

"Was the baby planned?"

I took a sip and shook my head no. *Damn*. That coffee was good.

"So I'm guessing it wasn't Pete's, was it?"

I shook my head again.

"Your lover's?"

I slapped him on the shoulder.

"Kidding, kidding. You're too prissy to have a lover."

I rolled my eyes, took another sip of coffee, and pursed my lips closed. Altan smiled, enjoying the game. "Do you know who the father was?"

Everything had been easy-ish until now, and I felt myself go pale as I shook my head again.

"Why do you look scared?"

"You said I didn't have to talk," I whispered.

"Right." Altan took a deep breath. "Did you have an abortion?"

I looked at him hard, trying to see if he had an opinion on the answer. His eyes were deep and brown and uncharacteristically caring in that moment—not a hint of mischief or malice to be found. My chin went up, then down. Just once. And I drew in a ragged, reluctant breath.

He reached for my hand on the table. "Does your aversion to having a baby now have anything to do with what happened then?"

I nodded. A tear snaked down my cheek, and I let it fall—for my almost baby, and for Altan's, and for our dinged-up hearts that were hail-damaged because of them. Jesus, why was I such a mess about this thing that had happened over ten years ago? That I still struggled with it felt like a weakness to me in the waking world, but in here, it felt . . . not right, but also not wrong. It felt appropriate, to feel, to grieve, to experience an emotion the way you eat an exquisite meal, really paying attention to the flavor instead of swallowing it down with a drink.

Altan gave my hand a squeeze. "I don't know exactly what happened, but I'm guessing it wasn't good. If you ever want to tell me the whole story, I'll listen. I won't make a single joke."

I nodded, my throat too thick to speak. I didn't exactly feel *better* now that Altan knew about the baby. But I did feel slightly less alone as we sat there, Altan rubbing his thumb along my knuckles, watching people walk past us while I let my sadness burn itself out like a campfire. And when the grief had petered out for the moment, Altan turned to me. "This is a really depressing dream."

I laughed the watery laugh of people mid-cry and dabbed a napkin to my face. Altan's smile was a half moon, and I felt a softness grow between us, like we were two sides of the same pillow. We spent the rest of the dream sitting quietly, lost in our own thoughts together

Wet dream about Ness in old-timey Paris. Not bad.

In fact, it was fucking fantastic. I didn't know people could have sex like that! I would take Ness over Mila Kunis and Natalie Portman any day.

I wonder if she's like that in real life. She doesn't really seem the type.

Must remember to avoid Pete for a while. Awkward.

THE PIRATE SATURDAY

When I opened my eyes, Pete was reading next to me in bed, propped up against the headboard with a pillow so thin my neck hurt just looking at him. But he was too absorbed in his book to register any discomfort. He chewed a thumbnail and scraped his eyes back and forth over the page. I watched him, wondering what his mind was like on the inside. I imagined it like a clockmaker's studio, all clean machinery and shiny brass, the *zizzing* of flywheels and the tinkling of chimes. I thought of it being cool and orderly, but I couldn't know for sure.

Altan, on the other hand: I'd seen the color of his memory, the dust it kicked up, the tin and tarnish rattling around his skull. I'd felt him. And as I lay there, warming up to the day, I understood with a slight concern that I'd never known Pete the way I now knew Altan. The discovery was like realizing you were using someone else's toothbrush and were now bonded to that person in a way few people were gross enough to try.

"Morning, Bug," Pete said when he caught me staring at him. He put his book down on the bedside table and snuggled close. "I was starting to wonder if you were going to sleep all day."

I smacked my lips together—my throat was dry—and croaked, "What time is it?"

"Ten," said Pete. "You were asleep when I got home last night. Are you feeling OK?"

It took me a moment to remember the lie I'd told at Altan's apartment about the cold, but now it seemed advantageous: the perfect excuse to stay in bed all day. "Now that you mention it, I feel like shit." I coughed dramatically. "Think I'll just lie here for a bit."

"Sure. Can I get you something?" Pete offered. "Tea? Coffee?"

"No thanks. I just want to sleep." It felt weird to be lying to him so soon after the previous night's fib. I'd shirked out of date night because I'd been tired from the week, but what excuse did I have after a full night's sleep? Maybe I'd know when I woke up.

Pete kissed me on the forehead and took his book to the living room, presumably to read all day—or maybe he'd go for a jog or grab a beer with one of his friends this afternoon. That was one thing I loved about Pete: we didn't have to do *everything* together. He was free to play pickup basketball with his work mates, and I was free to experiment with stolen drugs in the company of another man. Our marriage was solid. It was all good.

The bed was soft and warm, the sky outside a dull winter gray. Raindrops dragged snail trails down the windowpanes as I snuggled down, trying to doze off, trying to ignore that buzzing Morpheum energy that was trying to convince me to get out of bed. *Ugh.* The Altoid tin was sitting there on my nightstand, not hurting anyone. As I reached for it, I thought with the semi-guilty indulgence of people who order too much dessert, "Why not?" I deserved a treat.

In the dream I was nowhere; that's the best way to describe it. I stood on an infinite, seamless white space like I'd been drawn on paper. "Altan?" I said. There was a slight echo. "You here?"

He wasn't, so I sat down to wait, and after a half hour, I realized with some disappointment that he must have gotten up for the day. There I was: all drugged up, and no one to dream with. But there was still the noble science of our Morpheum mission to consider, so I picked myself up and walked, trying to think about anything other than how calm I'd felt in Marrakesh when Altan took my hand, how kind his eyes were, how deep his pain. It was unnerving to see him raw and honest, but I liked him like that, and I liked being that with him as well. I liked it so much it felt dangerous.

I walked for a long time trying to see what there was in this nowhere, but there was nothing—like the dream was in neutral: totally blank. *This would go faster if I had a bike*, I thought, and suddenly I was atop one of those elegant Dutch machines with chrome trim and a wide basket. I rode through the nothingness before I realized the basket would look better with some tulips, and suddenly there they were. I added a baguette, too, just to be basic.

There had to be an edge somewhere: the possibilities could not be infinite. So I rode and rode through miles of white. And when I tired of white, I changed the color of the room to red, then blue, then a whole damn sunset complete with streaky pink clouds—right before I made a massive full moon against a midnight sky so I could bike across it like in *E.T.* Altan would have been proud of the reference. *Stop thinking about Altan!* It was the one command I couldn't make happen in this world where everything else would.

But even alone, I began to enjoy myself as I focused on the art of bending the dream. It reminded me of this one time Pete had gone on a bachelor's weekend for one of his friends, and I, bored on a Saturday afternoon, found myself at one of those paint-your-own pottery places I'd always equated with women who were too fond of cats. I spent two happy hours working on a coffee mug, first brainstorming ideas for the design, then sketching them on a paper towel before copying onto the mug itself. And then there was the painting, the color mixing, the shading—the application of multiple coats to get everything just right. I was surprised by how much I enjoyed fussing over such an inconsequential thing: the tweaks I made, the perfectly good lines I erased just to redraw them again. Alone in the dream, I felt the same leisurely satisfaction, that warm glow that came from having nothing in particular to accomplish and all the time in the world to accomplish it. And I didn't have to be embarrassed if it came out wrong, because no one would know what I'd done. Here I could create, and no one would see.

In the big space of the white room, I practiced imagining objects into existence, little things at first. My house keys. My backpack, complete with the frayed seam on the right side. I made an exact replica of my camera before I upgraded the lens, and then I made trees to photograph—first a pine, then an oak. Around the trees I made a park within a city. I tried to convince myself it was a no-name place, one I made from scratch. But the longer I worked on it, the harder it became to pretend I wasn't trying to make Paris. Since I'd never been, the setting was limp, like a fallen meringue—nothing like Altan's rendering the first night we dreamed. My version had a hollow feel to it, the shaky, two-dimensional lines of a child's drawing. There were too many poodles being walked by too many ladies in Breton stripes.

When I tapped into a memory, however, everything came alive: the details were vivid and true, like my brain had recorded my entire life and stored every tape. I was able to recreate Coffee Talk with impressive accuracy down to the tangle of Coffeeshop Crush's topknot. I couldn't be positive that everything was 100 percent correct, but it felt real: the hipster-fresh soundtrack, the slightly burnt smell, the shuffling motions of my fellow caffeine addicts. Just for fun, I gave Coffeeshop Crush a haircut—he was still cute.

After sleeping and practicing these skills all day, I woke in the evening and checked my phone. A text from Pete said he'd gone out. One from Altan just said, *Hey.*

I smiled dopily like he'd said something clever or romantic. *What's up?* I typed back.

I was wondering how you were feeling, he said—odd, since he knew I was faking the cold.

Then I remembered what we'd discussed in Marrakesh.

So-so, I wrote. *Thanks for asking.*

Going to bed now. See you soon?

I chewed on a hangnail. Sure, I'd just taken back-to-back Morpheums and slept for twenty-four hours, but Pete wasn't here, so what was the use of being up? I thought of all the slept debt I had incurred in my thirty-ish years: surely, I was due for a catch-up.

Yep, see you soon, I replied trying to shrug off the guilt as I took another pill and felt it grab me like the bottom of a stiff drink.

I put my phone down and closed my eyes—I was on a clipper ship, a wooden one with four masts and countless sails. Beyond the deck a sunset splayed itself across a calm sea, a sailor's delight save for the silhouette of an approaching vessel. I'd never been on this ship before, but my brain was filling in the details (probably stolen from *Pirates of the Caribbean* movies) as lean, sunburnt women around me hauled on ropes and loaded cannons, shouting at each other as they readied the boat for war.

I didn't know why they were fighting or why I was dressed in knickerbockers and a tricorn hat, a saber bouncing along my hip as I crossed the wooden deck barefoot. The approaching vessel sounded its guns, and the sailors around me began to draw their pistols as our boat creaked through a turn and came about so that the two ships were rail to rail.

The frenzied crew poured onto the other boat, swinging on ropes and running across planks of wood, howling death threats and then making good on them. *This is weird,* I thought, thinking I should look for Altan or find someplace calmer to practice my dream-weaving. But the music of it was fantastic, the tympani of the gunshots, the clanging of the daggers. It was my favorite song, I thought, as I ran whooping beside them, bloodlust singing through my veins. I leapt onto the enemy vessel and sprinted through what felt like a real-life video game—everyone was punching, stabbing, swearing, as cannons went *boom* and wood splintered like confetti. A uniformed man came at me with his sword raised overhead. He looked suspiciously like Malcolm, and without thinking I drew my saber and slashed him through the middle. He fell over comically, like a "wounded" soccer player. There was no blood.

I started swinging with gusto then, taking out every man with brass buttons, leaping over their still corpses limp as body pillows. I fought all the way up to the highest deck, where there was an honest-to-god treasure chest looking like Scrooge McDuck's hot tub, filled with rubies the size of apples and emeralds round as limes and coins as bright and big as Hanukkah gelt. Just as I reached it, the fighting stopped, and my scraggly band of pirate women ("me hearties," if you would—and I did) gathered around me and screamed their throats out in jubilation.

I threw ticker tape strands of pearls like the fanciest Mardi Gras; I chucked a beach ball-size amethyst into the crowd and watched as it was passed around giddily like at a music festival. And I felt so . . . satisfied. I hadn't spared a single thought in fretting about whose gold this was or whether or not I deserved it or who I killed to get it and what they did back home. I wanted the treasure, so I took it: nothing had ever been simpler. The glittering weight of it in my hands was delicious.

THURSDAY, MARCH 7

~~Morpheum has mind reading capabilities~~
~~I think maybe I mind melded~~
Don't know how to write this down so I'm just gonna write it down:
Ness also had the Paris dream . . . Like, WTF?
What?
The?
Fuck?

She even mentioned that thing I did with the croissant. I was mortified but so was she, so everything is chill—all things considered.

I'm glossing over a lot of this, but frankly, it's just too fucking crazy to write down.

Yadda yadda yadda: we're now involved in this science experiment to figure out how dangerous this Morpheum side effect is. So we dreamed about each other again last night. We were attacked by a Sasquatch, and I was a total badass. I picked up this tree and was waving it around everywhere. And then I had a standoff with the monster so that Ness could get away, and she was like, "I love you," and I was like, "I know." OK, not really, but I felt heroic. And that was nice considering how hard I screwed June over. Maybe I'm not such a bastard after all.

Not likely, but neither is sharing a consciousness with your coworker.

None of this makes sense.

THE SUNDAY
BRUNCH

The rise and fall of the pirate ship on the ocean melted into the sensation of being gently shaken awake. Pete's voice said softly, "Bug?" I blinked my eyes against the white light streaming through the open curtains of our bedroom. He was sitting on the edge of the bed in the curve my body made when I slept on my side, holding a mug of coffee. "How are you?" he asked, putting his hand to my forehead. "No fever."

"What time is it?" I muttered.

"Sunday morning. Ten a.m. You've slept for thirty-six hours. Are you feeling better?"

"Yeah, I feel better." I stretched my arms over my head. "Must have been one of those, um, thirty-six-hour bugs."

Pete gave a half smile. "I was worried you were avoiding me because of the fight we had a few nights ago."

"Mad enough to sleep for an entire Saturday?" I tilted my head, like the thought *had* crossed my mind, and Pete's half smile graduated to a full one.

He said, "We still haven't made up officially. Can I take you out to brunch?"

I looked at the Altoid tin on my nightstand. How bad of an idea would it be to take another Morpheum? Bad, I decided. Probably very bad. Still, I bit my bottom lip guiltily and looked up at Pete. "I kinda wanna go back to bed."

He put the coffee cup down on my nightstand and took my hands to pull me to standing. I only protested a little. "Come on. Put on some clothes and let's get you a pile of bacon."

"Fine. But only leisurewear. I'm not putting on anything with buttons."

"All the easier to undress you later." Pete cocked his eyebrow as he shimmied backwards out of the room, and even I had to admit in all my unwarranted poutiness that he was cute when he got excited about taking me to brunch. I felt sheepish for sleeping through half a weekend, but how else was I supposed to miss him if we were always together? Absence makes the heart grow fonder— or at least that's what I'd been told.

I pulled on some sweatpants and a clean T-shirt, looking fashionably disheveled in the mirror. God bless Seattle for its complete lack of fashion sense. I brushed my teeth for the first time in two days as I checked my phone. The texts from Altan had come in at all hours of the night. *Where are you?*

I can't find you.

It sucks here by myself.

I miss you.

I felt a smile creep across my face and checked to make sure Pete was occupied in the living room. Altan Young was pining for me. Of course, what did it matter? It's not like we were going to run off together. But part of me still felt a small thrill of triumph, like I had leveled up in his esteem. Like I had power over him.

"Bug! You ready?" called Pete from the living room. "We're going to have to wait forever unless we get going."

"Coming!" I called back, stuffing my phone in my pocket as my stomach shrieked. It was then that I realized I hadn't eaten since Friday.

Pete and I went to breakfast at some hip spot in Cap Hill that would close in six months: it was only a block or so from Altan's place. The waitress led us to a table by the window—the best spot for watching hungover people stumble home—and as we waited for our waffle flights over ridiculously large coffees, Pete prattled on about the Billionaire X case. Of course, he couldn't tell me the true identity of Billionaire X, but he felt like he was allowed to gossip about the houses involved as long as he kept his voice low. "The bathroom fixtures in the master suite are all palladium," he said. "The faucets, the cabinet handles. We had to appraise those as a separate asset from the residence. Isn't that insane?"

"Totally," I said, one eye on the window as I caught a flash of plaid. I wasn't *trying* to look for Altan, but I couldn't help but double take any time someone looking like him came near—stupid when you factored how many fit, flannel-wearing guys live in Cap Hill. Why hadn't we seen each other in the dream? How did one create the Morpheum connection in the first place? I pondered as I watched Pete's mouth move. Maybe there was a proximity issue we hadn't accounted for: maybe we had to see each other in order for the Morpheum to work. Or maybe—

Pete's mouth had stopped moving.

"What was that?" I said.

"I said you seem distracted."

"Oh!" I blushed, realizing I'd completely zoned out and lacked a plausible excuse for doing so. "I had this crazy dream last night. I was a pirate. Can't stop thinking about it."

"Ooh! Did you have an eye patch?" said Pete the Irrepressibly Playful.

"Don't think so. The depth perception was too good," I replied thoughtfully. "Anyway, I was on this boat with my crew. And we attacked this other boat to search for treasure. And I was just—" Here I looked up to make sure Pete was paying attention, and he was, because he was the loveliest kind of man, the kind who would sit through someone else crapping on about their dreams. "I was just stabbing all these guys. Left and right. Slicing them in half. It felt *amazing.*"

"I knew it," Pete said, slapping the table with his palm. "I knew it was a matter of time before you snapped. Slaying people in your sleep."

"It's creepy, right?" I laughed along with him. "But it was so real and it felt so *good* to want something, and then to just . . . take it." My pulse quickened slightly from the memory: the lack of resistance when sword met stomach, the cheering of the throng, the weight of the opals as I threw them like baseballs. "Take the shit out of it. And kill everyone who disagrees."

Pete frowned. "Are you sure you're still not mad at me?"

I snorted. "I mean, kinda, but not enough to stab you."

"Oh. Well, that's a relief." He reached for my hand across the table. Briefly, I was reminded of Altan in Marrakesh. "Are we talking about babies yet?"

"*Please,*" I groaned. "I'm about to eat."

He sniffed a laugh. "You can't outrun me forever."

Here I took my hand back and sighed.

Why hadn't I just stayed in bed? Dreams were infinitely better than reality, I thought sulkily. In dreams there was no awkward dodging of subjects, no guilt twisting my guts. Hell, in the dream I wouldn't even be waiting for my waffle flight: I'd be chilling on a syrup sea using a pancake as a flotation device, and I'd be thrilled. The waking world felt dissatisfactory by comparison—sluggish and dull. Especially this moment, sitting across from my husband trying to avoid the baby-pink elephant in the room. I set my coffee mug down on the table with some authority and wiped my mouth on the napkin. "OK," I said. "Let's get this over with. You want to have kids?"

"Yes," said Pete. He was shifting into lawyer mode, suddenly all business. "Do you?"

I shifted into business mode, too, so it was easier to say, "I'm not sure."

"Why not?"

"Do I have to justify it?"

"I'd like you to. So I can understand."

"So you can understand or so you can change my mind?"

"Both," said Pete. He didn't smile, so he wasn't kidding.

"See, that's the problem," I said, motioning for more coffee from the waitress. "I don't want my mind changed. My mind is very happy where it's at."

"Your mind is happy not knowing what it wants?"

"It has to be."

"What does that mean?"

"It means—" I began, but I didn't know how to finish, how to explain that I had a hard time believing in what I wanted, because that night in college had crystalized for me in a very poignant way that what I wanted mattered very little to the world. My life forked at that point, and I went down a road paved with the truth that my safety and comfort were not as important as three drunk guys' pleasure. But I always wondered what would have happened had I not been assaulted, had my life been defined by the maxim that what I said actually went. Somewhere in another dimension there was a parallel Ness living that life. She was a travel photographer. She had long hair. She knew what she wanted, and I was left to want what she knew.

"Do you want to know why I want to have kids?" Pete asked once he realized I had no intention of picking up where I'd trailed off.

"Because it's all the rage?"

"You with the jokes," he said, dropping the lawyer act and reclaiming my hand across the table. He held it for a moment in his own as if it were a baby bird, as if it were infinitely fascinating and full of answers. "I want to have a baby *because* of your jokes. I want to make something with you—to collaborate on a masterpiece. It's just that I . . ." He was groping for words, and finally he bent his head and kissed my knuckles like I was the pope. "I love you so much," he said, and looked into my eyes with such intensity that I caught my breath. "I love you so much that I need to divert it into other people. There needs to be more of you. That's why I want to have kids."

Is it possible to sprain a heart? It felt like I had. It felt like my heart had leapt so high to hear this but flubbed the landing, and now it lay painfully in my chest, stuttering, stunned. "I love you, too," I said, looking into his clear blue eyes so he'd know I meant every word. "I love you so much. But having a baby will not create more of me. It will cut me in half."

"But you don't *know* that," Pete said.

"And neither do you. So why do we trust your intuition over mine, especially when I have more to lose?"

The waitress arrived with our waffles, and we were quiet as she placed the plates and poured more coffee, embarrassed to have been caught so obviously arguing in public. For a minute or two we did that thing couples do where they perform normal tasks a little more forcefully than usual to demonstrate they were having a fight. I set the syrup pitcher down louder than was necessary, and Pete sliced his food so hard the knife made an awful screech on his plate.

The waffles were delicious, though. So at least we had that.

After a minute, Pete put his knife and fork down with a clatter. "What do you call it when couples go on a trip before they have kids?"

"A baby-moon?"

"Yeah, we should go on one of those," he said, picking up his cutlery again. "I know you want to travel, so let's plan a trip. The catch is: we are not allowed to talk about having kids until we go. We can reflect on what we want, and then make a final discussion on vacation. Does that sound good?"

Was this a trick? That sounded *perfect*. "Can we call it a maybe-moon?" I asked.

Pete snorted. "Sure. Do you want to know where I think we should go?"

"Where?" I was practically salivating over the prospect of a trip—but maybe that was the hunger. I hacked off a slab of waffle and stuffed it in my mouth to make sure.

"I think we should go to . . . Quebec."

The waffle tried to claw its way back up my throat. "*Canada?*" I choked.

"They speak French! And the architecture is beautiful. You can wander around taking pictures, like you want. We'll eat poutine. We'll drink wine. We'll make love to accordion music." (More choking, as I remembered the Paris dream.) "Does that sound good?"

Hot coffee is not the best liquid to wash down a respiratory obstruction, but it works in a pinch. I kept drinking just to buy me some time. I knew Pete was trying to make me happy, but Canada wasn't going to cut it—especially when I had five thousand dollars in my closet that could take us somewhere better but no way to justify its existence.

"I know it's not Paris," said Pete, reading my reaction; he sounded hurt. "I know you're disappointed. And I'm sorry I haven't made your life more adventurous. But I'm trying to give us a little getaway without completely wiping out our nest egg. So, will it do for now?"

The look in his eyes was a sword to my stomach. Jesus, what was wrong with me? How could I make him feel like he'd failed? Pete was the man of my dreams—someone who worked tirelessly to make me happy. I was *lucky* to have him and his willingness to compromise, his steadfastness in these grown-up waters where all I wanted to do was squander our money and his love. And for the first time I wanted to change my mind for him, or at least try. He was giving me what I wanted: a trip and some space to think. The least I could do was entertain giving him something in return. Not that I would have a baby against my will, but maybe I could work a little harder to warm myself up to the idea instead of dismissing it outright based only on one night that I didn't like to remember.

"Ness? Please say something."

"It's a great idea," I said, putting the empty coffee mug down. "But let's do Vancouver instead so we can drive. Then you can afford to take me to two fancy dinners instead of one."

"Deal," he said as he sawed through more waffles. "You know, I went to Vancouver in high school for some chess competition. I remember it being cool. There was this botanical garden, and—"

Just then I saw Altan loping up the street through the window. I recognized his gait before I realized it was him: he had this hands-in-pockets, hunched-forward swagger that gave him a slight lean, like he was always walking into the wind. Judging by the duffel bag slung over his shoulder, he was coming from the gym, which might have explained why he was facing the cold with nothing more than a hoodie and a watchman's cap. Naturally, he was wearing sunglasses; he pulled them down his nose when he caught my eye through the window and jerked his chin up in greeting as he passed.

It was so brief and meaningless, just two friends recognizing each other out in the wild, but my pulse quickened ever-so-slightly. Pete didn't notice the exchange; he was too busy talking and eating his breakfast. But I realized that if Altan and I dreamed of each other tonight, maybe my theory about visual recognition forming the Morpheum connection would turn out to be correct. The thought of solving the mystery produced a kind of thrill that Vancouver couldn't touch, and even that excitement paled against the idea of spending another night alone with Altan.

FRIDAY, MARCH 8

Open Questions: Brainstorm with Ness

How does the pill work chemically?

How do you establish a connection with a person? Then how do you break it?

Are there deeper mind-control possibilities?

Is this the end of privacy as we know it?

Can I magic things out of thin air like I'm at Hogwarts?

Additional questions:

How real are the things you feel in the dream?

Have Ness and I gone crazy?

Is this dangerous?

What do we do if this is dangerous?

What are we doing?

Can she read my mind? Does she know how much I think about her?

THE
ONE ON ONE

Monday dawned groggily with more texts from Altan that had come in throughout the night. *WTF? Where are you? Are you even asleep? I can't find you.* And then finally, at 5 a.m., *Screw it. Meet me at Coffee Talk. 8:30. We need to figure this out.*

What we needed to figure out was why we weren't connecting in our sleep. Last night I'd dreamed about the white room again *sans* Altan, and while I waited for him to arrive I started baking. And by "baking" I mean magicking desserts out of thin air like Martha Stewart crossed with Hermione Granger, cakes complete with intricately detailed frosting and fondant that didn't taste like ass. Naturally, I had to photograph them, and somehow the plot of the dream overwrote my ability to control it until I was an Instagram celebrity with my own line of pastry bags. After a long and circuitous career as an Internet darling, the dream ended incongruously with my accepting an Oscar for directing a biopic about Arnold Schwarzenegger. When I woke, I was almost glad Altan had been a no-show so he didn't have to witness how dumb it had all turned out.

Pete was putting his tie on while I lay in bed trying to remember who had played Maria Shriver in my dream movie. "You getting up?" he asked. "You hit snooze seven times."

"I'm up, I'm up," I grumbled.

"Prove it. Put your feet on the floor."

I hauled myself up to sitting long enough to kiss him goodbye, and then I collapsed backward so that I was staring at the ceiling, wondering why I felt hungover when I hadn't even drunk. The alarm on my phone went off. I hit snooze.

At 8:45 I was stumbling into Coffee Talk fifteen minutes late, but as soon as I arrived I realized I'd still beaten Altan, which was annoying. Even when I chose to be cool and carelessly tardy, I could never be as cool and carelessly tardy as he. After ordering two Americanos, I grabbed a table by the window, just as he showed up in his sunglasses. He was wearing black skinny jeans and a green plaid button-down left open over a gray T-shirt. A black knit cap completed his disheveled ensemble. "So," he said, dropping into a chair across from me and claiming one of the cups. "Any discoveries?"

Shamefully, my face broke into a grin for no reason other than that he had appeared; this habit was getting embarrassing. "Really? That's how you greet me?" I teased. "No 'How are you?' 'What did you do this weekend?'"

"I know what you did this weekend. I saw you at brunch." Despite this brusqueness, there was warmth to having him around, a comfort in the predictableness of our banter. Apropos of nothing, he grinned at me over his coffee, like he felt it too. "Why are you smiling?"

"Dunno," I said goofily. The air felt spiked all of a sudden— like the dream in real life. "Why are *you* smiling?"

He pulled his cap off his head, embarrassed; his hair was plastered unfashionably to his forehead until he ruffled it with one hand so that it resumed its normal bird's nest. "I guess I'm happy to see you. I thought about you this weekend."

I re-crossed my legs and leaned forward; subconsciously, my fingers found their way to the collar of my shirt. "Oh yeah?"

Altan was radiating excitement, his hands spread in front of him so he could mimic the art of building a scene. "I was creating landscapes from memory, and I'm getting pretty good at it. But the trick of it is that sometimes a story starts forming—like what happened with the Sasquatch. As long you can keep from getting sucked in too far, you can control everything."

"So how do you do that?"

He waited a beat to build anticipation. "I put the coffee maker next to my bed."

I stared at him like he was crazy. "You're joking."

"No. I set the coffee to brew around an hour after I take the Morpheum. The smell is enough to pull me out of the dream, just a little bit, so that I can keep directing." He leaned back in his chair, smug in his own cleverness. "Anyway, I thought of you, since you like coffee so much."

The scene came to me unbidden: Altan's loft; me—naked, sex-sweaty, and rumpled in his white sheets, as he poured me a cup of postcoital coffee from his nightstand. "You thought of me in bed?" I said before I could register how flirty this was.

"I think we've established that," he replied, his voice low.

Our usual acerbic banter was changing flavor profiles; things were getting spicy. "If you get a girlfriend, she's going to think your loft coffeepot is very weird." I said this to establish the fact that he was supposed to be actively searching for a new partner.

Stretching his arms overhead cockily, Altan yawned. "Good thing that won't be a problem."

I took greater note of this than was probably appropriate, while he pulled his notebook and pen from his back pocket. He cleared his throat—twice. "So, we still don't know how to make the connection. Is it safe to assume it's proximity-based, considering we only dream when we're together during the day?"

"I think that's fine," I said. It was good to talk science. Hypotheses. Chemical reactions. "Though we can probably rule out visual cues, because we saw each other yesterday through the restaurant window and couldn't find each other last night."

"Think it's audible?" he asked, scribbling notes. "Maybe I can call you next Saturday to test since we won't see each other on the weekend. I'd suggest we do it sooner but I'm not sure either of us should risk taking a sick day with Malcolm hanging around."

Ugh. I'd almost forgotten about Malcolm. "Think he'll be here this week?"

"Of course," said Altan. "Why wouldn't he start regularly showing up the minute we start stealing pills?"

The thought of having to spend the day in the office with our boss made me want to throw up. Why couldn't he just go back to sailing the Mediterranean where he belonged? "Think he's still pissed about what I said last week?"

"Oh yeah. You definitely misread the memo." Altan stood with his coffee cup. I did the same, following him to the front door. "Malcolm wants you to *blow* him; not blow him *off*."

"That's a good joke. I'd laugh, but it's too true."

"I know that. That's why I'm not laughing either." Altan pulled open the door and propped it with his foot so I could pass through.

Outside, the gray was oppressive, the sky was stacked so thick with clouds it felt claustrophobic, like a ceiling on the verge of collapse.

I had just finished with a patient and was updating my files when Malcolm landed his pinstriped ass on the corner of my desk with a thud like an albatross falling out of the sky. "Can I see you in the conference room? It's about your performance review."

I caught Altan's eye over the cube wall and tried not to make a sound like *gulp*. "OK," I said. "When?"

"Now."

"Right now?"

"Yes."

"Um . . ."

"Great," said Malcolm, putting his hand on my shoulder to steady himself as he stood up. The casualness of his contact was supposed to be fatherly, or like that of a coach who likes to swat his players on the ass for some reason. I could tell it was designed to not arouse suspicion, but the question remained: why did he keep touching me after I'd specifically asked him to stop?

I followed him to the conference room, where he took the seat at the head of the table, forcing me to sit to his right, like I was valuable. "About your intake interview with Sam last week," he began, leaning back in his chair. "I've been talking to Diana, and she seems to think we shouldn't have signed him up for the trial. His case is too risky."

I blinked at him, unbelieving. "That's exactly what I said to you last week."

"Well, then why did you sign him?"

Quickly I pinched the back of my hand under the table to make sure I wasn't caught in some kind of stress nightmare. Nothing changed. "Because you told me to."

"*No.* I told you to make a decision, and you made the wrong one. You need to take accountability for that."

Even in my shock, the middle schooler in me flipped through files and files of retorts trying to find the one that would appropriately convey what a butthead I thought Malcolm was, but the adult professional in me came up empty-handed. There was no point in arguing about Sam when we weren't really arguing about Sam. Still, damage control was needed: that much was clear.

"Anyway," Malcolm said, "since he's so risky, I want to make sure our interactions with him are by the book moving forward. No corner cutting or ad-libbing like you do, and for god's sake don't chat with him all day about whatever it is he does in his free time. You don't have to ask him about his favorite book, OK? It could skew the results."

I addressed my hands on the table when I said, "Of course."

"Your little stunts could cost us the trial. Stick to the script and our interview protocols; they're there so you don't screw up with something unapproved."

"I understand. I promise to work on it."

But he wasn't appeased. "Well, you'd better, because this drug is too important to have to shelve because you were too flighty to follow the rules."

With that I looked up. "Are you upset about what I said the other day?"

Smiles don't usually have a scent, but this one did. Malcolm's smelled like the Styrofoam tray of a raw chicken breast that's been sitting in the trash too long. "Why would you think that?"

"Because you're coming down pretty hard on me for asking a patient about a book."

"I'm coming down hard on you because your performance is crap."

This stung, even though I didn't want it to. Part of me was usually so ready to admit I'd done something wrong, but I was unshakably sure I was in the right when it came to Sam. I'd done hundreds of intake interview since starting my work with WellCorp, and while I didn't always go by the book, I'd yet to make a bad decision when it came to accepting or denying a patient access to our drugs. Still, I refolded my hands on the table and parted my gritted teeth to say, "Regardless of my performance issues, I owe you an apology."

Malcolm nodded as if this was acceptable. "Go on."

How could I word this without completely letting him win? "I'm sorry for being harsh when I declined your lunch invitation. It was rude."

"I was just trying to be friendly, you know," he sniffed. "I only want to get to know my staff better. Find out what you like to do, what makes you tick."

What color my underwear is, I supplied in my mind. *How low I'm willing to stoop for my job.* I lowered my eyes, trying to look modest, confused. "Why don't you ask Altan to lunch?"

Malcolm snorted. He made a lot of noises with his nose. "That's because Altan is a slacker and not long for this job. All he does is crack jokes and take coffee breaks."

"He's good with the patients, though. They trust him."

Malcolm uncrossed his legs and leaned forward over the corner of the conference room table. I fought the instinct to push my chair back. "But I don't. I think he's up to something."

My face, like my mind, was blank. "I'm not sure what you mean," I replied, convincingly, I hoped.

He settled back in his seat and chuckled, like he didn't believe me but was willing not to give me a hard time about it—for now. "Tell me a secret, Nessie," he said. "What's something about you that no one else knows?"

I'm stealing medication from work. I've had mental sexual relations with my colleague. I'm terrified of you. "I take pictures," I confessed. "In my free time." Boy, I was really bringing that up a lot.

"A photography hobby!" Malcolm said brightly, and then he wrinkled his nose. "Cute."

I bristled. "Not a hobby. I sell my photos in the market."

"Well, obviously not enough to quit your day job," he sneered.

This response was the very reason I didn't tell people about my photography: I didn't want it demeaned or taken as less-than-serious, when I was already forced to downplay it in my mind and in my life. Of course, I wasn't Ansel Adams or Annie Leibowitz. But that didn't mean I was totally without merit. It also didn't mean I was "cute" for knowing that. "No one can afford to quit their day job in this town," I countered.

He smiled with perfect teeth that probably cost more than all the cars I would ever buy in my lifetime. "I can afford to do anything."

"How kind of you to remind us all the time," I snapped.

It was official: I had definitely gotten too used to the truth serum of the dreams, but saying what was on my mind for once just felt so damn *good.* Clearly, Malcolm disagreed. His expression went hard, like he couldn't stand anyone not kissing his ass for more than a second.

"Let me remind you of something else, then." He leaned even more forward, and I jumped a little in my seat as I felt his hand on my knee. "I am in a unique position to make things happen. I can make them happen *for* you or I can make them happen *to* you. It all depends on how you play your cards"—his hand squeezed—"if you catch my drift."

My heart was a bird trying to fly through a cage. My fear was a Gatorade cooler of ice being poured over the winning Super Bowl coach. All my middle-school comebacks withered and died where they grew. This was a power play that I was powerless to stop, and for some reason I thought of Altan, sitting just outside. I remembered the Sasquatch dream and how he said he liked my brain, but what use was it to me if I could be so easily turned to stone? *Think, Ness! Do something!*

I did nothing. Malcolm's hand was warm through the denim, and his thumb pressed a little harder than his other fingers. I managed to whisper, "Are we done here?"

He nodded, his eyes sharp and cold as icicles.

I stood up and walked to the door, hoping my knees wouldn't give way.

SATURDAY, MARCH 9

Dreamed about Marrakesh again last night, only this time Ness was with me. It was nice to be there with her—to talk about what had happened. It made me feel better, which is sappy, I know. But true.

Turns out poor Ness had to get an abortion when she was in college. Not sure she took it well, since she seemed pretty banged up about it. Not like I can judge: I was crying like a baby myself.

In terms of what this means to my wish-fulfillment theory, I guess the dream is trying to tell us we need to come to terms with our pasts? Necessary, but heavy. Kind of miss the sex dreams, but I'm glad I'm dealing with my issues.

Just hope Ness is, too.

THE
NIGHTCRAWLER

I was waiting for Altan that night in the white room, busying myself with this magic camera I'd concocted that showed scenes through the viewfinder so I wouldn't have to make a full landscape. In effect, it was nothing but a glorified View-Master, one of those red binocular-looking toys with the discs of film, but it was enough to keep me occupied as I waited, imagining what the world looked like outside of Washington state.

Eventually Altan popped into the room next to me, his hands in his pockets, sunglasses on. He looked even more casual than he usually did, as if he were trying to be cool about being happy to see me. I knew because I was trying to do the same. "'Sup?" he said.

I hitched my chin up a little to acknowledge his greeting without spending a word. "You doing OK?" Altan asked as I rose from my chair.

This was an interesting question, considering I'd had to throw my jeans in the washing machine the minute I got home to get Malcolm's fingerprints off the knee, and then I'd gone straight to bed at six. I didn't wait for Pete to come home. I just wanted to be somewhere where I could think about something other than the weight of my boss's palm.

"Fine," I said. The air around us shivered just a bit to absorb the lie.

Altan furrowed his eyebrows. "Why don't I believe you?"

I didn't want to talk about Malcolm. I wanted to forget about Malcolm. What was the point of having these fantastic drugs if you used them up worrying about regular things like you weren't asleep at all? Besides, I wanted to see what Altan had learned over the weekend. "Got the coffee on?"

His face split into a wide smile, and he rubbed his chin. "Nah. You have my undivided attention tonight."

I tried not to recognize that we were flirting, even as I wondered what he wore to bed. "Alright, hot stuff. So show me what you got."

Altan's coolness slid off him like an avalanche. "Wh— what?" he stammered before recovering sheepishly. "Oh! The landscapes! Of course." He shook his head as if to clear it. "I thought you meant . . . never mind."

I arched an eyebrow as he put two fingers to his temple like Professor X. For a moment nothing happened, and then the white room began to vibrate as if there were a washing machine above us. Suddenly, a hole opened up in the ceiling, and through it poured a liquid green like paint, except it was all shades of green at once, hunter and kelly and olive and lime. It pooled around our feet and began to organize itself until we were standing on a terraced mountain looking up at a tremendous stone peak. The air was crisp, and small wisps of cheerful white clouds drifted overhead, all of it electrified beneath a brilliant summer sun that felt close enough to touch. I squinted, recognizing the scene from *National Geographic*. "Is this—"

"Machu Picchu?" finished Altan. "Fuck yeah, it is!"

He ripped off his shirt and whipped it over his head in a disgraceful frat-bro move that I would have truly frowned upon if I wasn't too busy trying to confirm that his abs in the dream matched his abs from the photo in his apartment. (They did.) "Machu fucking Picchu!" he whooped, going apeshit. "I did it!"

"But how?" I called after him, floored as I bent to touch the grass; it was as real as my hiking dream, but intentional. I'd only managed to make places like decoupage, putting pictures of things in the white room. I'd never conjured a UNESCO World Heritage Site from scratch.

"You have to concentrate really hard to change the scene. Picture it in your mind, and *poof*." Altan was electric. "I got close this weekend, but this is the first time I got all the way."

That's what she said, I thought, as Altan tackled me around the waist and lifted me in a bear hug, running around with me still gripped in his arms. His manic enthusiasm was endearing, if slightly dangerous on a mountain this high.

"Put me down before we go over!" I shrieked, feeling like Fay Wray in *King Kong* (but not totally minding it).

He dropped me onto my feet and spun to face the cliff edge. "Wait! Do you think—?"

He sprang for the void at full tilt. I saw him go over, his arms and legs wind milling before he disappeared, and I heard myself shout "NO!" as I chased him to the lip and crumpled on all fours to thrust my arm over the side, like I could catch him, like I could bring him back. "ALTAN!" I screamed down a sheer rock face pocked with jagged gray ledges and bird nests. "ALTAN!"

"What?" came his voice from behind me. I turned so violently that I lost my footing and, watching Altan's peering face shrink above the cliff's edge, I fell into the dark, screaming.

I woke up in bed with a start, my heart threatening to trampoline through my sternum. Pete was snoring softly beside me, and the sound was comforting, because it wasn't the wind slicing my ears as

I plummeted off a cliff. I reclaimed some of the covers (a gentleman by day, my husband was a selfish blanket hoarder by night) and settled, slightly shaken, back into my pillow.

When I found Altan again, he was still shirtless on Machu Picchu, flashing in and out of the scene. He'd disappear on one tier of the mountain and then reappear magically another three levels up. "Look at me!" he shouted, a sugar-high child. "I'm Nightcrawler! You know, like in the X-Men?"

He popped up in front of me, scaring me half to death. "You don't have to X-Man-splain to me," I grumbled. "I know who Nightcrawler is."

"Where'd you go anyway?"

"I woke up, after you were dumb enough to sneak up behind me on a cliffside," I said, trying not to be aggravated that he'd been happily learning new skills instead of wondering if I was OK. "Weren't you worried when I went over?"

"Not particularly. I thought you'd Nightcrawl back up—like this!" He flung himself off the cliff and was instantly back where he started.

I narrowed my eyes at him. "How'd you do that?"

"Just imagine yourself where you want to be—and ta-da!"

He resumed popping in and out of the scene. It looked cool as hell, and I was frustrated I couldn't do it—that I was the kid who'd frozen at the top of the slide. He noticed me watching. "Pretend you're not going to die," he said like he ran the punch bowl at Jonestown.

"The trick is to not hit bottom!" he called.

I poked my nose over the cliff edge and looked down to see the topsides of birds, their wings flapping through stringy clouds. I dipped my toe into the air like I was testing the temperature of a swimming pool. And then I put it back on solid ground. "That easy, eh?"

"Sure!" shouted Altan from fifty feet away. "Try it!"

He was all hale and shirtless, panting from excitement and exertion and his own innate bravery. I wanted to be like that, I thought as I squeezed my eyes shut and hopped off the cliff as casually as possible. My mind spun wildly trying to think of another place to be besides smashed into a thousand blobs of goo.

The sheets were hopelessly tangled when I came to.

Now I was *really* scared—not of the cliff but of the possibility that I couldn't change my mind, that I wasn't mentally agile enough to enjoy all that Morpheum (or even life) had to offer. I punched my pillow for comfort and catharsis, wishing I could be as unencumbered as Altan; he had no fear, when it felt like that was all I had. I was sick of it, of having to lug all this terror around with me like a sack of laundry. Every time I had a drink in public, or walked alone in the dark, or had a meeting alone with my boss, or closed my eyes—there was so much fear. How could I reprogram myself to feel safe when I still wasn't convinced that I was?

Don't think about Malcolm, I scolded myself as I settled back into bed, but I did, and my fear of him warred with the Morpheum for a long time. When I finally drifted back to sleep, I found Altan still at Machu Picchu, riding a cloud that was bucking bull-like beneath him as he screeched, "THIS IS AWESOME!" while holding on with one hand.

Cracks were forming in the dry landscape of my fondness for him; my crush was officially in its death throes. "ALTAN, CAN YOU FUCKING HELP ME?" I screamed.

"Sure," he said, chipper as a Boy Scout. The cloud disappeared beneath him, and he dropped to the mountain and landed on his feet. "You just had to ask."

"And put a fucking shirt on. It's distracting."

He snapped his fingers and he was wearing a flannel buttoned all the way up like Billy Bob Thornton in *Sling Blade*. "What's wrong?" he said, suddenly serious. "Are you OK?"

"I'm freaking out," I told him, experiencing that shedding feeling that came with coming clean in the dream. "I'm totally freaking out."

He pulled me into a friendly, reassuring hug. "Hey, it's OK—you just gotta breathe."

But I couldn't breathe. I was gasping like a fish. "I'm. Scared," I gulped into his chest.

"Of heights?" Altan asked.

"No. Of me. Of myself. What if I can't change? What if this is what I am?"

Altan tipped my chin up and put his forehead to mine so he could look me in the eyes, and I felt my crush resuscitate. His hand gripped the back of my neck to steady me. "What you are isn't bad," he said.

"But what if it's not enough? For Pete? For our family?"

"You're freaking out about too many things! *Breathe*, Ness!"

"The air. It's thin."

"Shit." He clutched me to him and as he did his Professor X temple touch Machu Picchu drained below us like he'd flushed a toilet. We were in the white room again. The air felt better, which was funny, because I was asleep and the air hadn't changed at all. *That* was how powerful the mind was: it could trick you into feeling like you were dying even when you weren't, and I hated that I had no control over mine at all.

"Thanks," I said, sitting on the floor, embarrassed to be having panic attacks in my medically induced antidepressant-infused dreams. These were some next-level issues.

Altan took a knee next to me so he could rub a flat hand between my shoulder blades. "I shouldn't have ignored you like that. I got too excited. I should have checked in."

He stood and with his finger drew a circle on the white floor around where I was sitting and another roughly the same size about ten feet away. He went to stand in the opposite one. "You're a photographer, right? So take a picture of this circle with your mind, then close your eyes and look at it. Do you think you can do that?"

I imagined my Nikon, heavy and smooth in my hands. I pretended to bring it to my face, recalled the crosshairs of my viewfinder, the small glass window through which I liked to focus on the world. In my mind I took a picture of where Altan stood, and then I closed my eyes. And when I opened them, he was standing next to me, nodding. There was no grand applause, no fanfare that I'd been able to perform this small trick. Altan's reaction suggested that he knew I could do it all along, and so there was no need to make a big deal out of the fact that I had.

"Now," he said, magicking a box the size of a shipping crate out of thin air and sending it twenty yards across the room. "Do the same thing. Take a picture of the box and then go there."

When I found myself on top of the crate, I shrieked and clapped my hands like Julia Roberts in *Pretty Woman* after Richard Gere tried to chop her fingers off with that jewelry box. Altan was grinning now to see me get it, and he jacked the height of the box until it was as tall as a three-story building. We kept upping the stakes, getting progressively higher and faster, until I was standing on top of what looked like WellCorp's office tower, my toes at the edge.

Altan tilted his ant-like head up. "Just don't hit bottom!" he called.

I took a step off the edge and felt my stomach try to cram itself into my mouth as gravity kicked in with a vengeance. A memory forced itself to the front of my mind: once, in a nightmare, I'd gone skydiving, and just as I thought of it a parachute popped out from behind me and jerked me upward, slowing me so that I had time to aim for the circle and float down to nail a perfect bull's-eye.

The cords and parachute vanished just as Altan ploughed into me, whooping his excitement. He cupped his hands to my face and kissed me then, the joyous, sexless kind of kiss you force on city strangers when wars end. I was laughing when he pulled away, still high on my skydive. "What was that for?" I asked, hoping my blush would pass for excitement.

"You did it!" said Altan, holding me by my shoulders. "You didn't die!"

"But I also didn't Nightcrawl." I groaned as I felt my vertebrae go out of alignment beneath another of Altan's frat-bro bear hugs.

"But you changed your mind!" said Altan. "Do you know how great that is?"

He set me on my feet and opened the ceiling again so the green could pour in all around us. Before it was even done coagulating, Altan was tearing through the terraces of Machu Picchu, his arms open wide. I flew after him as a cocktail of chutzpah and adrenaline coursed through me, but it was the relief that felt the headiest of all: I wasn't saddled with a rusty brain cobwebbed shut with terrifying thoughts. I was capable of reconditioning, of growing. My mind was a house that would allow for sprucing, instead of the teardown I'd feared it was. That was more than I could ever hope to learn from a drug like this—and it was Altan who had shown me, who had taken the time to convince me I could change.

And if I could change this way, in what other ways was I capable of evolving?

I caught up to Altan just as he pulled short at the lip of the cliff. He was shining with excitement, breathless and windswept, his hair a mess from the speed of his flight. Wordlessly he took my hand, and together we went over. I felt his fingers steady and warm through mine, and even though we'd run out of ground, my heart soared instead of fell.

SUNDAY, MARCH 10

Couldn't find Ness in the dreams Saturday or Sunday. Super weird. There must be some kind of event that creates the connection, but I have no idea what. It's not visual because I saw Ness at brunch yesterday morning with Pete but I didn't dream about her last night.

Side note: I miss brunch.

Without Ness around I decided to test my coffeepot theory and was able to make the dream a little less deep so I could reverse-engineer a few concepts. I'm so close to learning how to make a place. The thought of getting out of Seattle, even if it isn't real, is so hot it makes me hard.

I also learned how to throw the dream into gear. Like, there's this white room where everything is in neutral, and that's a space I can experiment in. And when I'm tired of having to plan everything, I can sort of switch the dream to autopilot, and a story will start playing.

Which is how I ended up in Paris with Ness again—only it wasn't her. It was like a hologram of her—like Princess Leia in *A New Hope*. I knew it wasn't the real Ness because she didn't talk. (The real Ness never shuts up, but in a charming way.) She and I were just walking around Montmartre holding hands. No sex, but that's fine. It would have been weird knowing it wasn't really her.

Anyway, I hope we link up tonight, because everything's a bit more fun with her around.

THE MISSING LAB COAT

The alarm was going off for the millionth time, and I smashed a pillow over my head, groaning, "What the hell?" to no one from the cocoon of the bedding, as I recounted all the times I'd woken up last night in my attempt to master the art of being Altan. So much for a good night's sleep.

"You're awake!" I heard Pete say. Peeking out from under the pillow, I watched as he sauntered out of the bathroom in his undershirt and boxers. He'd already showered.

"I feel sick."

"That 36-hour bug again?" he teased. "Can you call in?"

It was tempting, especially given the groping Malcolm had dealt me. But ducking work would only prove that I was afraid—which I was, but I didn't want Malcolm to know because that would just give him leverage. Also, if I called in sick, I wouldn't see Altan.

"I'm not sure I'm sick enough to warrant staying home," I said.

"That's too bad," said Pete as he donned his suit pants. "You look awfully cute in that bed."

When I overhanded my pillow at him like a ninja star, he caught it and tossed it into the bathroom. "Now you *have* to get up."

"That's what you think." I hauled his pillow to my side and buried myself beneath the covers again.

The edge of the bed depressed as Pete sat down; I felt his hand through the blankets as he rubbed my back. "Seriously, though. Is everything OK? I feel like I didn't see you yesterday."

He hadn't, but he didn't know why, and I didn't want to go into it, to answer the questions that would follow *Well, my boss got sexually aggressive and low-key threatened to fire me, so I went to sleep instead of telling you about it.* "Work is wearing me out," I said instead, my voice muffled by the covers. "Having Malcolm in the office is stressful."

"I guess you're not used to having a boss around, right?"

"Something like that."

"Well, let me know if you need anything," said Pete. He kissed my shoulder through the blankets; I could hear the worry in his voice, but to his credit he assumed I was capable of handling my shit.

"I will," I said from beneath the quilt, hoping he was right. I was guilt-sick to be keeping so much from him—the extent of Malcolm's creepiness, the depth of my infatuation with Altan, all those stolen pills—but not enough to stop. Wasn't I entitled to a few secrets here and there? Wasn't fostering the richness of my personal life better than being one of those limp and codependent women that never left the house? *Sure it was*, I justified—and I almost believed it, too. I wasn't doing *anything* wrong! I was developing a hobby. I was spending quality time with a Platonic friend. I was being my own person, and that was completely fine.

"What the hell are you doing?" Altan hissed when I stumbled into the office at 9:20. It wasn't quite the greeting I was expecting. While I knew he and I weren't trading in any kind of suspicious camaraderie at work, still I was hoping for a softness from him after the experience we'd had last night. I thought of his hand in mine as we flew off the cliff, borne on the currents of our mutual excitement. "You're late!" he said.

"For what?" I replied as I set my backpack on my desk.

"Your appointment with Sam."

"That's not until 9:30."

"Are you sure?"

There was worry in his face. Through the window of the conference room, I saw Sam waving his hands as he prattled on to Malcolm, who frowned, banging his pen on the table. I snapped my eyes back to Altan and finally understood his panic. *Shit.*

"Thanks for joining us," said Malcolm seconds later when I flew through the door, apologies nocked like arrows. "We've been waiting."

"I'm so sorry," I said. "I thought we started at 9:30!"

"We were supposed to," replied Sam. "But I was just telling Malcolm here that I've been sleeping so well and getting up at six every morning, so I end up being early everywhere I go. I tried to wait. Ironed my shirt. Tidied up the house. I even made breakfast! Just toast and eggs, but Mary would have been so proud. I haven't had a hot breakfast since she passed on, and—"

Sam's clothing, I noticed, was neater than it had been last week. He'd even put a pink rosebud in the buttonhole of his tweed jacket. "I like your boutonniere," I interrupted, hoping to get him on task— or at least distract Malcolm from my lateness.

Sam looked down to admire it and then straightened his jacket. "Just because my passengers can't see me from the front doesn't mean I don't have to look nice. Besides, I thought I'd dress up for the doctor."

I smiled, playing along. "I'm not a doctor."

"I know, but you still make me feel good." He flashed a megawatt grin.

Malcolm cleared his throat to make his annoyance known. "Let's proceed, shall we?"

I took my seat on Malcolm's side of the table but left an extra chair between us, then turned my full attention to dapper Mr. Stevens and his boutonniere. "So, Sam, how are you feeling?"

"Even better than I'm looking. I feel spruced up! Been having the best sleep of my life!"

I noted this in his file. "Did you take the Morpheum for the first time Friday night?"

"Sure did. And I took it the past three nights as well."

"And how were your dreams?"

"Perfect," he said. "I dreamed about Mary, that we were reading books in our living room on a Saturday afternoon. We used to sit next to each other on the sofa with our feet on the coffee table and hold hands while we read. When she got too weak to hold up a book, I bought her one of those little e-readers so we could still do it. Worked a charm for her for a while. I remember this one time—"

My palms broke into a sweat. Sam had dreamed about his wife—his *dead* wife—on Morpheum. Were they interacting with each other the same way Altan and I could? Was Sam communing across planes of consciousness and into realms we didn't know? "Did she talk to you?" I interrupted.

"I'm sorry. What?" Sam looked confused.

"Was she talking to you? Did she say anything?"

"No, we were just reading, side by side."

"Did she have the e-reader in the dream?"

"No!" said Sam. "She had a *real* book. A *hardback*. Must've weighed a ton. That's how I knew it was a good dream—because she was well."

"Did you recognize the title? Was it a book she'd read before or one you'd never seen?"

Sam chuckled a little, looking embarrassed. "I don't know, Doc. I didn't know I'd be expected to pay that close attention."

"It's OK," I said, trying to make him feel better, trying to calm my own intensity. Maybe the dream Mary was just a hologram, a memory thrown up by Sam's brain, like my bear cub. "And you're sure she didn't talk to you. You two just read books."

Malcolm interrupted with his unctuous chuckle, "Nessie, Nessie." I hated when he called me that. "This isn't an interrogation. This is just a follow-up exam to make sure Mr. Stevens isn't having any new side effects. Let's stick to the script, shall we? Like we discussed."

Sam ignored him. "We didn't talk," he told me, addressing the table. "I would have remembered hearing her voice again."

"Did you consciously try to dream about your wife or do you think it was a fluke?"

Malcolm barked, "Nessie!" But I ignored him. *Let me do my job*, I thought. *Let me control something, even if it's just a conversation.*

"I don't think I dreamed about her on purpose," said Sam conversationally. "I was thinking about her before I went to sleep— I always do—but I don't know if that had anything to do with it. Didn't feel like it anyway."

"Interesting," I said, noting this down. "When you woke up, did you feel happy?" Malcolm unclenched a fraction, since this was in our script.

A cloud passed over Sam's face but disappeared almost immediately. "Well, the mornings are hard, you know, because I have to remember Mary has passed on. But I'm hopeful I'll see her again in the evenings, so I look forward to that. Gives me something to get me through the afternoon rush hour."

"Last question: any side effects?"

"My face hurts from smiling," Sam said with an exaggerated *What can you do?* shrug. "But that's about it."

"Good," I said, smacking the table with my palm. Despite Malcolm's reign of terror, I felt triumphant. I couldn't in any way take credit for any of Morpheum's development, but I was proud to be associated, even in a small way, with something that had the power to make Sam iron. "I'm really glad you're feeling better," I told Sam, and he said, "Me, too."

I closed my notebook. "So, I'll give you two more pills, and we'll see you Friday for your weekend dose, OK?"

"Well, that's the thing," said Sam, rubbing the back of his neck so he wouldn't have to look me in the eye. "I have to go out of town tomorrow, last-minute. Going to visit some old friends in Vancouver. Been meaning to do it since Mary passed but I just couldn't seem to manage. Anyway, I didn't want to miss out on my medication, so I was hoping I could get my pills now."

That's the problem with relief: when some people put a burden down it's impossible to pick it back up. "I'm sorry, Sam, but we can't do that," I said, feeling slightly guilty as I did. I knew I couldn't give him extra pills if I wanted to play by the book, but I was certainly in no position to prevent someone from abusing Morpheum, considering I'd done it and loved every second.

"Oh, well, that's too bad," Sam said as he twisted his wedding ring on his finger. "Because I can't really cancel the trip. I have a client that needs me to drive him up to Vancouver, see, because his car is in the shop. And he's a germophobe: can't stand buses. Only uses Uber—"

"Nessie, why don't you go get Sam a week's worth of medication so he can be on his way?"

I snapped my head toward Malcolm. "What?"

His face was a mask of politesse, but I could sense the undercurrent of his aggravation at just about everything: my tardiness, Sam's chatting, my questioning him. "We don't want to waste Sam's time making him come in here every other day so he can talk our ears off! The man has important things to do!"

"But what about the protocols?" I said, dumbfounded.

"Sam's pretty trustworthy. I think we can rely on him not to overdose, right, Mr. Stevens?"

Malcolm turned to Sam, whose eyes were glinting greedily. "Oh yes," he said. "I promise to do everything to the letter."

I cleared my throat and looked at Malcolm, careful to avoid Sam's eyes. "I don't feel comfortable with this."

"That's why I make the decisions around here," he said icily. "Now off you go."

When I returned with seven pills for Sam, I found him rambling on about this time he went camping with his daughter. Malcolm's angry-looking vein throbbed at his temple, and it struck me that if he wanted to get out of the conference room so badly, he could have gotten the pills himself. But then he couldn't have ordered me to do it, and thus wouldn't have met his daily degradation quota. Maybe his bonus was based on how many times he could make me feel small.

When he saw me reenter, he sprang to his feet. "Here's Nessie now with the pills!" He snatched the packet from me and thrust it into Sam's hands. "Diana!" he called out the conference room door. "Can you escort Mr. Stevens out? Ness and I have to chat."

"Thank you, Doc," Sam said to me as Diana arrived in the doorway.

"We'll see you in a week? Next Tuesday," I said. "Not before."

He offered a mock military salute as he left me alone with Malcolm, who closed the door and said sharply, "Sit."

I sat—away from the table so that my knees were in full view of the windows.

Malcolm eschewed a chair and instead leaned back against the table in front of me in what I'm sure he hoped was a casual, fatherly pose, but in reality put me in eyeline with his crotch—which probably wasn't a mistake. My mind, my body, my whole self tensed like I could brace myself against his bullshit.

"I'm disappointed in your performance," he began in the same tone my dad used when I got caught breaking curfew. "You've been slipping. You were late today. You deviated from the script. You were asking personal questions—after I told you we have to do everything by the book."

While Malcolm had a proven history of giving me grief as boner fuel, suddenly I wondered if he was right: I hadn't been my best self lately. I'd been my laziest self, sure, but I'd been neglecting things that mattered—Pete mostly, but also my job. And maybe it was the guilt that caused me to stammer, "I'm sorry, Malcolm. Really. I've been trying to stick to process—"

"Then where the hell is your lab coat?" he said, raising his voice.

I looked down at my sweater and blanched. "I saw you and Sam in the conference room, and I was in such a hurry to get in here—"

"This is what I'm talking about, Nessie. I used to think you had so much potential, but these days . . ." He trailed off, dripping concern. "Is there anything going on you want to tell me?"

"No!" I said a little too quickly.

Malcolm leaned forward and dropped his voice as if we weren't alone. "Is everything OK between you and Altan? I know we talked last week about how much time you two spend together, but I realized maybe his attention is . . . unwanted."

I pursed my lips together and shook my head. "I wouldn't say it's unwanted. I mean, it's also not *wanted*—it's not like I *want* to

173

spend a lot of time with Altan. You know, because I have work to do. It just . . . happens."

Malcolm sat on the table and spread his knees to drop his laced fingers between them, a different crotch-forward pose. "When was the last time we had a round of drug tests?"

I felt that same sensation I did when I was falling off Machu Picchu, that wild panic that accompanies all your organs trying to climb out through your mouth. "What do you mean—drug tests? Like for cocaine or something?"

"Yeah," mused Malcolm; he rubbed his chin thoughtfully like all of this had just occurred to him. "Or you know—just full panel drug test. Over the counter. Illegal. Morpheum. It would be good to baseline everyone's pharmaceutical profile, in case there are side effects from even handling these drugs."

"Or we could all wear gloves?" I said, knowing how shady this sounded—then realizing we probably should have been wearing gloves all along. Would physical proximity be enough to account for the Morpheum that would light up my drug panel like a menorah?

Malcolm's body went through the motions of laughing, but no sound came out. "You're hiding something."

I only liked having secrets when no one suspected me of having secrets. I looked at the door: I physically itched to go through it, like my skin was crawling off my body and trying to get there without me. "No, I'm not."

He ignored this. "So, do you think we should have some drug tests around here?"

"You're honestly asking me?"

He nodded.

"No, sir," I said, trying to convey health and sobriety. "I think we're all fine."

Malcolm smiled another of his signature stinky smirks, and I couldn't tell if this was the answer he wanted, or if he knew about Altan and me, or if he was just trying to make me uncomfortable because that was his favorite pastime. "Anyway, let me know about Altan. If someone on the WellCorp staff is harassing you, I want to hear about it. Is anyone here harassing you?"

So *that* was the deal Malcolm was offering: my silence for his, for as long as I was willing to play along. What choice did I have but to climb into bed with this arrangement? Considering I was taking liberties with company policy, I didn't want to get into a pissing contest with Malcolm, especially when actual piss could be involved. I could lose my job, I could go to jail.

I looked Malcolm dead in the eye, refusing to flinch. *Don't let him under your skin*, I thought, and I said, "No one is harassing me at all."

"Good," replied Malcolm. "We understand each other."

We understood each other completely.

MONDAY, MARCH 11

Last night's dream was killer. Ness and I were doing parkour on Machu Picchu, and I was going nuts, doing all these crazy tricks. Ness wasn't good at it at all, which is weird since she's practically better than me at everything (except dressing herself).

Out of nowhere, she had a mild panic attack—something about being afraid she couldn't change her mind—and I had to help her calm down. Reminded me so much of June, how she'd get upset every month when she got her period—and I would be all, "Why are you crying? Why do you have feelings?" Like because I didn't understand where she was coming from, I thought I didn't have to care.

But that's not how it works, is it?

Anyway, I was able to tutor Ness in Nightcrawling, and it was nice that she could lean on me for help. Once she got the hang of it, we spent the rest of the night extreme skydiving. She held my hand every time we jumped.

THE SIGNATURE

"So what the hell are we going to do about Malcolm?" Altan said after work.

I'd called an emergency debrief session about our boss's recent interest in both our goings-on and my knees. We were at The Signature, this swanky cocktail bar near our office that featured literary-themed drinks: The Adventures of Huckleberry Finnlandia, Bour-bon the Road, Gin in the Time of Tonic-a. The place reminded me of pictures I'd seen of Hemingway's house in Key West, all light paint and taxidermy antelope heads and neatly organized bookshelves. Very masculine. I wondered why no one ever designed a bar after the Bronte sisters' bedroom.

"I don't know," I said before draining the last of my Oedipus Rex on the Beach. "I don't know how to get him off our backs without getting *on* my back."

Altan snorted. "Gross."

Motioning the bartender over, I ordered a Tequila Misérables despite my normal leeriness around drinking in public. But my Machu Picchu cliff diving episode had taught me that maybe I needed to let go of some of my fears. Besides, I trusted Altan the same way I trusted Pete. One had access to my brain and the other had access to my heart: when you start letting people that close to your favorite organs, you should be fairly certain they will do no harm.

"So what exactly did Malcolm say again?" said Altan, chewing on the straw of his Campari in the Rye. I tried not to fixate on his oral fixation: the workings of his tongue, the angles of his jaw. Oh good! Here was my drink.

"He said I've been slipping because I was late and not wearing the lab coat. Then he asked if you'd been harassing me. And then he—"

"Seriously? All he does is ogle you. Every time you turn around or bend over, he stares at your ass. I mean, I do it too, but at least I have the decency to be discreet."

"—threatened to drug test us."

Altan harpooned his ice with his straw. "Shit."

It shouldn't have scared me, the risk of losing access to this pill I'd been taking for less than a month, but I thought about how bereft I would be if I had to stop. The dreams were fun, of course, but more than that was the feeling that I was doing something important, unprecedented, top secret. In only a week I'd grown addicted to the adventure, and maybe even doing it with Altan. Our little experiment was the zing that made the waking day tasty enough to chew through. Altan must have been contemplating this, too, because he said out of nowhere, "I'd really hate to lose what we have."

It was always safer to err on the side of humor. "You mean a bunch of stolen pills and a risk of developing bedsores?"

His hand lifted from the bar and landed lightly near mine— close enough that if he spread his pinkie it would have made contact with mine. "That too," he said to the bar.

His proximity, the impossibility of our attraction, vibrated from my arm to my heart, my brain, my groin. There was this feeling that

I was going in over my head, that I was being swamped by what we were doing. I felt this thing between Altan and me sucking me down, pulling me toward some gravitational center, and I didn't know whether to be excited or afraid.

Altan laughed out of nowhere just to break the tension. "Are you sure you can't just sleep with him? I mean, not full intercourse. Just a hand job."

"Oh, a hand job? Sure, no problem," I said, making a jerk-off motion to prove I was kidding.

"See? You're a natural. Malcolm will love it."

"I know I do," laughed a voice behind me.

My heart spasmed when I turned around. "Worm!" I said, throwing my arms around Pete's neck, and I felt him stumble back a bit from the force of my greeting. "What are you doing here?"

"Some guys at work decided we needed a break from Billionaire X." Pete motioned to one side of the room, where ten suited men were arranging themselves around a twelve-top. "I sent you a text. Didn't you get it?"

I really had to start keeping better track of my phone. "I didn't, but I'm happy to see you."

"I'm happy to see you standing up! Can't remember the last time that happened." He deposited a quick kiss on my lips before releasing me so he could shake Altan's hand. Considering I'd never seen them together, it was easy to forget they knew one another and had, ostensibly, spent a lot of time talking about Altan's personal life. "Hey, man, how's it going? You still in Cap Hill?" said Pete.

"Yep. Same shitty studio," Altan grumbled—which was unlike him. Not that Altan wasn't disparaging: but when he was, it was usually funny. Now it just sounded . . . sad.

"We should grab a beer sometime," Pete went on. "I've got a lot of free time on my hands now that Ness has decided to take up

Olympic-level napping." He put his arm around my waist and drew me into him, and I wiggled out of his embrace in protest.

"I've been run down too," said Altan, and I was grateful he was fueling my alibi. "Work has been a nightmare."

"Sounds like it. Now *who* are you giving a hand job to?" Pete asked me mischievously.

"No one," I said. There was a slight slur to my voice.

"Our shitty boss," piped up Altan. I widened my eyes at him in alarm, and he shrugged, like he was entitled to butt his nose into my business. "He put his hand on her knee in a meeting."

"*What?*" cried Pete—who then proceeded to freak out and pepper me with approximately seven thousand questions like I knew he would: was I sure? What exactly happened? Could I call HR? Was I in danger?

"Maybe I misunderstood," I said, glaring at Altan and registering how Pete hadn't been this fussed about Malcolm when *I'd* brought him up on Cole Porterhouse night. It was only when *Altan* suggested Malcolm might be moving in on Pete's territory did my husband take note—and that was annoying. Did men even recognize the ways they wrote women off?

Pete raked a hand through the back of his hair, and I wondered if he did that in the courtroom because it made him look so boyish. "Is this the reason you've been acting weird?"

"Yes," I replied, knowing an out when I saw it. "I've just been so anxious about going to work these days. I know but Malcolm will go away again soon—maybe get promoted and taken to HQ if the trial goes well—and then this won't be a problem anymore."

"Ness, this isn't right," said Pete looking to Altan for confirmation, but Altan looked away, suddenly embarrassed to be witnessing a conflict he started.

I took Pete's hand and looked at it in mine. "I know, but I can't afford to lose my job right now: we might need the income, for . . . you know, day care, strollers, things like that."

After the clean conversations I'd been having in my sleep, the mouthfeel of this was disgusting, like a loogie dipped in motor oil. But it only complemented the high-quality tension of the moment: here was Pete, the man of my figurative dreams, face-to-face with Altan, the man of my literal dreams, discussing what to do about my nightmare of a boss—and the push and pull of the three of them was giving me heartburn.

"So I just want to ride it out," I finished. "I can put up with Malcolm for a few more weeks."

"But, Bug, you shouldn't have to—"

"I *know*," I said, leaning on the last word. "I know. But let me handle this, OK? I can take care of myself."

I could tell Pete wasn't convinced, but he squeezed my hand in solidarity and let me have my way. "Fine. But if you want to press charges, I'll do it for cheap."

"You don't do anything for cheap," said Altan to break the tension.

It worked. "Hey, I'm a generous guy!" Pete replied, all smiles, like he was trying to prove everything was alright—or at least would be with another cocktail. "I'll prove it: next round is on me."

"Oh goodie!" I said almost too brightly. I needed something to get the taste of all this nonsense out of my mouth. "Get me a Bloody Mary Shelley. Altan, what'll it be?" But when I turned to ask him, I saw his eyes had dropped to Pete's arm around my waist, and a brief sadness settled into his face before he said, "Actually, I'm going to go home."

Pete stuck his hand out as a way of saying goodbye, like he wanted Altan to go, like he understood. "I guess third-wheeling is the divorced man's nightmare."

"Something like that," Altan admitted with a rueful smile as he gathered up his backpack.

"You know what? I think I'll go home, too," I told Pete. If the swiftness of my changing my mind was suspicious, I didn't notice after two cocktails. I told myself it was perfectly acceptable to go home early with a colleague rather than spend an evening out with my husband whom I'd barely seen in days.

Pete smiled. "Sure thing, Bug." My nickname in front of Altan felt as gross as a dog turd left in the middle of the room. "Let's get an Uber."

"No!" I insisted. "Stay with your work friends. I'm just going to go home and veg out with some HGTV." By that I meant, *Take some sleeping pills and trip balls in my dreams*. "It'll be very boring."

Pete ping-ponged his eyes between me and his coworkers uncertainly. "Are you sure?"

"I'll share an Uber with Altan," I said and squeezed Pete's hand, unwilling to kiss him all of a sudden. "I know how much you hate *Flip or Flop*. It's Tuesday night. Almost Friday. Live a little."

"Ok, love," he said, picking up my backpack and helping me into it like it was a coat. "Feel better, OK? Don't stress about Malcolm too much."

I promised I wouldn't.

In the car, Altan wasn't talking. He was suddenly fascinated by the storefronts and restaurants of Capitol Hill, staring out the window so I could sit there in silence and pay full attention to the guilt ballooning in my stomach like wicked gas.

I shouldn't be doing any of this, I thought: lying, sneaking around, blowing off my husband to take some experimental sleep medication with a colleague. It was bad—very bad—and that I was doing it probably spoke to a very serious flaw in myself that would infect my marriage. But at the same time, I *needed* to do it—to be excited, challenged, terrified, enchanted. I needed a break from the email and the takeout and the "How was your day?" conversations that always ended with a shrug and "Fine." I needed to escape being fine. I *deserved* it, I told myself through the booze. And since I wasn't going on any thrilling trips any time soon, this would have to do.

OK, so this attitude wasn't sustainable, but it also wasn't a problem: in a few weeks, once Altan and I figured out what to do about the trial, we would stop taking the pills. And then I'd go back to being "fine" with Pete, having scratched this itch and come out richer for it.

"You shouldn't lie to him, you know," said Altan like he was reading my mind. He was still looking out the window, and the ghost of his reflection frowned in the glass.

"I know," I said.

And suddenly I realized with dreamlike clarity that I wanted him. Very much. Maybe it was the cocktails and the way they made me understand things I didn't know while sober, but I wanted Altan then—his body, his heart, his hurt. Not forever. Not more than Pete's. But still I wanted to rent him for a night, to fall asleep in his arms, to rake my fingers through his hair and jerk his head backward so I could kiss his mouth. I imagined for a moment how he would taste, the smell of his bed, the sounds he would make—and as we got out of the Uber in front of my building (Altan insisted he make sure I got in safely before walking home) I pictured myself pulling him into my apartment by his shirtfront and fucking him right there where we kept our shoes.

But I didn't. I unlocked the door to my building and said "Goodnight," which was silly since we'd be seeing each other in a little bit—a fact he pointed out as he lingered on the mat, before turning to stalk off to his own bed with that step of his that made my blood boil. Who knew a person could be sexually attracted to a walk? I watched him until he turned the corner, and then I closed the door.

See? I could control myself. And it made me feel better, to know there still were lines I wouldn't cross, to know I wasn't coming completely undone.

I went straight to my apartment and opened a bottle of wine and put on HGTV, like I told Pete I would, so that I hadn't lied to him entirely.

WEDNESDAY, MARCH 13

Ness and I bumped into Pete at drinks after work. Awkward AF. All I could do was think about the Paris dream. Pete had his hands all over her—not in a gross way, but, like, in a husband way. I thought I'd just be jealous of Pete's happiness, but I realized I was jealous he got to be happy with Ness. It made me sick to watch.

What's weird is that when I went to go, Ness insisted on sharing an Uber with me back to the Hill. I dropped her off at her place first. She was acting *super* thirsty on her doormat; wouldn't go inside, kept leaning in to me like she wanted me to kiss her. The scene had prom-night levels of sexual tension. Of course, I wanted to kiss her. Ever since that dream, I've been dying to fuck her from scratch. But that would be wrong I went home and called Sarah With the Nails to see if she wanted to come over. She did. I got laid. It was . . . fine.

No Ness in the dream last night. Maybe she was too drunk to take the Morpheum? Either way, I dreamed I won the lottery. I bought a company that developed an eco-friendly jet that you could fly anywhere. I was designing the prototype, so I could pick all the fixtures. All the upholstery was purple velvet. The faucet handles were palladium. Never even heard of palladium.

Woke up feeling good, until I rolled over and saw Sarah sleeping there. For a moment I thought it was Ness—but then I realized it wasn't. And *then* I realized I was broke and hungover and late for work and in no way close to being able to travel the world in a private eco-friendly jet. It was slightly depressing. Sometimes Morpheum does more harm than good.

THE HANGOVER, PART 1

I didn't "wake up" as much as I "came to": still on the couch, still in my work clothes. My phone on the coffee table read 4:30 when I touched the screen, illuminating the bottle of wine, which was now empty. Pete must have turned the TV off at the same time he tucked a blanket around me to make sure I wouldn't get cold. Wrapping the throw around my shoulders like a cloak, I stumbled back to the bedroom. Pete was facing my side of the bed, and when I hit the mattress, he automatically reached for me in his sleep. In the half-drunk stupor of the almost-morning, it felt like returning to the good warmth of home after a wacky trip. With Pete's arms around me, his breath soft against my neck, I went out like a light.

I hadn't moved when the alarm went off two hours later. "Hit the snooze," I groaned, pulling Pete back into bed when he tried to get up. He didn't fight me.

"How are you feeling?" he asked, pulling me close. "You were asleep on the couch when I got home. Did you drink that whole bottle of wine by yourself?"

"Don't remember. But my headache says 'probably.'"

"Aww, Bug," he said, like I had the flu—like I hadn't done this to myself. "It's OK. You're allowed to have a night off from consciousness." He kissed my forehead, which rattled in my brain like a gong, and I loved him for not making me feel worse than I already did. "I'm so sorry you're having a hard time at work. We need to get away. Have you given any more thought to when we'll go to Vancouver?"

Honestly? I hadn't thought about much besides avoiding Malcolm and what Altan would really be like in bed. "No. Not yet. Even though everyone knows Vancouver is for lovers."

"It will be once we're there," said Pete. He rolled on top of me, supporting his weight with his arms, and kissed my neck.

"What are you doing?" I groaned.

"Trying to seduce you. Is it working?"

Despite my terrible hangover, I felt my mouth slide into a smile. "Not really."

"Then by all means. Tell me how to improve." I felt his fingers creeping up the hem of my shirt. "I'm open to feedback."

"Worm, I can't. I feel like death, and I don't want to have sex until we figure out the baby."

"Fine. No baby. I don't want one," Pete said, trying to peel my shirt up. "Now bring me those gorgeous breasts of yours."

I squealed, pulling the shirt down. "It's not that easy."

Pete was wearing his loose, easy grin. I envied him that, that it took so little to make him happy. "I know, Bug. I was joking." He kissed me one last time and clambered out from under the covers to dress. The moment he was gone, I realized I wanted him back, that I needed to remember his weight, his warmth, the feel of his hands—because I was getting dangerously close to forgetting. It was too late, though; I'd missed my chance. Pete was already in the bathroom brushing his teeth. I hauled myself out of bed, lurching as I caught myself on the nightstand, waiting for the room to stop spinning. When it didn't, I stumbled for the bathroom anyway.

Altan was at his desk when I arrived at work with two giant Americanos from Coffee Talk—both for me. He had his earbuds in, and he didn't take them out (or even wave hello) when I sat down, to which I thought, *Well, good morning to you, too.* I was checking my email when my messenger app blinked on. *Where were you last night?* Altan had written.

I fell asleep before I could take aspirin, I wrote back. Fell asleep. Passed out. Same thing.

Not surprised, wrote Altan. *You were wasted.*

My hands hovered over the keyboard as every improbable fantasy I'd entertained came flooding back to me in Technicolor. Did I mention any of them? Out loud? *What did I say?*

The cursor blinked at me, like a tapping foot. *Don't worry,* Altan wrote. *You were cute.*

Cute? Oh god. The only other person in this world who would ever accuse me of being cute was Pete, and only because he was legally obligated. I felt my face flush.

Anyway, typed Altan. *I missed seeing you last night. That's all.*

I wasn't sure exactly what this meant. Did he miss me because I was good platonic company or did he miss me because he was secretly in love with me? And what would it mean if he was? Was I still drunk? Was I cute? I couldn't parse Altan's hidden messages hungover, and then to make matters worse, Malcolm barreled through the front door with his briefcase in hand.

"Ness!"

I jumped in my seat, unable to handle the strain of my obnoxious boss-*cum*-mortal enemy screaming at me—so much drama before coffee. "I thought we went over this!" he yelled. "You *cannot* keep our patients waiting."

I was too woozy to defend myself; it was easier to assume I'd messed something up, considering I was barely alive. "What are you talking about?"

"Sam Stevens is in the waiting room! How long has he been there?"

I hadn't seen anyone in the lobby when I came through ten minutes ago, but when I rushed to the front door there was Sam sleeping across two chairs. He was a mess, shirt untucked, sweater unclean. He was using his jacket as a pillow; the rose was crushed.

I went down on one knee to try and wake him up, wondering how Malcolm could think to yell at me before checking to make sure Sam was even alive. "Sam?" I said, touching his shoulder. Even through the hangover, my voice was bright on the edge of panic. "What are you doing here? You're not due for a check-in."

His eyes when he opened them were dull like old nickels. "Hey, Doc. You said come Monday."

"Today is Thursday. You said you were going out of town."

"Oh, right," he said sleepily, pushing himself to sitting. There was something childlike and innocent about how he blinked against the light. "Well, the trip got canceled. But seeing as I'm here, you don't happen to have any more Morpheum, do you? I lost some of the ones you gave me. They, um, fell down the sink."

He was lying, and not even well, but before I could send him home, Malcolm said, more gently than I'd thought him capable of, "Sam, why don't you come and wait in the conference room while Ness gets some more medication?"

My mind was a bird that had flown into a window and now lay twitching on the lawn as I watched Malcolm lead Sam deeper into the office, my feet following a few paces behind of their own accord. I barely noticed Altan sidling up next to me as I stood in the middle of the office. "Is there a problem?" Malcolm asked, coming out of the conference room.

I thought I would have difficulty standing up to Malcolm, but the dullness of the hangover blunted the reality of what I said. "We can't give Sam more pills. He's clearly abusing them."

"And whose fault is that?" he replied, eyes flashing. "Have you told him how to take them?"

"I gave him the same training I've given everyone else," I said.

"Well, you must be doing *something* wrong." Malcolm pinched the bridge of his nose like he was infinitely annoyed, and then he smoothed out his voice like a duvet. "I need you to prove to me that you can be trusted."

"I'm trying, Malcolm," I said. Altan shuffled a bit closer to me in solidarity. Normally I'd be strong enough to realize this was another one of Malcolm's games, but I was weak from the hangover and worried now that a man's well-being hinged upon my ability to do my job. "I can't make Sam cooperate."

"Well, you'd better figure it out. Now go get some pills. Give him a week's worth."

I stood there, working my mouth open and shut. And just when I felt my resolve crumbling from the sheer nonsensicalness of the situation, Altan stepped forward. "Do you want this whole trial to tank? Because that's what will happen if you keep going down this road. We'll have to throw the whole thing out and start over if he overdoses."

Did I imagine Malcolm's smile? "If you won't do it, I will. Either way, it gets done. The question you have to ask yourselves is, do you still want to be employed by the end of the day?"

Altan looked at me, eyes boring into mine as if to convey some secret message. And though we were awake and I couldn't truly read his mind, I could still without a doubt read his expression. *Don't throw this away,* he was saying. *I'm not ready for us to end.*

God help me, I wasn't either.

In the conference room, I placed a packet of seven pills next to Sam on the table and spun his swivel chair so that we were facing each other. I was close enough to smell him, and the result wasn't good: stale sweat and morning breath, like he'd just gotten up. "Listen to me, Sam," I said, looking into his eyes, which were wobbling, his gaze bouncing around so that he didn't focus on anything. "I want to go over how to take the pills again. This is important. I need you to take just one a night. OK? Just one."

His head listed a little to the side as he studied me. "You remind me of my daughter."

I didn't know what that meant, but I sure knew what to do with it. "Her name's Maria, right?" I said, making my voice soft. "I bet she'd hate to see something happen to you."

Sam looked down at his hands. "She would, yes."

"So take care of yourself, OK, Sam? One pill a night."

He sighed, still refusing to meet my eyes. "I'll try."

I walked him to the elevator, knowing full well he wasn't going to listen, hoping I'd be wrong. When I got back to my desk, I had a text from Pete telling me that Billionaire X had decided to proceed with his divorce, which meant his firm was all hands on deck for the foreseeable future. *They've sent an intern out to buy us all toothbrushes, so I think we're pulling an all-nighter. See you tomorrow?*

I looked up and saw Altan staring at me across the cubicle wall. He flicked his eyes to his computer a second too late, and the realization that he'd been studying me lit my skin on fire. It was dangerous to be alone at night, I thought. I might not be able to stop myself.

SUNDAY, MARCH 24

It's been ten days since I last updated—which isn't great, I know, but between work and the extracurricular drug use, I've been busy as fuck. So here's the recap.

First, the awake stuff: Malcolm is still hanging around work every day. Turd. Wish he'd go back to the Seychelles or wherever. Not only is he a general douchebag to have around, he's also got a big hard-on for giving Ness shit. I swear he's had, like, ten meetings with her about her "performance," while I sit there dicking around on Tinder all day.

I've been interrupting the shit out of their meetings. I don't know why, but sometimes when I'm sitting at my desk I'll get this feeling like I have to go to the conference room and offer to go get coffees for everyone. Some kind of sixth sense, maybe. Who knows?

So yeah, Malcolm sucks. Sam sucks even more. He keeps showing up, asking for more pills, claiming he dropped some down a random open manhole—or they were eaten by his dog, who doesn't have a name. For some reason, Malcolm keeps forcing Ness to give Sam more pills, which is VERY shady considering how obviously he's abusing them. She's in a panic about the whole situation—not just because of her job, but because she's worried about the guy. I am, too. I mean, on the one hand I wish he'd just take the damn pills correctly so we didn't have to deal with any of this, but on the other . . . hell, I get it. I'm not exactly the poster child for dealing with your absent wife.

If he's in over his head, that'll mean it's possible to get in over your head, and that's scary. Sometimes I wonder about Ness and me, if we're swimming or drowning.

Either way, it's been great. Dreaming with her has been the most fun I've had in a long time. Scientifically speaking, our experiments are worthless: I'm not sure how much we can rely on the drug working the way it's meant to since we're manipulating so much. But then again, maybe that's Morpheum at work. Maybe we need to feel like we have power over something. Because this whole work situation—ok, maybe life situation—makes it very clear that we don't. So here's what we've been dreaming about:

Saturday/Sunday: No Ness dreams. Still can't figure out how to create the connection. Spent the weekend practicing Nightcrawling in Angkor Wat. It was sick.

Monday: Ness was Sherlock Holmes and I was Doctor Watson, and we were trying to solve a murder by beheading. Judging by the suit, I think the victim was Malcolm, but without the face we couldn't be sure. We ended up infiltrating some masquerade ball, but we kinda forgot we were supposed to be solving a crime because we had too much punch and ended up making fun of everyone's costumes. My only beef is that Ness got to be Sherlock instead of me, but she has the right intensity so I guess I'll allow it.

Tuesday: We've been experimenting with recreating movies since memories make the best dreams. Tonight was *Jurassic Park*— we did the scene in the kitchen hiding from the raptors, and then outran the T. rex in the Ford Explorer. It was terrifying, but in a Haunted House kind of way. Ness kept grabbing my hand in the kitchen. Her face was hilarious every time the pots and pans came clanging to the ground, like she was being electrocuted.

Wednesday: Low-key dream. I was pulling beers in this crappy college joint when Ness came in to study, and we ended up just shooting the shit all night. For some reason there was a copy of *The Great Gatsby* on the bar. I hated that book in high school. I didn't recognize the bar, so it must have been based on her memory. If it meant something, she didn't tell me.

Thursday: In an exercise of scientific worthiness, Ness tried to jailbreak my memories in case anyone decided to use Morpheum as some kind of spy weapon. She was able to pull up the entire tape of my life—all thirty-four years of memories, recorded in real time. There were no date stamps, and you had to fast-forward to get anywhere, so while it would be possible to extract secret information, we determined it'd be too time consuming. Best to browse. Anyway, we ended up laughing over footage of my teenage years. Ness about peed herself when she saw what I wore to prom, but I maintain the zoot suit was very on-trend back then.

Friday: We were tired, honestly. It's hard to be thinking all the time; I worry we're doing our brains actual harm by not taking breaks with natural sleep, but we're only doing the experiment for another week, so I guess it'll be OK. I dreamed up a beach from Fiji—super deserted, except for a cabana boy who would bring us drinks in coconuts—and some hammocks and shit. Sometimes Ness and I talked but we mostly just dozed in the sun. It was weird to sleep while sleeping, but not bad. It was nice to be together.

The good news about dream beaches? No need for sunscreen!

The bad news about dream beaches? No need for sunscreen. I tried to convince Ness to let me rub some on her back for purely scientific purposes, but she didn't buy it.

Today is Saturday, so no Ness tonight. Not sure what I'll do. Might go out with some guys from the gym. Maybe I'll call Sarah? Maybe I'll just save my Morpheum for when I can dream with Ness?

Fuck it. I have tons of the stuff. More soon

THE PIZZA GUY

It was Monday—the beginning of the third (and last) week of the experiment—and Altan and I had gotten no closer to figuring out how to make the dream link. We'd taken our research to the Seattle Public Library during lunch, and there we were: seated at a community table with a stack of books beneath a ceiling made, pointlessly, out of windows. The fog outside was the pea soup variety; a heavy cloud of it swirled on the glass. I swear I heard the panes creak with the weight.

I looked up from *The Interpretation of Dreams* by Freud and watched Altan pore over some Wiccan tome about sleep magic. His fingers swept across the page like he was dealing with braille, like he had to touch the words to read them—and for some reason I found this endearing.

I was finding a lot about Altan endearing these days.

He looked up from his book to catch me mooning over him like I had LOVE YOU written on my eyelids. "Why are you staring at me?"

"I'm not staring!" I lied, wondering if he could tell. Ever since we'd started dreaming together Altan had been more in tune with my fibbing—with all of my states, really.

"You *were* staring," said Altan, returning to his book, his fingers drifting across the page. "Stop perving on me. I'm more than just a beautiful body, you know."

"You're barely just a beautiful body," I quipped, settling down again with Freud. For someone with so many sex theories, you'd think he would have been hotter. But there was nothing foxy about Sigmund—with that frown and that beard and that phallic cigar of his. Nothing like Altan: the gold of his skin, the sinew of his movement, the play of his fingers as he read, caressing his book like a lover.

"You're doing it again." He didn't look up, but still I thought I could detect the corner of his mouth flick upward in that signature Altan Young smirk that made me feel sixteen again.

Altan and I, god we were in deep. The borders between us had been completely smudged out. Before Morpheum there were fences, salt trails like coke lines to keep the slugs of our thoughts within the mazes of our minds. Now our fears and fantasies were thundering between our brains like mustangs, and I wasn't always sure we had to be asleep for it to happen.

Take Malcolm and the "performance reviews" he'd been hosting for me all last week in the conference room with the blinds drawn and the door closed. I swear to god he poured cement in the air conditioning ducts, too, because I couldn't breathe at all during these "coaching sessions" designed to help me "raise the bar"-slash-"feel so afraid of losing my job that I might blow him in an attempt to save it." It was fairly obvious that's what he wanted, judging by the way he kept rubbing my shoulders while he explained how I wasn't being a "team player" and how I didn't represent the "WellCorp ethos" and how wrong I was to not wear my lab coat all the time but how I was also wrong to wear it into the bathroom.

He was wearing me down in that room. Any time he came toward me, or walked past me, or was generally a distance less than five feet away, I broke into a sweat. And just when I'd think my nerves were at risk of fraying completely, here would come Altan, throwing open the conference room door, asking if we needed coffee. Or if anyone had heard the fire alarm go off. Or if Malcolm had the number for IT (he didn't). Sometimes I wondered if Altan could feel me freaking out—or maybe he was just being thoughtful.

Either way, it was heroic of him, and I noticed. I noticed everything he did, how he distributed dollars to panhandlers when we went out to lunch. How he typed with a pen clamped between his teeth like a cigarette. How he'd taken to running to the kitchen to fix coffee every time Sam Stevens came in trying to score more Morpheum. On Friday Altan had showed up to work with granola bars, because it was clear that Sam wasn't eating anything except pills.

Which didn't concern Malcolm; he'd order me to get Sam more medication every time he came in. I'd try to stand up to him. I'd say, "This is bad," or, "We're jeopardizing the trial," or, "We're killing this man." But I never said no. I couldn't risk losing my job, or the pills. Or Altan.

Because the dreams were worth it. They were worth everything: the guilt, the lies, the angst, the shame. The dreams were the most astounding experience of my life. I'd flown over the ocean, I'd explored space, I'd learned magic—all with Altan laughing by my side. The night I broke into his memories, I was able to feel so much of what he'd felt growing up: the death of his childhood dog (a collie named Sprinkles), the joy of playing in the surf, his insecurity at school, his first kiss, the day he went to college. It all played for me as if on a movie screen, and I'd never known anyone as deeply.

And every night I became more and more enamored with my coworker. I rationalized that my feelings for Altan were strictly for my sleep, but sometimes I'd catch myself watching him at work as he sat at his desk with his spreadsheets, or when he met with his patients in the conference room. Sometimes I'd catch myself wondering what he was thinking now that I'd seen the colors and contours of his mind. It was weird to be awake and not to know.

Altan looked up from his book. "Got anything useful?"

I shut Freud and shook my head. "No. You?"

He sighed. "Only some weird smell spells. Maybe the connection is scent-based? We could experiment Saturday when we don't see each other."

"That means we'll have to extend our experiment," I said. "Since it ends this Friday."

Part of me knew we were going to keep taking Morpheum, though I was still dreading this conversation in case I was wrong. I couldn't help but worry I was misjudging Altan's feelings for me, but when we slept together I could feel them. He wanted me as much as I wanted him.

"I guess we could give it another month," he said, not meeting my eyes, like he was afraid to let me see how hopeful he was for me to say yes.

I shifted uneasily in my seat, knowing I'd have to come clean about just how much I'd been enjoying my Morpheum lately. "In that case, I'll need more pills."

Altan nodded, trying not to smile now that I had agreed. "I can bring you some tomorrow."

"No, I need some tonight. I'm all out."

His head snapped up so I could see the alarm on his face. "How did that happen? You were supposed to have enough to last you until Friday."

I batted my eyelashes, trying to look innocent. "I dropped some down the sink?"

It was here that I expected Altan to be all California chill about my recreational drug use. But instead he furrowed his brows, dad-like. "You've been doubling up," he accused.

"Only on weekends!" I said, like that somehow made it less bad. With Pete working so much lately, I was catching up on all the sleep I'd missed in my entire life.

Altan shook his head, exasperated. "What does Pete have to say about any of this?"

"How the hell is *that* relevant?" I spat, my anger flaring white hot.

"It's not. I shouldn't have said it," he replied, backing down immediately—not because I was angry, but because he meant something else. "I'm worried about you, and I was hoping he'd been keeping tabs on you."

"Because I can't do it myself?"

"That's what I'm afraid of, yes."

I'd noticed that our conversations had become franker since we'd started dreaming together. There had always been a bluntness to our interactions, but now we were practically cudgeling each other with our thoughts. What was the point of pussyfooting around when it would all come out in the wash of sleep? "Pete's been busy at work, so I haven't seen him," I confessed, trying to address Altan's fear instead of his accusation.

"Are you OK?" Altan said.

"Yes," I said, wondering if I could get away with this in a Morpheum dream or if the air would betray me by trembling. "So can I get some more?"

Altan hesitated a beat. I knew the feeling: it was how I felt every time I handed more pills over to Sam. "I don't keep it on me anymore—not since Malcolm started coming in," he said.

"Oh, that's no problem. I'll come over after work?"

Altan looked away. "I'm not going home after work."

"OK. I can come by later. Just text me when you're home," I said chipperly.

"Ness," he groaned. "I can't see you tonight. I have plans."

"Fine," I said, putting my palms up to show I didn't care. "Just bring me some tomorrow. See? No problem. No problem at all."

That night was a different story. I'd gotten into bed at six, which was becoming my custom now that Pete was living at the office, but I couldn't fall asleep. I tossed and turned for four hours, thinking about Pete, worrying about Sam, dreading Malcolm, wondering what Altan was doing, reminding myself that Morpheum was made with non-habit-forming ingredients and that I was not addicted to it: I just really, really liked it.

Look at me, thriving without Morpheum! I thought as I microwaved a second mug of milk.

I thought about where in the world would be the best place to take pictures. I tried to imagine having a baby. I planned the dreams I would have the next time I got Morpheum. I had a third cup of milk. I had two fingers of scotch. I was contemplating the cooking and consumption of an entire Thanksgiving turkey just to get the tryptophan when I texted Altan to see if he was awake, and when I didn't hear from him I decided to go bang on his door and insist on more pills. I couldn't afford to be a zombie tomorrow, was what I'd tell him—not with Malcolm on my ass. I could get fired, just like that, and it would be his fault. I threw on my raincoat and some sweatpants and trudged through the rain to Altan's.

When I punched the button next to his name, the door clicked open immediately. Inside, the hallways smelled of the fug of warring spices and ghostly onions. Who knew you could cook so much in apartments this small? I was panting disgracefully when I reached the third floor and rapped on Altan's door. "Coming!" came Altan's muffled voice from within the apartment. That's what she—

He swung the door open and stood there in his boxer briefs: only in his boxer briefs. He was shirtless and, by the looks of things, engaging in some type of physical activity. Beads of sweat on his stomach caught what little light there was.

"Shit!" he swore, shutting the door so that it opened only wide enough to accommodate his head and an elbow he pinned to the doorframe in an attempt to look casual. I went momentarily dumb at the sight of his biceps. "What the hell are you doing here?" he hissed.

"You buzzed me in. Why are you whispering?"

"I have company."

I appraised his naked torso, and something roared in me then, something like hunger and anger mixed into the same feeling. "Why'd you even answer the door?"

"I thought you were the pizza guy."

"You ordered pizza?"

Altan raked his hand through his disheveled hair. Downstairs a commercial for soda blared through the walls. "We needed a snack. What do you want?"

I pictured Altan with the unseen woman, his hands on her body, her head thrown back as she fisted his sheets. I pictured Altan fucking her so hard they needed pizza to recover. "I didn't know you were seeing anyone," I stammered. Was he sleeping next to someone while dreaming with me? "I came for more *aspirin*."

"Jesus, Ness." He ducked into the darkness of his living room, leaving me in the hall, shifting guiltily under the hum of the fluorescent lights. I didn't feel like a medical pioneer. I felt like an addict in a bad part of town. He returned with an aspirin bottle in his hand, appraised the rattling; there were more than a few pills. "Here," he whispered, giving me the entire thing in his haste to get rid of me. His fingers brushed mine in the handoff; when he drew back, I felt the ghost of his touch. "Now go home and sleep. I'll see you in a bit."

I stood there as he was closing the door, trying to think of something good to say besides "Good luck!" like I didn't mind that he was sleeping with someone else at all. I *wanted* him to have great sex. That's what friends wanted for each other.

The door shut. And then Altan ripped it open again. "Are you OK?" he asked.

I tried to answer that scientifically. "Yes, ultimately."

"Let me rephrase that." He dropped his voice to a whisper. "Are we OK?"

"I didn't know you were seeing other people at night."

"Does that matter?"

Here was that crazy truth between us again. "It shouldn't. But it does."

"That's completely irrational."

"I know, Spock. You don't have to tell me."

But he told me anyway, hissing into the hall so his visitor wouldn't hear. "You're married! You sleep with 'other people'!"

That wasn't exactly true of late, but I still said, "I know."

"So why can't I?"

"I'm not saying you can't." I looked at him, half-naked like my own private dream, and I blurted, "It's just that I'm feeling things for you that maybe I shouldn't."

When Altan looked at me, I could feel the Tesla-coil snapping of energy with no place to go. "I know what you mean," he said, after a moment. "I feel the same way."

And that was it. That was all that could be said. There was no "yes, *and*" to this situation—there was just yes. Yes, we have feelings for each other. No, there wasn't anything we could do about them.

"Maybe we should stop," I said finally.

"I don't want to."

The door out was open. I was free to walk through it, to put down the pills and go back to Pete with a secluded mind and a loyal heart. But because I'm both a sadist and a masochist, I said, "Me neither."

"So this is the way it has to be," he said heavily, his eyes pleading with mine for something I wasn't willing to give, and then I heard a woman's voice call from the dark of his apartment, "Is that the pizza?"

"I have to go," he told me, but I was already saying, "I should leave. Have a good night." And we muttered over each other until the door slammed shut.

I put the pill bottle in my pocket and made my way slowly down the stairs, trying to measure my feelings. If I were dreaming I'd have an easier time of it—my subconscious wasn't exactly subtle under the effects of Morpheum. But awake I had a harder time putting things into words.

The closest I could get was "jealousy," but how could I be jealous? I was happily married, wasn't I? Could I be happily married if I was falling for another man?

Outside, the pizza man was pulling up. I held the door for him, then walked home, put the pills in my nightstand drawer, and lay in the dark for a long, long time.

TUESDAY, MARCH 26

So Ness showed up in the middle of the night while Sarah was over . . . yikes. Big time yikes. I'm still cringing but not sure why. After all, I'm completely within my rights to sleep with Sarah. Ness is married—to my <u>divorce lawyer</u>—and she's just a friend. So why did she look like I'd stabbed her in the back when I opened the door? And why did I feel like I'd done the same?

Dude . . . it's getting complicated with Ness. I think about her a lot, which is funny because we're only apart for maybe the hour a day I shower. But still—I think of her in the shower, and it's not always innocent. And then I think of her on the way to work, wondering what she's doing, what she's thinking, if she's alright.

She showed up because she needed more pills—told me earlier yesterday that she's out because she's been taking too many on weekends. So now I'm worried about her need to escape.

Anyway, after she left, I dreamed about her—the fake her, that R2-D2 hologram that passes for Ness when Ness doesn't take her Morpheum. In this dream, Holo-Ness was trying to seduce me, and I'm ashamed to say, I let her. It wasn't nearly as good as our first Paris dream, but it was better than real-life sex with Sarah.

Is it weird to have sex with someone in a dream after you've had dream sex with them—and this after you've just had real-life sex with someone else?

God. I need to lie down.

WEDNESDAY, MARCH 27

Been thinking about the smell connection I read about in the library. Remember when June was researching babies, and she read that thing about how you should swaddle the infant in a blanket that smells like a parent so it sleeps better? I figured Ness and I could do the same thing with T-shirts: if we got the same one in the same size and wore it all week, we could trade on Friday to see if we could dream about each other on Saturday.

I told this to Ness, and she was good to try it, so we went down to Pike Place Market at lunch to buy some shirts. As we're walking along, this lady with dreadlocks calls out. Turns out, her name is Debby, and she's the lady who prints Ness's photos on T-shirts and shit. Ness's photos are *really* good, and famous! I see people wearing those shirts all over town. Debby even had an *Us Weekly* photo of Dave Matthews taking out the trash while wearing one.

I was stoked AF. I was like, "Ness! This is so fucking cool!" And she was all, "Meh, not really."

I wish she'd be nicer to herself. I wonder if I could convince her to take her photography more seriously. I mean, maybe that's what the Morpheum would be doing if I wasn't slumming around in her dreams. Sometimes I wonder if I'm doing her any favors.

Anyway, we bought two of the Dave Matthews shirts: same color, same size. Today is Wednesday: hopefully we can wear them to bed tonight and tomorrow and then swap at work on Friday to see if we've figured it out. I hope we do, because my weekends are kind of boring.

THE DORM ROOM FIRE

It was Saturday, and I was sitting on Altan's and my beach in the dream, playing with the sunset, trying to get it *just* right. It was the same beach we'd dreamed about last Friday when we were tired of doing Morpheum tricks in our sleep, and it was a good one, based on one of Altan's memories of the South Pacific. The sand was white with a touch of pink, and there were palm trees impossibly close to the water that he'd uprooted and replanted just so we could string a hammock between them. I was lying in it now, staring up at the sky, wondering if I liked it more purple than orange, wondering if I'd see Altan now that we had traded the T-shirts we'd bought in the market after wearing them for two nights.

He'd put his in a sandwich bag so the musk would be especially strong, and with Pete at the office through the weekend, I'd fallen asleep breathing Altan's scent. I'd always been bad at picking out flavors: Pete's lawyer friends could tell you if a wine tasted like oak or sadness, but I couldn't do it to save my life. Which is why I couldn't tell you what exactly the T-shirt smelled like, only that it smelled good. It smelled like a younger me, one who'd steal her high school boyfriend's T-shirts to sleep in. It smelled like a time before sex when closeness was the epitome of arousal.

I looked out at the ocean and saw a sail appear on the horizon. My heart surged as I watched it grow closer, noting it wasn't the pirate ship of my previous dream but an altogether smaller vessel—rigged similarly but miniaturized. The boat sailed straight for the beach and even pulled itself onto the sand, and from the deck dropped Altan, barefoot and shirtless and grinning like he'd eaten the world's biggest canary. "So the connection *is* smell-based!" he crowed as he sauntered over to my hammock and hoisted himself into it.

"Get your own," I fake complained as he shoved into me.

"Nah," he said. We flailed in a tangle of limbs, threatening to tip over. The hammock swung wildly. "The trees look happy. I don't want to move them."

We steadied in the center of the netting, Altan's arm beneath my neck, my body curled into his. I hooked a leg over him like we were actually lovers, and though we hadn't specifically discussed a new arrangement between us in the dream, I felt us tacitly agreeing to pretend we were. It was the closest we'd get without resulting in actual adultery. Altan buried his nose in my hair. "I never realized you had a smell."

"I guess it's one of those things you take for granted," I said, snuggling closer into his shoulder without second thought, doing all the things I wanted to do with him when I was awake. The connection between us was so strong—was it because of the T-shirt? Regardless, I couldn't fight the urge to reach up and stroke the stubble of his face. "This is nice," I said.

He pulled me closer and began twirling his fingers through my hair; it felt as good as I'd always thought it would. "You should see the real thing," he said idly. "Fiji is the most beautiful place I've been. It's probably even prettier than this, though the sunset is especially nice here."

"You like it? I made it."

I could feel Altan smile, the movement of his face against my hair. "It's beautiful, like you."

It was tempting to counteract his compliment with some wisecrack, but I didn't. We lay there drowsing happily in the sun of our fake drug-induced vacation, blissfully ignoring how we were saying things now we never could when awake. "I'd like to go Fiji someday," I said.

"Why don't you?"

I shrugged like I didn't know. The air shivered with the lie. "Too expensive."

Altan was thinking: I could feel the machinery of his mind whirring. "What if we Slugworthed the Morpheum to Merck? We could sell them the formula. Tell them what it does. Then you could go traveling."

"Assuming I didn't go to jail for breach of contract?"

"Oh, right." He was quiet for a moment. "What about your photo money? That's got to be enough for a ticket!"

Why was he ruining our dream with talk of the real world? "It probably is, but Pete doesn't know about it, so how do I explain that I've been hiding my photography hobby from him for no reason without coming off as a complete weirdo?"

"Well, go without him. Tell him you have some sort of work meeting in the South Pacific. The airfare is the most expensive part. Once you're there, the hostels are pretty cheap."

Altan could feel my body tense warily at the prospect. "I don't do hostels."

His chuckle was lazy, half-hearted. "Prissy, are we?"

I heard a sizzling sound, like hair catching fire. Just when I thought he knew me completely, there were these ugly reminders that he didn't. I turned my head to plant the point of my chin on his pectoral muscle. "I don't sleep anywhere where the door doesn't lock. It's not safe."

"Says who? I've traveled everywhere! Half the time there weren't even doors."

"It's different when you're a woman. You're more . . . vulnerable."

"To what?"

Suddenly I couldn't be there. I swung my legs over the hammock and got up to face the ocean. Behind me I heard Altan repeat, "To what, Ness?"

I looked out at the water, all the infinite possibilities that lay across it. "To people taking things from you."

I heard the shifting of the rope as Altan got up and came to stand next to me. Together we studied the calm, unceasing roll of the waves, the long, low sound of them like the world's *Om*. "OK, show me," he said without turning.

"Show you what?"

"Show me everything: what's in your head, what you're afraid of, why you won't travel."

"I can't." I felt him take my hand. Even with the truth serum of the dreams, it took me a moment to land on the right words; I spoke them to the surf. "It's ugly, and I'm ashamed."

He pulled on my hand so that I had no choice but to turn toward him. "When I showed you places from my past, like Marrakesh, I felt better for doing it, for confronting the memory with someone by my side. I don't know if it would feel good to you, but it felt good to me. And if you would like to try, I'm here for you."

But Marrakesh wasn't the same, I wanted to say; it wasn't his blood or pain but June's. "Even if I wanted to show you," I said. "I— I wouldn't know how."

"It doesn't matter. Just close your eyes and think of it."

God, I was tired. I was so tired of keeping the secret, of pretending I was OK, that it didn't still burn. I could show him— why not?—and maybe it would feel better. "Promise not to leave?"

He took my other hand so that he was holding both, and he unfurled my fingers like wadded pieces of paper and flattened them on his chest where his heart was. "I swear."

I leaned into him, and instead of nervousness I felt nothing: cold, clear nothing. It was the nothingness of abandoned mines, a darkness with no bottom. I looked into it, and then I let go.

The beach dissolved around us, the warm sand and the pastel sky hardened and bled out their colors until Altan and I were standing at the start of a long, gray hallway lined with jail cells on either side. He looked at me confused, like he hadn't expected Alcatraz. "What's this?"

I answered, "I don't know."

But I kind of did. The dream was more of a feeling than a memory. It was the fear I felt in public ever since the college incident: in public, at night, alone. I hated it, but it was familiar, like an old wound that aches when it rains. I shivered as we walked past the cells. Their bars framed the leering faces of cruel men, their eye-whites not exactly white but yellow, like old teeth. One was bald, and huge, his knuckles like cinderblocks as he wrapped his fingers around the bars. "Hiya, sweetheart," he growled at Altan, not me.

There was a malice in his look, his voice. The way he licked his lips and looked down the slope of his nose conveyed that this man would not be satisfied by the mere act of hurting. He had a cruelty intent on breaking, burning, demolition. This was a man who wanted to destroy. Instantly Altan knew it, and I felt the fear I felt all the time grip him by the spine and squeeze. It was an intense feeling, like we were *connected* by the same terror—not one made in the moment like in the Sasquatch dream, but an ancient one as much a part of me as my own limbs.

Altan started to jog down the hallway as more men appeared, pressing their faces between the bars so hard that their heads popped through like they were being born into their violence, grinning. Their arms snaked through the bars to stroke him, the way one might caress a saint as she glided past. He broke into an honest run when he felt the fingers catch at his clothes, but their grasps held as their arms spooled out from the cells like fishing line. The men oozed after him from between the bars, limber and sinister as eels.

He shouted, "Ness! Make it stop!" But I couldn't make them stop. I couldn't make anything stop—not then, not now, and I knew it with a sadness so heavy it left me numb to the horror unfolding all around. There was Altan, a man I cared about, being tormented by the same wickedness that had wrecked me all those years ago. I was so paralyzed with fear and despair that I could only watch as a man with Malcolm's face launched himself at Altan's feet. My hands were useless, my stomach a crushed-up soda can. My fingers twisted in each other like roots.

The inmates finally caught him, not with their arms but with their bodies, their thick torsos wrapping around his ankles. He tumbled toward the concrete floor, landing belly-up on an extra-long twin bed—the kind commonly found in college dorms. There were band flyers and kung fu movie posters tacked to the walls. The bodies slithered over Altan's face, around his belly which, despite the sit-ups, did not feel so hard anymore. "Shhh," they were hissing. "Everything's fine. Just relax."

Their tails crawled up his nose, down his throat, across his forehead, binding him to the bed. He watched me watching and widened his eyes so I could see his fright. "Stop," he said, but it came out like, "Suh," his throat so full of muscle, his stomach full of fingers, pulling. He felt his bones creaking and giving way, the softness of his guts torn like bread. "Neh! Suh!" But I couldn't, or didn't, or something—I just stood there, frozen to the spot, wishing I was braver, stronger, smarter, whole.

He squeezed his eyes shut and disappeared as he woke himself up.

I was alone with the fear, and immediately I thawed from the heat of knowing that. In blind panic, I set fire to the room and watched the snake-men blacken and convulse. As they burned, they smelled like cigarettes and rum and beer. I took extra time singeing the one with Malcolm's face, and when they were all good and crispy, I set fire to the bedspread and the band posters and the Sony Vaio on the peeling desk.

I burned the Red Hot Chili Peppers T-shirts spilling out of the bureau and the dirty socks on the floor. I burned the bike helmet and the worn sneakers and the textbooks, backing out of the doorway into a blank white nothingness from which I watched the charred remains of the men go up a second time as the carpet caught. I watched it all burn, my stomach roiling, my heart clenched like a fist, before I finally closed the door. I took a moment to dust off my hands, waiting for a relief that did not come. That fire would burn and burn and never put itself out. This knowledge made me tired even in my sleep. I sighed once and woke myself up.

My phone had vibrated itself off my bedside table; that's how many texts I'd received from Altan. *WTF? How could you do that to me? Are you insane?*

You left, I typed, feeling oddly detached. *You left when you promised you wouldn't.*

I left because you wouldn't stop. Why didn't you stop?

I couldn't. I thought of the Sasquatch from our hiking dream, all the monsters in my mind. *No one stops when I ask them to.*

Three dots appeared. Then disappeared. Four times this happened. I waited for Altan's reply, composing my retort in my mind. The memory of the inferno was fresh, and I still felt like burning. When his reply finally came, I leapt as if holding a match.

I'm sorry, he wrote. *I'm sorry it was like that for you. I had no idea.*

I settled back in the dark, cradling my phone. I reread the text. I read it ten more times, and every time I felt my stomach loosen another centimeter, like someone was dialing down a torture I didn't know could end. Altan believed me. I was livid at myself for needing someone else to corroborate my truth, but I was also relieved that someone had. I wasn't crazy. I never had been. My treatment had been one big pile of shit, and now someone was admitting it.

Anyway, I typed back. *That's why I don't travel alone.*

SATURDAY, MARCH 30

So good news: the smell theory is right. Ness and I dreamed about each other after the T-shirt experiment.

The bad news: Ness was raped in college, and I was foolish enough to ask her to replay it for me. Jesus, it was awful. How does she live with all that in her head?

THE KISS

I didn't want to go back to sleep after that.

I didn't want to face Altan, to have to feel bad about what I'd done or watch him feel bad about what had happened to me. And because it was Saturday turning into Sunday and I wouldn't have to work, I went out into the living room and watched HGTV until I was sure he was up, and then I took a Morpheum and went back to bed. When I woke in the late afternoon, Pete was still gone, so I grabbed my camera and went down to the market to take some pictures for Debby, of the ferries going back and forth across the Sound at sunset, the mountains sleeping in the distance. It was a good winter day, cold but sunny, and everything had a steeliness to it that could pass as silver in the right light. It had been too long since I'd taken pictures. I'd forgotten how much it calmed me to look at something else.

Altan texted me all day, but I never replied. Pete texted too, and I replied enough to make sure he didn't worry. I went to bed Sunday night without Altan's shirt. I took Morpheum alone and dreamed about setting that dorm room on fire all night.

I only felt marginally better on Monday morning when I stopped in at Coffee Talk. Altan was waiting for me, which was weird because he never beat me anywhere, and when he saw me come in, he leapt up and pulled me into his arms right there in the rush-hour crush of the coffeeshop. His body was solid and strong; mine felt deflated, brittle. He held me in silence for what seemed like forever while people jostled us on their way to and from work. I watched them from the cave Altan made for me with his body. I took my time in letting go.

"Where have you been?" he asked, leading me to the table he'd snagged for us. There were already two cups of coffee present. "You didn't go back to sleep Saturday night, and I kept texting you Sunday. Are you OK?"

He was so worried about me; it was almost cute. "No worse today than I am on any other."

"But it's like— I mean—" He was spinning his coffee cup in his hands, agitated that the words wouldn't come. Things were so much more fluid in dreams. "How do you cope with *that* every day?" he finally spat out.

"It was a long time ago."

"It didn't feel like a long time ago. That dream felt *fresh*."

I felt myself struggling, too, with the words, and then I let the truth spill out as it would in the dream. "It feels fresh, every day. Not that specific incident, but everything that came from it: why I try not to drink in public, why I don't travel. I don't feel safe when it's dark, when I'm alone with Malcolm. I don't want to have kids. My life could have been so much different, and I hate that. When that night happened, it hurt, of course. But all the things that have been stolen from me because of it are just as shitty."

"I'm sorry," said Altan. He took my hand across the table, and I flinched slightly, horrified about what would happen if Malcolm walked by—or, god forbid, Pete. But his hands were warm and steady and mine were cold from being outside and the chill of my memories. "I'm so sorry. And that's how you ended up pregnant?"

I nodded.

"Did you ever tell anyone?"

"You're the first." I smiled then to keep myself from crying: it was a move straight out of the Sam Stevens playbook. "And I blame myself for that, too—for not getting help."

"It's not your fault. None of it is your fault."

"I know." I sniffled. "And I don't know. And I'm so broken over it, and there's no fix."

Altan faltered again and finally closed his mouth. He moved my hand under the table so he could hold it without being seen. It was a great gift, how he we sat there in silence, our time in Marrakesh in real life. There were no answers, and he didn't try to find any. But he gave me what he could.

We finished our coffees. We went to work. Malcolm was an asshole. Sam came to ask for more pills. Pete worked late. It was business as usual.

When I fell asleep that night, I was in Paris again. I found Altan scampering around a long stretch of nighttime lawn beneath the Eiffel Tower, lit up like a Christmas tree. Altan was humming what suspiciously sounded like "Be Our Guest" from *Beauty and the Beast* (must have been some sort of ironic hipster remix) as he fussed over a picnic blanket and a bottle of champagne in an ice bucket. "What's all this?" I asked.

"Ah! *Bon soir, madame,*" he oozed in a ridiculously French accent. "*Bienvenue* to your vacation." He took my hand so I could sit on the blanket, then poured me a glass of champagne.

I snorted. "The last time you were a French waiter we had a hard time looking each other in the face the next day."

"Wasn't that the best?" he said brightly as he sat beside me with his own champagne. "But no, I'm not looking for that any more than I usually am." Here he winked. "Tonight, we are traveling.

Anywhere you want to go. If I've been there, you have free rein over my memories."

He clinked his glass with mine. "Altan, that's very sweet, but you don't have to—"

"I'm not 'having' to do anything. I *want*. I want you to see things and feel good." He took my hand, interlacing our fingers in the casual way of lovers. "It's not the real thing, but it's what we have for now. Will it do?"

It took me a moment to realize he was talking about traveling, but yes, it would do—him, this, the dreams, whatever crumbs we could glean in our sleep. It was ridiculous and crazy and romantic and needed, and I let him pull me to my feet and take me in his arms completely unironically, and he asked me, as he put his hand to my cheek and looked me deep in the eyes, "Where can I take you, *madame*?"

We went to Rome. Cambodia. India. It was a whirlwind tour of Altan's favorite spots, and he tailored them all to me, made sure I saw the things I wanted to see, ate the things I wanted to eat. "But this must be boring for you. You've done all this already," I said.

"Not with you," he replied. "Not like this."

We toured the Louvre—no lines. We saw the Taj Mahal at sunrise. In Istanbul we ate the greatest baklava I'd ever had. "No, it's not quite right," Altan was saying, trying to correct it. "It was stickier than this. Here, try it now."

It was sweet—both the baklava and the gesture, how Altan kept asking, "Is this good? Is this what you like?" It felt like my birthday, or rather what I would love my birthday to feel like: like I was entitled to anything I wanted. "I'm bored of India. Let's do Fiji again," I'd say, and Altan would squeeze his eyes shut and we'd be on the beach, eating lobster tails, drinking the coldest beer I'd ever tasted. Sure, it wasn't the real world, but it was the closest I could get safely for free. And it felt real enough to someone who would never get more, and I was touched that he knew it and made it so just for me.

We finished our world tour at the Parthenon, sitting side by side on its crumbling marble steps, looking out at Athens while she slept. The Acropolis was lit only by the full moon, which dipped the stones in silver, and I lay my head on Altan's shoulder, exhausted from having seen the whole world in an entire night. Altan was looking at the stars overhead, and I craned my neck so I could watch him watch the sky, knowing he was wondering what it was like out there, all those planets he'd yet to see. His wanderlust had no border: it would go on and on as long as there were places to visit, minds to explore. And I loved him for it.

Oh my god, I loved him for it—for all of it: his curiosity and his sense of wonder, and his kindness and his humor. And, of course, his eyes, as they searched the heavens and then, dipping downward, found mine. Without speaking, I shifted so that I was kneeling on the step below him, leaning into his body, reaching for the back of his long neck so I could touch my mouth to his. Without fighting he tipped forward into the moment. It felt inevitable, like we'd been hurtling toward it as a comet zings through space, fast and fatal and white hot in an otherwise frigid world. We were nose to nose, and I felt his breath on my lips and his body tighten beneath my hands, and we were so close and then—

I woke up alone in bed to the sound of my alarm, and it was all gone: the warmth of Greece, the platinum of the moon, and Altan. It was raining on the other side of the window and time to go to work. I fought the urge to cry.

THE OVERDOSE

On my way to work, Seattle was tense and exasperated as it waited for spring. The raw, cold morning had a desperate feeling to it as puddles that had been there for months just kept taking on more water. I could relate to the feeling: it had been winter forever. And just when I thought it was going to warm up? More rain.

What do to about Altan? The man had wormed completely into my heart, and our little game had become a big problem. I was head over heels for him in a way I used to be for my husband—who wasn't at all a bad guy, by the way. His only real flaw was that he hadn't happened to stumble upon a sleeping pill that would allow him to understand me perfectly. I was so ashamed that I'd gone and fallen in love with someone else, but that love for Altan felt so good, like the first hit of a cigarette, like a piece of New York cheesecake. Like being completely seen for the first time in my life. What was I doing to myself? To Altan? To Pete?

"Good morning," I said quietly over the cube wall when I got to my desk. I could barely look at Altan after our almost-kiss—my heart was still pulsing with the memory of it—but still I chanced a glance. He was in his chair, staring straight ahead, his elbows propped on his desk, his nose resting behind his clasped hands. By the way his computer monitor was shaking, he was doing that nervous leg jiggle high school boys do during finals. "What's wrong?" I asked. "You look like shit."

Then you look like ten shits, I wanted him to say. But instead he looked at me, anguish in his eyes. "We just got a call from Harborview." I knew why instantly, even as he said, "Sam overdosed. He's in a coma."

"Oh, god," I groaned, sinking into my chair. The weather was inconsequential, as was my shitty boss, and my little love triangle: none of it mattered. It was stupid to think that they did. I looked up at Altan in shock. "I— I didn't know that was possible."

"It shouldn't be, according to Diana. The chemicals don't usually react like that. But somehow Sam found a way." He ran his hands through his hair seemingly just to give himself something to do. Altan was shaken; it was so unlike him. "He left a note. Said he wanted to be with his wife."

"Jesus." I sank my head in my hands and stared into the carpet. I thought of Sam in his blazer with the crushed boutonniere, hooked up to a dozen machines. Was he dreaming of Mary? Was he dreaming at all? "I should have never let him in the trial."

"This isn't your fault," I heard Altan say. There was the sound of his pushing back from his desk and walking over to mine; the toes of his boots drifted into my view. "This was all Malcolm. You did everything you could."

"Did I?" I snapped my head up. "Or did I just kill a man while I covered my ass so you and I could—"

"Shh," Altan warned me with his eyes to shut up.

But it seemed a little late to be discreet, now that I was protecting a job I couldn't stand for a second longer. "Where's Malcolm? Is he in today?"

"No. When the call came in he blew out of here for HQ. Diana's been in her office with the door shut. And I've been sitting here, wondering—" He broke off, cleared his throat. "Wondering if you were coming in. Or if you'd also taken too much."

With a mind of its own, my hand reached for his as if we were asleep. Altan's palms were warm and dry; his long fingers felt reassuring when locked with mine. "Hey, we're OK."

"No, we're not. This is too dangerous. I—"

Diana's door opened then, and Altan and I dropped hands. Immediately, I missed his touch. Poor Diana, she looked like twelve shits. Her eyes were bloodshot, and she looked small bundled in her coat, her purse over her shoulder. "I guess you heard, then," she said, her voice thick from crying. "Fucking Malcolm. I warned him."

"I know," I said, swallowing tears and bile and hatred and regret. "I warned him, too."

Diana nodded, more to herself than to me. "I'm going home. I can't be here today. I can't be in this disgusting place with its shitty policies." She fished a tissue out of her pocket and swiped her nose with it. "You two should go home, too—take the rest of the week off. Malcolm won't be here and I canceled all our appointments. Either we'll regroup Monday, or I'll come to my senses over the weekend and get brave enough to leave this horseshit company. Who's to say?"

Altan reached over the cube wall to get a box of tissues from his desk. He held it out to Diana, and she took one gratefully and dabbed her eyes. "Thanks," she sniffed. She was quiet for a moment, and then she said, "The worst part is, I believed in this one. I really thought Morpheum was going to help people. I was proud. But now—" She looked like she would have shrugged if she wasn't so weighed down. "Anyway, see you Monday?"

"Sure," I said, surprised she was taking it this hard. I didn't think Diana cared about anything except her plants. "Feel better, OK?"

She nodded and shuffled for the door. Altan and I stood there staring at each other; I couldn't remember the last time the office was so quiet. "So what do we do?" he asked.

"I don't know." I felt empty except for the guilt. The thought of doing anything was torture. "Go home? Go back to bed?"

Horror crossed his face. It was mixed with disgust and disbelief with a dash of pity, and that's how I knew everything was about to change. Altan and I couldn't go back to dreaming and pretending we weren't hurting anyone. The point was being forced, and that was just as upsetting as the idea of slipping into a sleep from which you could not wake up. "Are you serious?" he said. "A man goes into a coma and you want to go home and take the drug that did it?"

I laughed hollowly to cover my tracks. "It was a joke."

"That's a pretty bad joke, Ness," he said, sounding, briefly, like Malcolm's disappointed-dad voice. It stung. "Go home and sleep if you want. I don't feel comfortable leaving the office unattended. What if one of our patients comes by freaking out?" I hadn't thought of our other patients. I hadn't cared. When did Altan become so responsible? "I'll stay for a little while. Maybe update my resume, just in case. I don't know what else to do."

My desire to be near Altan outweighed my need to get into bed and dream about anything except Sam on a gurney. "I'll join you," I said. "I just need a minute."

I went to our office's small one-hole bathroom to splash some water on my face, and I stood there dripping wet, gripping the sink until my knuckles were as white as the porcelain. I really looked at myself for the first time since I'd started taking Morpheum, and I barely recognized the swamp creature staring back at me: pale, blotchy, damp-skinned, bug-eyed. I'd lost weight. I'd been taking liberties with my hygiene. I'd slept through my haircut last Saturday, and now my hair was overgrown, unbrushed. Worse than that, though, was the fear in my eyes, twitchy, harried, like a field mouse in winter. I'd turned into a careless person. I'd started thriving on destruction.

When had I last looked for the beauty all around? It was there. My life was so goddamn pretty. Why was I sleeping it away?

My back hit the wall opposite the sink, and I slid down it to crouch over my phone, texting Pete. *I got tomorrow off all of a sudden. Can you go to Vancouver this weekend?*

My phone buzzed almost immediately with Pete's reply. *Cool! I'll make reservations.*

It was so quick, and that's when I started to cry. I cried for Sam, and for Altan, and for Pete—for how terrible I'd been to all of them. I had love with Pete—a liquid velvet love, the kind Sam had tried to kill himself for—and I'd neglected the greatest thing in the world. *I love you*, I texted. *I love you so much.*

I love you, too, he wrote back, cheerful, oblivious. I only had to hold out my hand, and Pete would catch me like a trapeze artist, swift and sure and smiling. *Can't wait for the weekend!*

I cradled the phone to my chest like it was an infant, and then I lay down on the tile and sobbed and sobbed and sobbed.

There were wires everywhere when I woke up; they were drooping across my vision like jungle vines. For the briefest moment, in the half-light of this unfamiliar bed, I was terrified I was in a hospital— but then I recognized the blue-gray carpet I was lying on. Altan's jacket was draped over me like a blanket, and my backpack, still slightly damp from the morning's rain, was serving as my pillow. "What am I doing under my desk?" I said mostly to myself as I crawled out of the tangle, pushing my chair out of the way and heaving to my feet. "Oh. You're here."

Altan was seated at his desk, typing calmly. He stopped to look at me as I stood there, blinking under the fluorescent lights. "You fell asleep in the bathroom. I didn't want you to get cold on the tile."

"You brought me out here?" I joked. "You carried me out here like *The Bodyguard*?"

He didn't laugh at my movie reference, but his voice was soft when he said, "You didn't even flinch. I've never seen anyone sleep like that."

I looked away but I felt Altan's worried eyes on me, like he wanted to say something but couldn't bring himself to. *Since when?* I wondered. *When did we start pulling punches?* Did he know I was coming apart? Could he smell it on me? "What time is it?"

"Four," said Altan.

"Has anyone come by?"

He shook his head no.

"Want to go to The Signature?"

He sighed for some reason, like he was disappointed, but then he said, "Sure."

If I couldn't have Morpheum, alcohol was the next best thing. It warmed me up, made me feel happy, loosened my tongue, forced the truth. I took the first Moby Dicktail in one swallow (that's what she said) and then ordered another, which lasted about five minutes. I signaled the bartender for a third, realizing as the booze hit my empty stomach that I hadn't eaten anything all day, so I was going down fast. *Good.* I was bringing my A-game to this errand. I had a heart to break, and I needed the strength.

Altan was sitting next to me at the bar, only halfway through his first beer. There was a casualness to his posture that undid me, how he hunched his lean frame, how he'd refused the glass and pulled from the bottle, tilting it all the way up. He was wearing his beanie inside—it was that cold—and his coolness like a jacket. And while he'd raised an eyebrow as the bartender handed me my drink, he hadn't said anything about the speed of my imbibing. Which was annoying. I hated when men respected my wishes when I was spoiling for a fight.

"So I texted Pete," I said, apropos of nothing. "We're taking that trip to Vancouver I told you about awhile back."

"Oh?" Altan said into his beer. The word popped cheerfully like a bubble, but it felt false. "That's nice."

"I've been ignoring him," I said. "It's not right. You're the one who said that."

"I know," he replied evenly. "I'm glad you two are going on your Baby-moon."

Altan leaned a little harder on that last word, and I could feel it happening: the fight I was trying to manifest was gathering speed. "Maybe-moon," I corrected. "Sam wanted to die for his wife. He's a good man. So is Pete. It's time I start treating him that way." My voice slurred.

"You don't have to explain yourself," said Altan curtly. "I understand."

"Of course, you do. You always understand. You're so goddamn perfect."

I wanted his rage then. His disgust. His grief. I wanted him to scream at me because he loved me and couldn't stand the thought of my leaving. I wanted to break his heart, because then I would know it was mine. But he wouldn't let me, either because he was too cool or he didn't actually care after all. "You're so goddamn perfect, Altan!" I repeated louder. My drunkenness had gone from zero to sixty faster than Malcolm's BMW, and it felt good to be making a scene. It felt true, like a dream, like I was doing whatever I wanted.

"Maybe you should slow down with the booze. Remember the last time you came here?" Altan said. There was in concern in his eyes but I told myself it was condensation.

"Do you love me?"

"What?" He physically recoiled from the question, grinning, like it was a joke.

"Altan Young, do you love me?"

He eyed the bartender, smiled into his lap, licked his lips. It was too early in the evening for conversation like this. "Do I have to?"

"Answer me? Yes. You have to answer me."

"No," he said, quieter, leaning toward me on his barstool. "Do I have to love you? I mean, what's the point if I say yes? Are you going to leave Pete?"

No, I thought. *Maybe.* My vision swam in and out of focus. "Depends on your answer."

"So you want me to make some kind of declaration, so you can know what to do with your life." He was chuckling, incredulous, and then he leaned over to clap a hand on my back like we were chums having a laugh over some kind of movie pun. That was what made me snap, that he could think we would ever be friendly again. That he could think we would go back to being coworkers who rolled our eyes at the clock while we waited for it to hit five.

"Don't touch me!" I shrieked before I even knew what I'd said.

The bartender, practiced in these arts, slid over in a flash. "Miss, is there a problem?"

"No," I replied, then changed my mind. "Actually, yes. This man won't leave me alone."

The bartender leveled a look at Altan. "Sir, do I have to ask you to leave?"

Altan leaned back and poured the rest of his beer down his throat. He set the bottle roughly down and took out his wallet. For some reason I was reminded of when I'd accused him of stealing "my" Moleskine: he'd looked at me then like he couldn't believe I would stoop so low. Now there wasn't even an ounce of surprise on his face, like my despicableness wasn't shocking at all.

"Will you make sure she gets home OK?" he asked the bartender, tossing four twenties on the bar. After a moment, he took out a fifth and put it in the tip jar. "Please," he added.

The bartender nodded as Altan snapped his jacket on and slung his backpack over his shoulder. "Bye, Ness," he said as he passed me without looking. "Take care of yourself. Have fun in Canada."

As he went, I felt no satisfaction, no sense of triumph. I didn't even feel the bittersweet tinge of an old dog's death—the sadness that accompanies a necessary ending, the comfort of knowing there was marginally less pain in the world, that he'd be better off. I watched Altan shove the door open and then slump past the window with that walk of his, thinking I'd dug a hole so deep I'd never see the sun.

That was the last thing I remember.

Everything is very bad right now.

THE HANGOVER, PART 2

When I went to the student clinic in college, there was a white noise generator outside the examination room so no one could hear what was being said within. That's what it sounded like when I came to—indiscriminate noise, like an ultrasound machine, the whooshing of my sluggish blood as it dragged poisonously through my veins. I opened my eyes and saw a low ceiling, and there were walls close on either side of me. I was either in a morgue drawer or one of those Japanese capsule hotels. I didn't know which would be worse.

I stretched my arm out and winced when it collided with something, *clang*. The empty carafe of a coffeepot, knocked loose of its base, rolled lazily near my face. *What the hell?*

Sit up. Nope: lie back down. Everything was blinding white—the light coming through a window at my feet, the sheets, the paint. For a moment I thought maybe I was in the blank room of my dreams until I remembered that room didn't have a mattress on the floor. I craned my neck and saw an opening behind me, so I flipped over with walrus-like elegance to crawl toward the mouth of whatever I was in—and that's when I saw Altan below in his living room.

He was fully dressed in his flannel and jeans, crammed into his one IKEA chair, asleep. Somewhere my sober mind was freaking out—how had I ended up here and where were my pants (oh shit—near the door). But another drunker, dreamier part of me watched him sleep with a tenderness that surprised me. He had his arms crossed over his chest like he was giving attitude even in his dreams, but his face was softer, like a child's, weightless without the gravity of life pressing ever harder on the seams.

As if he felt me watching, Altan twitched awake, unfolded his arms with a long inhale, and looked up to see my head thrust over the edge of his loft like the cliff on Machu Picchu. "Oh good. You're alive," he said without enthusiasm. He got to his feet and stretched backward, arms over his head, unintentionally revealing his navel and the front of his jeans.

"Um, hi," I said. "I don't know how I got here."

"No shit. You called me hammered around ten o'clock and told me to come get you from The Signature. You left me a voice mail when I was at the gym."

This was news to me. "I don't remember," I said sheepishly.

"It's probably better that you don't. You were a mess," he replied, aggravated and disapproving—bold considering he used to show up karaoke-hungover at work. "I didn't want you going home to Pete like that so I texted him and said we were pulling an all-nighter."

My brain was a bass drum, and his words were sharp as pins. "Shit. Altan." I covered my face. "I'm so sorry."

He crossed to the kitchen, poured a glass of water from the tap. His movements were short and swift, like he was pissed. "Don't be. Friends fish each other out of bars and go on crazy capers together. That's what they do."

"So we're friends—is that it?" I said from behind my fingers.

He banged the glass on the counter and marched over to the ladder to put one foot on the bottom rung, hauling himself up so he was looking into my face. It was almost romantic, like Romeo and Juliet, except there was a passion in his eyes that seemed more interested in killing than wooing. "I don't know if we're friends, Ness. I don't know *what* we are. You made a pass at me last night, which I had to decline—multiple times."

I felt my chest constrict with something akin to panic. The footage was gone, but I could have recreated it easily enough: me, a sloppy mess. Altan, trying to protect me from going home to Pete and saying something that would have wrecked my life. Me, closing on Altan in his loft, whispering in his ear, my breath hot, my hands wandering. Altan, saying no. Doing the right thing. Tucking me in. Stroking my hair. Gritting his teeth.

"I said no, not because I didn't want you, but because I didn't want you like *that*. Drunk. On pills. I want you clear-eyed and awake, Ness—*all* of you, not just the part of you that sleeps." He dropped his voice to a growl, he was so angry. "I love you, OK? That's what I couldn't tell you in broad daylight at the bar, but I love you. And there's no point to it. And I'm *furious* that we were so stupid to let it get this far, that I let you fuck with me so freely."

I covered my mouth to stifle a sob, because I loved him too, but if I said it out loud then there would be decisions that would have to be made. Altan looked up at me in anger, but I could tell it was softened by hope—a selfish, childish, completely valid wish for me to leave Pete, one that I couldn't fulfill without tearing myself in half. He was waiting for an answer I could not give, and when he realized it wasn't coming, he looked at me with grim resolution, the kind of face you'd wear to a funeral. The kind of face that says goodbye. "Go home, Ness. Pete is waiting for you."

"I can't." My voice wobbled like a theremin.

"Well, you can't stay here." Altan hopped off the ladder, grabbed my jeans by the door, and tossed them into the loft. "I'm going to the gym. There's coffee in the cupboard next to the fridge. Put some on, have a cup, get yourself together, and leave. I don't want you here when I get back."

I nodded, my whole face cracking like a dam after a flood.

He glowered at me like he wanted to say more, then shook his head, grabbed the duffel bag by the door, and left without looking back. The door slammed behind him like a gunshot, and I collapsed back into his pillow. Even with my running nose, I could smell him, and I cried harder.

I don't know how long it took to wring myself out, but when I was done I felt no better—just thirsty and tired.

Eventually I pulled on my jeans and climbed down the ladder with the coffeepot tucked under my arm. Sniffling, I plugged it into a kitchen outlet and yanked open Altan's cupboard to find a couple of bags of nice coffee from local shops—and then, incongruously, a can of Folger's in the back, which I grabbed as a kind of self-flagellation. I didn't deserve nice coffee. I didn't deserve nice things. I'd broken Altan's heart, which was what I'd set out to do, but I hadn't thought I would also destroy mine in the process.

I struck something hard when I dipped the scoop into the grounds, and when I shook the can like I was panning for gold, the coffee fell away to reveal the top of a sandwich bag. I fished it out, and it was chock full o' Morpheum. There were hundreds of pills in there—enough to allow me to avoid reality for months.

I didn't think, and I didn't bother making coffee: I took the bag and stopped at Starbucks on my way home. Altan already hated me; he could go ahead and add stealing his pills to my tab. Maybe when I ran out of them, I'd be ready to face what I'd done.

WEDNESDAY, APRIL 3

Sam overdosed and is now in a coma. Mother. Fucking, Shitballs.

I'm sick over it, but Ness took it super hard. We went to The Signature when we heard, and she downed three drinks before flipping out, asking if I loved her—like she didn't already know.

I left her and went to the gym. When I was done, I had a voice mail from Ness saying she needed to be picked up. She sounded sloppy AF, so of course I went—only to find her three sheets to the wind sitting in some dude's lap. She was out of her mind, and the guy was taking full advantage of it: had his hands on her thigh, started shit with me when I tried to get her out of the bar; I had to play the voice mail for the bartender to prove she'd called me.

I tried to put her to bed but she was a mess; kept grabbing me and trying to kiss me. God, I wanted to kiss her back—but not like that, you know? I wouldn't do that with anyone, but especially not Ness. Not after what she's been through.

Still. She said she loved me. And I know she was high and didn't mean it, but I wanted it to be true. And then I had to tell myself repeatedly that it wasn't: what we have, it's all in dreams.

The worst part was that she wouldn't believe me when I told her we were awake; she thought it was a dream, like she couldn't tell the difference, and she moaned and teased and begged me to fuck her. And when I wouldn't, she demanded I sleep next to her, and she dozed off in my arms, murmuring about the places we would go, the children we would have. And I just lay there listening to all the things we'd never see.

THE CANADA TRIP

I slept off the bulk of my hangover in the car as Pete drove us to Canada; he chalked my tiredness up to the all-nighter I'd allegedly pulled. "Altan mentioned you had a patient overdose?" Pete asked, after waking me up so I could experience the thrill of having my passport checked (but disappointingly not stamped) at the border. "Was he one of yours?"

I'd been so heartbroken over Altan that I'd forgotten to be heartbroken over Sam. "Yeah, he did it on purpose. His wife died last year, and he missed her too much." My voice caught then as I realized maybe I'd gotten it all wrong: maybe Altan was the great love of my life. Maybe I was supposed to be traveling with him.

"Hey, Bug, don't cry," Pete said, taking my hand in his as he drove.

"Sorry." I wiped my eyes with my sweater cuffs. "I'm so tired. Yesterday was a long day."

"Go back to sleep if you want," said Pete, and I reclined my seat and dozed off again.

When I woke up, it was late afternoon, and we were pulling into the portico of a swanky hotel. I followed Pete miserably past giant urns of flowers to the check-in desk, and then up the elevator to a beautiful room with a king-size bed and at least fifteen feather pillows. A bottle of Maker's Mark on ice sat next to a bouquet of what smelled like mint on the sideboard, which got my attention. "Most guys would have gone with champagne and roses," I quipped weakly.

"But most guys aren't nerdy enough to remember the part in *The Great Gatsby* where everyone goes to the Plaza in New York just to order—"

"Mint juleps," I finished for him. My brain was sluggish but not enough to misremember the scene where Jay Gatsby and Tom Buchanan square off over Daisy on a hot day. Gatsby loses when he insists Daisy say she never loved her husband. But she couldn't lie. She did love Tom: the two of them had a history that a third party couldn't compete with.

And maybe so did Pete and me.

"Worm," I said, feeling my chest grow tight again. I'd made the right decision. "That was really thoughtful."

He looked alarmed when he saw me tearing up for the second time that day. "If you're going to lose it over some bourbon, you're going to have a hard time with this." He pulled a cloth-wrapped bundle from his weekend bag and handed it to me. The box was swaddled in a T-shirt—"I didn't have time to get paper," he said—and when I unrolled it I found a Canon AE-1 in a tattered (but original!) box. "Oh my god!" I squealed, dropping the T-shirt to admire the grandfather of the mass-produced home-use camera. "They stopped making these in the '80s. Where did you find it?"

"Craigslist," he said, grinning at me. "I got you some film, too. The guy said 35 millimeter. Is that right?"

He'd crammed five canisters into the camera box. "Holy shit! I haven't seen film in ages!"

Pete shrugged like he was trying to be casual, but I could tell he was pleased. "You said you wanted to take pictures."

I leapt into his arms, which tipped both of us onto the bed, laughing. "I love you," I said, and it wasn't a lie. I didn't need to read the air as I would in a dream: I felt it steady in my heart.

"And I you," he replied, kissing me on the lips. "And as much as I like where this is going, we have a dinner reservation in fifteen minutes that I think you're going to like."

I felt my stomach unspooling, the knots coming undone, the rope going out like an anchor to drag my churning mind to stop here. In Canada. Which was suddenly more romantic than I could ever have hoped.

We went to dinner at a restaurant in the hotel, this dark and swanky spot with white tablecloths and tufted velvet banquettes dotted with posh-looking people in suits and cocktail dresses. Pete and I were clad in our PNW finest—which was to say we looked like forest rangers. This was funny. Everything was funny: the way the waiter put my napkin on my lap, how many choices of water there were. How light and free I felt to be on a cheesy romantic date with my husband, as if I had remembered all the good things we had and the Morpheum episode was behind me now, like one of its dreams. It all felt destined, like I was heading in the right direction, called by the correct lighthouse like a rowboat on the Sound.

"So, is this what you expected when you envisioned a life of travel?" Pete teased.

"Oh yes," I said, exuberantly. "It's very sexy in Vancouver now that we've arrived."

Pete smiled. "It'll do for now. We'll go farther someday."

"When the kids are grown?" I joked.

"Let's get a bottle of wine in us before we start on *that* topic."

I was still hungover from the night before—the kind of hangover that could only be cured by more booze. So I was game when Pete called the waiter and said, "I'd like a nice bottle of wine. But not too nice—we might need day care money. Time will tell."

It was fun that he was joking about this, and I felt nervous for some reason, but in a good way—like a first date. "But of course," the waiter said. He pointed at something on the wine list, and Pete pulled a face at the price but then shrugged, good-natured, and the waiter was off.

The wine was good; we ordered another bottle with steaks. We talked about everything—work, books, the news, TV shows, our families. I couldn't remember the last time we'd talked, really talked, about nothing and everything at the same time. It was like we'd gone back in time, back to the beginning of our relationship—or at least to January before we'd started the baby business.

"This is nice," I said over dessert. "Just the two of us. You sure you want to give this up?"

"Oh man, we're going to do this!" said Pete. He was loopy and so was I. "You know the last time we drank and talked babies, we ended up in a three-day fight."

"You ruined Cole Porter for me."

"Fortunately, I can still eat steak."

I laughed as he reached for my hand across the table like he was proposing, and in a way he was. He took a deep breath and exhaled to clear the air and asked, "Have you given more thought to having kids?"

The wine sloshed in my stomach as I realized one of the things I loved about being with Altan was our radical honesty, the way we didn't hold back. It was time I came clean with Pete. "Before I answer this, I have something I want to tell you."

"OK," he said, dropping my hand and leaning back in his chair. "I'm all ears."

I glanced at the people dining around us and suddenly realized I didn't want to say what I had to say in front of them. "Can we talk about it when we get back to the hotel room?"

Pete frowned, his eyebrows almost touching across the bridge of his nose. "Ness," he said, "I thought we agreed: no more putting this conversation off. I want to do this now."

"I'm not putting anything off!" I thought the wine would calm me, but I could feel panic creeping out from the corners like an army of ninjas backflipping across the restaurant. "It's just that this is a delicate subject—"

"I don't believe this," he huffed. "I thought the whole point of this trip was to talk about starting a family—"

"And I want to, it's just— I was pregnant once before," I stammered. The words sailed over the table in a graceful arc to land with a *thwack* in Pete's wine: I felt like I could actually see the splash. "In college. Before I met you," I added, so he wouldn't think I'd ever cheated on him. It was instinct to worry about him, to wonder if what I did hurt.

His face was unreadable—neither angry nor surprised, but merely confused, like I'd suddenly started speaking French. "You were pregnant?"

I nodded, and Pete waited for me to go on, like I was capable of elaborating. My hands shook when I reached for my wineglass. "I think I need a bit more of the story here," he said.

I felt myself shrinking as my fingers fumbled with the clasp of my own personal Pandora's Box. "It's hard for me to talk about. Can you— can you ask me some questions and I can nod or shake my head?"

Pete's tone was escalating in alarm, and I couldn't blame him, but I also couldn't soothe him. "Enough games, Ness. Tell me what happened already!"

The problem with living in dreams is that you get used to the surreal quality of them, the ridiculousness without consequences: the ability to do whatever you want to do all of the time. This does not exist in the waking world. You can't just start screaming about sexual assault in a nice restaurant on a date with your husband, but for some reason I felt entirely entitled to it. For a moment it was like I couldn't tell if I was dreaming or not. "I was raped!" I said, louder than polite conversation called for. "I was raped, OK?"

The couple next to us glanced up from the menu worriedly, but I was focusing on Pete, how he was making a face I'd never seen before: one of complete and horrified shock. "It was at a party, and there were three of them, and—" I started to cry for the seventy-fifth time that day, hot, wet, fat tears, the blubbering, hyperventilating variety. I wasn't even remotely ashamed.

Pete blinked, open-mouthed, three times. And then he rushed to my side and knelt by my chair, pulling me into his arms. We looked like an engagement gone horribly wrong. "Oh my god, Ness—" he said. "I'm sorry. I'm so sorry—"

"And I got pregnant!" I shrieked through the tears and the snot. "And I couldn't have it. I was young, and it would've just reminded me of that night. I would hate it, you know?"

"Shh, Ness," said Pete. His arm left my back, I assumed to flag the waiter for the check. It didn't matter: I could see the hostess consulting with a man in a suit, who was rushing over.

"So I got an abortion," I went on, practically unintelligible. "I know I'm not supposed to feel bad about that but sometimes I do. And I think about that baby all the time. And I'm sorry," I howled.

Somehow I was on my feet; Pete must have pulled me up. "I'm so goddamn sorry!"

The manager was coming in hot, and Pete was doing his well-meaning chokehold that drove me up a wall. "Calm down, sweetheart," he said, trying to hold me tight. "It's OK."

"It's *not* OK!" I reared back and slapped Pete across the face. It was the sound that made me realize I'd done it, a crack like a baseball bat. The manager backed up. "Don't you *ever* say it's OK."

"That's not what I meant," stammered Pete, holding his cheek. "I was trying to say that you're safe now—"

"I'm *never* safe. Never. No matter where I go. I can't even go to work without my boss—"

The manager leaned over to whisper in Pete's ear, and Pete spat, "You sonofabitch. Can't you see we're in the middle of something here?" More muttering, hardly audible above my keening. "We're going! We're going!" Pete shouted, but I was already running out the door into the hotel lobby to the bank of elevators, punching the UP button furiously, tears pouring down my face like the rain back home. "Come on come on come on," I begged as I jabbed the button—that's how Pete found me. He tried to put his arms around me but I threw him off. The elevator opened and we both got in and I collapsed onto my hands and knees to better support myself as I sobbed.

"Ness!" Pete was pleading with me now, his own voice cracking as he tried to take my hands in his, but I wouldn't let him.

"I can't," I said. The elevator opened at our floor, and I half-crawled, half-ran to our room like a TV zombie. There was no thought. I was all impulse and adrenaline, and my instinct was telling me that if I wanted to survive this moment I had to knock myself out immediately.

Pete ran faster than I did. He sprinted ahead so he could unlock the room, and the door was open by the time I reached it. I kicked off my shoes and rushed to my backpack, to the Altoid tin in the front pocket. I dry-swallowed two pink pills and threw myself face down on the bed.

"What was that? What did you just take?" Pete asked. I could hear the alarm in his voice but I squeezed my eyes shut until I felt the pills hit the wine and burst like an Alka-Seltzer.

"Ness! Talk to me!" I heard Pete's voice but it faded away like a stereo turned up loud in a passing car on the freeway, and soon it was gone.

Altan was sitting on the floor of the white room, doing nothing in particular. He had the listless look of the preoccupied, like he was sulkily throwing rocks into some unseen pond. "Ness," he said, standing when he saw me. "What are you doing here? I didn't think—"

"Shut up," I said, crossing to him. I pulled his face toward me and kissed him greedily.

When he groaned, I could taste it. I could taste everything: his anger, his desire, his hurt, his love. "Ness, stop," he said, when I freed his mouth to focus my attention on that beautiful throat of his. "Don't do this to me."

"Shut the fuck up." I grabbed him by the scruff of the neck and dragged his face toward mine. I was trying to fill my field of vision with him; I wanted to blot out everything but his eyes. "Are you mad at me?"

He flicked his gaze toward mine, and I felt the electric zap of his fury. "Livid."

"*Then fuck me.*"

I was on a roll with shocking men today. "I'm sorry, *what*?" Altan said.

"Show me how mad you are. Tear me a new one."

He pushed me away slightly, but not enough to mean it. "Ness, come on."

"*You* come on." I jerked him forward by the front of his shirt so he had no choice but to stumble closer. "The only thing I want to feel right now is your dick in me."

"Jesus!" he swore somewhere between shock and disgust. "Where'd you get that mouth?"

"Why?" I shoved my hand down the waistband of his pants. "You like it?"

It was clear that he did. I could tell with my fingers, by the hunger in his eyes.

"Altan, I've treated you like shit, and I hate to be here asking for another favor because I don't deserve one, but I need you to fuck me. All night. Like you did in Paris. I want you to fuck my brains out so I can't think anymore. Will you do that for me?" I begged, touching my forehead to his, my breasts to his chest, my hips to his groin. I pressed myself into him like a flower, this fresh pain in need of drying. I needed someone to keep me, and I knew that he would.

He licked his lips, hesitating, and for a minute I thought he was going to turn me away. But then his mouth was on mine, and I burst into flames.

Ness showed up in the dream last night, said she needed me to have sex with her. She was in a panic about something but wouldn't tell me what. And even though I'd told her that morning I wanted her for real, I settled again for fake.

The sex was incredible, even better than Paris. It was everything I knew it would be. We're so goddamn good together, but why can't we have it when we're awake?

THE
MORNING AFTER

When I left Altan and the dream, Pete was already awake, curled on his side, watching me with his blue eyes, silent. And when it was clear that I wasn't going back to sleep, he pulled me into his arms and held me. We lay like that for a long time, watching the sun creep across the ceiling through the gauzy hotel curtains. I knew there were things I should have been thinking about—Did I just cheat on my husband? Did I really want to have a baby? How fast could room service deliver an Americano, or a Canadiano or whatever they called them up here?—but I was completely wrung out, incapable of doing anything but wait for something to happen, for life to become pretty. Around midmorning, Pete finally asked, "Why didn't you tell me?"

"I don't know," I said. "You never asked."

Silence hung between us like a curtain, and then Pete chuckled. I did, too. The awkward tension we'd been carrying around—him for weeks, me for years—was oozing from us like a lava flow, and we laughed along with it, rolling around the bed like we were being tickled by invisible fingers. Smearing his tear-stained face across his pillow, he finally gasped, "When was I supposed to ask—the first date?"

"Second, actually. Everyone knows that. You know the drill: *What's your favorite movie? Have you ever been sexually assaulted? Do you like to snowboard?* That sort of thing."

"Christ, Ness," he moaned, pulling me close as the giddiness in the room dissipated slightly. "I wish I'd known. I want to have been there for you."

I patted the strip of skin above his sternum. "There's nothing you could have done."

"Not true. I've been thinking about all these years, the shit I'd have done differently. The things I wouldn't have said, if I'd known. Like this baby situation? I've been such an asshole."

"You have not. You've been a normal husband treating me like a normal wife—which is what I've always wanted. Maybe that's why I didn't tell you." I inspected my cuticles, just to give myself something to do. "Maybe I didn't want you to treat me like damaged goods."

"But you kind of are, and I mean that in the nicest way." He kissed me then to prove it. "This thing that happened haunts you, and rightfully so. I hate that you've been carrying it alone." His throat got thick, and he stopped talking for a moment. "But now that I know, I want to help. What do you want to do?"

For the first time in a while, the answer was immediate and right: "I think it's time I get a therapist."

"Totally agree," said Pete, all business—in a good way. "We'll find you someone the second we get home. In the meantime, what do you want to do today? Right now?"

I appraised the growling of my stomach. "Are you hungry? We could get breakfast."

"Don't ask me what I want. What do *you* want?" He smiled his glorious toothy smile. "I asked you that the night we met, remember?"

Of course I did, but I wondered if my answer now would be the same. Back then all I'd wanted was not to be abused, and true to his word Pete had never done me wrong. But years later, I realized my needs had evolved since that night. Of course, I still needed a partner who would respect and cherish me, but I also needed excitement, adventure, the opportunity to be creative, to sow a little mischief—and I wasn't sure Pete could give me these things. I'd never thought to ask.

Maybe I could start?

"You know what I want right now?" I threw off the covers and stood on the mattress, infused with the energy that came from a new project. "Coffee."

"No-brainer. And what do you want after coffee?"

"I want to use my new camera," I said, bouncing on the bed. "I want to take some pictures."

Pete tackled me mid-jump so that I fell back to the bed, laughing as he kissed me on the lips. "You'd better get dressed."

After coffee, we went to the Butchart Gardens so I could photograph the flowers. It was a warm, beautiful day, bordering on spring even though early March was still raw and rainy elsewhere in the Pacific Northwest. Pete and I walked through the most beautiful rose gardens, holding hands like we were on our first date. And in a way, we were. Even though we'd been together since college, we were finally getting to know each other without a wall between us. It was sweet and exhilarating and fresh, like wind on wet hair, like sex without a condom.

In the afternoon, we went back to our hotel room and talked over mint juleps and room service. I told him everything: about that night in college, about what followed, about the photos I sold to Debby, and how I had some money saved up, and that I wanted to use it to take a real trip. "And then maybe we can try for a baby," I said shyly.

"You don't have to say that now," said Pete. "Get your heart and your head sorted out. We have plenty of time to try for kids."

"But what if we run out of time? What if it's just you and me?"

"Would that be so bad?" he purred, crawling up to where I sat against the headboard. He was like a cat. (A very *sexy* cat.) "Sometimes it's nice, just the two of us." When he kissed me, my eyes fell shut.

We made love for what felt like the first time, just the two of us: no doubts, no memories, no worries—just Pete and me the honest way it was always meant to be. And when it was over, we lounged in bed napping, watching TV, chatting, enjoying the other's proximity and the sheer pleasure of doing nothing. We were winding down for bedtime, and my head was on Pete's shoulder, his fingers in my hair. He yawned, rolling over to face me. The blond scruff of his day-old beard caught the lamplight, and he had dark circles under his eyes courtesy of Billionaire X. "What do you keep in that Altoid tin?" he asked.

Oh shit. I was only surprised because I'd thought I was being discreet. "Which one?" I asked, like I personally owned twelve different tins of Altoids.

"The one by the bed."

"Oh, *that* one! Prenatal vitamins." The lie was instant, like a reflex—crazy considering I'd come clean about the rest of my secrets today. Why was I still hoarding more?

Pete raised an eyebrow. "Really?"

"Yep. I read you're supposed to take them if you're thinking of having a baby. So I thought it couldn't hurt. I put them in an Altoid tin so you wouldn't get the wrong idea."

"That brain of yours," he said, like he was impressed by my thoughtfulness and ingenuity. "Always scheming."

He kissed me one last time, switched out the light, and fell asleep immediately, leaving me in the dark to itch with guilt. I thought about Altan for the first time that day, how we'd slept together the night before, how it had completely wiped my mind clean the way I'd wanted it to. *Don't think about Altan,* I told myself. I was moving *forward*—with *Pete*—and I had to control myself when it came to where I spent my attention. But around 2 a.m. I was no closer to sleeping than I was at eleven, and I took a Morpheum just so I wouldn't be a mess the next day. The dream I had was a replay of the previous night's session with Altan, and I didn't mind reliving it at all.

When I woke up the next morning, Pete was already dressed in jeans and a button-up, sitting on the edge of the bed. He held his head in his hands, like he had a migraine. "Hey, Worm," I said, my voice husky from sleep. "What's up?"

"Oh. There you are. Kind of you to join me," he said flatly. When he turned to look at me, I saw his eyes held none of the warmth or sparkle of yesterday; they were lifeless and dull, like he hadn't slept. He reminded me, briefly, of Sam, and I caught my breath. Pete never looked at me like that.

I slid out of bed and went to the bathroom, unnerved by his crabbiness. What the hell happened? "Did you sleep well?" I asked, putting toothpaste on my brush.

"Not at all."

"Oh no!" I said all chipper. "You were snoring by the time I nodded off, so I just assumed you were out. I slept like the dead. You wore me *out.*" Here I turned my head to give him as saucy wink, but he continued to stare at me blankly, like I was a movie he'd lost the plot to. I returned to my reflection in the mirror. "I had such a great time at the gardens yesterday!"

"You did?" He sounded confused.

"Yeah! The roses were fabulous." With the toothbrush in my mouth it came out like "A ro-ra a ha-ba-ba."

"Did you say 'roses'?"

I spat into the sink. "Yeah! All those colors?"

His reply came after a long pause. "Roses don't bloom in winter."

"Huh, you're right," I said, brushing my hair, attempting to remain breezy, beautiful, unconcerned. "I wonder how they get them to come out in March?"

"They didn't," Pete said. I didn't know what this meant, but I let it go as I came back into the bedroom and started going through my duffel bag, looking for a clean shirt. Pete didn't move.

"What's wrong?" I asked. "Is everything OK?"

"Peachy," he said in a way that suggested it wasn't. What was the opposite of peachy? What's that big spiky fruit that smells like shit? Durian. Durian-y. "What's in the Altoid tin," he said. It wasn't a question this time.

"I told you last night," I said, trying not to tense. "Prenatal vitamins. You know, in case we . . ."

I trailed off, partly to keep from accidentally signing myself up for pregnancy, and partly because the fury on his face was unprecedented. We stood there standing at each other, like we'd just met. Like we didn't know each other in the slightest.

"The other night, when you said you were assaulted . . ." Pete's face was twisted, like the words in his mouth were scorpions. "I'm just wondering . . . did it really happen?"

An inferno erupted in my chest, but my voice was quiet; my breath felt like smoke. "Why would I make that up?" I asked him, horrified.

"I wouldn't have thought you would, but . . ." He blew out a huge sigh. "You're different these days, and . . ."

"I can't believe—" I said, groping for words. Everything was red. There was nothing in my mind except the panicked flashing of a strobe light and a shrieking that sounded like baboons. "Seriously, are you accusing me of—of *lying?*—about my . . . my . . ."

"No, of course not," Pete said quickly. He stood and started packing his bag, not looking at me at all. "I know you're telling the truth. I just wanted to make sure you were sure of your story. That's all."

The three-hour drive home was silent. I fell asleep in the car.

Diana texted this morning to let me know Dean Jacobs is coming in tomorrow to get to the bottom of this Sam mess. I bet Malcolm is shitting his pants.

Took a Morpheum but I didn't dream anything. Literally, there was nothing. Maybe because I have no idea what I want.

Wait, that's not true. I miss Ness.

THE CLIMAX

Pete and I got home late Saturday and I went to bed immediately. I slept all of Sunday, too; it was easier than being awake. All I did with my eyes open was worry about Sam and Pete and Altan and my own deteriorating ability to deal with stress like a functioning adult. The noise in my head was terrible, and while I knew I shouldn't be drowning it out with Morpheum, I couldn't help myself. It was so easy. One pill, and it was all gone.

Sunday night, Altan texted me to give me a heads-up that Dean Jacobs was coming in the next day to investigate who was at fault for Sam's coma, and I texted back *Cool* because I was pretty sure it was me. I took another Morpheum and went to bed. He didn't text me back.

I didn't know how to talk to Altan about our freak-fest because I didn't know how to say, "I care about you, and I enjoy our sexy times, but I'm trying to make it work with my husband even though he's acting weird, so maybe we should cool it, even though I don't want to, because I'm attracted to you mentally and physically in ways I've never felt for other men." Funny that there wasn't a greeting card for that—I even checked Bartell Drugs.

That's a lie. I didn't go to Bartell's. I didn't go anywhere. I slept all Sunday.

To say I was dreading work on Monday was an understatement, but I hauled myself out of bed and knuckle-dragged downtown. A cardboard box filled to bursting with Diana's houseplants met me when the elevator doors slid open on our floor. I stepped awkwardly over it as I heard her shrieking in the back. "This is bullshit," she said, chasing Malcolm out of her office; he was holding her violets in one hand and the ivy in the other, intent on dumping them on one of the empty desks in the cube farm. "You can't kick me out of my office just because your daddy is coming to visit and you need to look competent!"

"As your boss, I can do whatever I like," answered Malcolm, and it was nice to know he treated everyone like shit and not just me.

When his eyes came to a rest on me, he drank me in like a beer in the tropics. "Well, well," he sneered, and my skin did that thing where it tries to slink out the door with the rest of me still in it just to avoid his touch. "If it isn't the lady of the hour! Can you join me in my new office so we can have a little chat about how thoroughly you've fucked this trial up?"

Before I could even fully register the harshness of his words, I heard Altan say, "Malcolm, that is completely uncalled for."

I hadn't even seen him at his desk, but he was there, slouched behind his monitor, as disheveled and sexy as ever—even more so for standing up for me, even though he was sitting down. My heart leapt to see him.

"Shut up, Al. This doesn't concern you. A man is in a coma because of *her!*" bellowed Malcolm. "So tell me, *who's* out of line?"

The wind left the room, because Malcolm wasn't wrong. I knew it not with fear, but rather calm. I thought of Anne Boleyn's execution, how, when she stepped trembling onto that grassy patch inside the Tower of London, part of her must have been relieved. It sucks to die, but at least you can stop worrying about it when it happens.

"Thanks anyway, Altan," I said, and then gathered myself up and marched to Diana's—I mean, Malcolm's office. Malcolm followed me inside, and when he shut the door he fiddled with the lock on the knob—*holy shit* had that always been there?—and then came to stand toe-to-toe with me—*literally,* like he was trying to see how much of my personal space he could invade before I crumbled. He reached up to tuck a strand of hair behind my ear just to prove he could, and I hated him. That hate gave me strength. I knew I was screwed; all was already lost. There was nothing to fear. "Have a seat," he said with venom in his voice.

He gestured to an armchair across from Diana's desk, and I sat, assuming he'd plotz himself opposite from me on the furniture so I could converse with his crotch like I usually did. But instead he took a seat in Diana's swivel chair and steepled his fingers on the desk like a classic Bond villain. He was really overselling the whole "evil boss" thing.

"Let's cut to the chase, shall we?" he purred. "Your name is on all of Sam's paperwork, and my father will be here in thirty minutes. I can save your job, but you haven't been terribly nice to me lately, so I think it's time to make amends."

The calmness of his voice made me shiver. "What are you talking about?"

"I want to give you a job." He leaned back in Diana's chair and unzipped his pants slowly enough that I could count each individual tooth release. I couldn't see exactly what he was doing since I was seated, but I had a pretty good idea that he was stroking himself. My mind was static, like it couldn't even comprehend that this was happening. It was almost funny, in that "I'm laughing so hard because I'm on the verge of a mental breakdown" kind of way.

"Let me get this straight," I said bluntly, because what's the point of being delicate when genitals are on (or under) the table? "Your father is on his way here to investigate you for negligence because a man fell into a coma under *your* watch, and you want me to *blow* you?" This was weird, even for Malcolm.

There was that smile again, so confident, like he had me in a checkmate but I hadn't figured it out yet. "That's exactly right."

I tasted bile then. And blood. And copper. And asphalt. Malcolm locked his eyes on mine as he continued to move his hand under the table, panting slightly. "I had a feeling you wouldn't be too keen on this *particular* job offer, so just know if you refuse, I'll pin Sam on the three of you and you'll all get fired. I know you don't care because your husband is a hotshot lawyer who probably makes at least double your shitty salary. But think of Diana and her children. Think of Altan and his alimony payments. They would leave here empty-handed: no severance, no recommendations, no prospects. Nothing."

He let that sink in. "Or, you do what I say. And no one gets hurt."

He was really breathing now; the glint in his eyes was metallic. "Look, I'm already halfway there. It'll be so easy. All you have to do is kneel down and open your mouth. It'll be over in seconds, and then all your little lives remain intact. Either you go down or everyone goes down. You have about thirty seconds."

I shook my head, which rattled words out of my brain; they tumbled from my mouth like gumballs: "Malcolm, you're a fucking piece of shit."

"Yeah, tell me."

"I fucking hate you so much—"

"That's it, Nessie. Talk to me."

I was tearing up now. "I cannot believe you think you can do this."

"Oh my god, Nessie! Are you *crying*?" Malcolm yanked four tissues in quick succession from a box on the desk and then pressed them under the table. He shook and emitted a low groan, his face contorting and turning lavender. I wanted to kill him, to grab him by his throat and keep squeezing until he turned eggplant and then maroon and then died. That was the kind of job I had in mind: his neck was the only part of him I'd squeeze.

When it was over, he sighed contentedly. Then swift as a fox the tissues were in the waste bin, resting atop one of Diana's plants. Malcolm was zipping himself up as a knock sounded at the door, and for a moment I had to question if it all had really happened. "Nessie, would you get that?" Malcolm chirped.

Whoever was on the other side was twisting the knob in vain by the time I undid it. I found Altan standing on the threshold, looking confused that the door was locked to begin with. And then he inspected the map of my face. He saw where streams had sprung and dried, and I watched his eyes go black. "What the hell is going on in here?" he said.

"Nessie and I were just discussing meeting tactics," Malcolm replied, squirting Purell on his hands.

"That true?" Altan asked me.

I nodded weakly, though it wouldn't have fooled anyone, much less someone who had part-time access to my mind.

For a moment, I thought Altan would forget himself, that he would act as he would in a dream: punch Malcolm in the teeth, sweep me off my feet, and rescue me from all this shittiness in a dashing white Uber—but this wasn't a dream. This was real life in all its cruel and ugly unfairness. "Happy endings" meant something different here.

For a moment I thought Altan would make a scene, but he didn't, and I didn't blame him. In real life, we weren't nearly as cool as we pretended to be asleep. "Malcolm, your dad is on his way up," Altan said. His eyes didn't leave mine.

"Jesus!" exclaimed Malcolm, checking his watch, rising from his desk. "Assemble everyone in the conference room! And get your damn lab coats on!"

Altan turned to go, and before I could follow him, I felt Malcolm's hand on my ass, followed immediately by his breath in my ear. "You're finished," he whispered as he strode toward the lobby.

THE CONFERENCE ROOM KERFUFFLE

The active lifestyle of most Seattleites, in combination with the city's complete lack of sun for 75 percent of the year, has a way of freezing certain folks in amber age-wise. Dean Jacobs was one of those people. He was in his late sixties, but he didn't look a day over forty, with his barely creased face and a head of thick hair that he wore Brylcreemed to one side in a style that was either ironically vintage or an earnest attempt at a grandfatherly dapperness—it was hard to tell. Regardless, in dark jeans and a V-neck sweater, Dean was authoritative without being intimidating, engaging without being creepy. He was everything his son was not as he stood to shake my hand when I entered the conference room. I didn't hear anything he said. Everything sounded like the flapping of wings, a flock of pigeons taking off.

I sat down across from Altan, who was next to Diana. Neither was schmoozing Dean or his sundry toadies who were fluttering around worrying the pens and distributing papers. "Are we ready to get started?" Malcolm asked, and instantly everyone settled into seats. One of the toadies had brought a platter of bagels to my execution! Super. I slathered one with an unholy amount of cream cheese to serve as my last meal.

Malcolm began: "I know our thoughts right now are with Sam's family,"—*bullshit*, I coughed in my mind—"but we must also consider what this new development means to our trial. As you know, we've invested a lot of time and effort into Morpheum, and we're really proud of what this drug does. Diana, do you mind walking us through the findings so far?"

"Sure," said Diana with a megawatt smile. She launched into a PowerPoint that was bone dry and full of data—purposefully, I assumed, so Malcolm would look like an idiot when he didn't know what any of it meant. She went on about patient satisfaction scores and dropout rates, then included a really dynamite graph about the different kinds of diarrhea that had been recorded as a side effect. Malcolm chuckled nervously, eyeing his dad. "Let's skip forward to the part where Sam Stevens overdosed."

"You don't want the comparison of stool firmness in latter trial stages?" Diana asked sweetly.

"Actually, Ness," said Malcolm, "why don't you talk about Sam? You knew him best."

"*Know* him," I corrected. I'd finished eating the bagel ten minutes ago, but for some reason it still felt like there was cream cheese gumming up my throat. "I know him best. He's not dead."

"Of course," said Malcolm. He extruded a smile from his perfect teeth. "My mistake."

Everyone in the room turned to look at me, hands folded in their laps, beatific expressions on their faces, like they were churchgoers ready to daydream through the sermon. I hadn't prepared anything, and frankly, even if I had, it would have all been wiped the minute Malcolm took his dick out. My panic was manifesting itself in an urge to babble, so I did. "Sam Stevens is a seventy-year-old male in good health. He lives in Ballard and drives for Uber. A former English professor, his favorite book is *Fahrenheit 451*. His least favorite is—"

"Nessie," interrupted Malcolm, a slight chuckle to his voice. "I think we can skip the bio."

"*The Great Gatsby*," I finished, directing this to Dean. "He has a daughter, Maria, in her mid-thirties. Presumably named after her mother, Mary, who died last year after a long battle with cancer."

Malcolm hissed a frustrated breath. "This isn't important."

"It's *extremely* important," I said, slapping the table with my palm for good measure, which caused the toady next to me to jump. "This man is in a coma because of what we gave him."

"What *you* gave him," said Malcolm. "After all, you're the one who signed him up for the trial, aren't you?"

My instinct was to defend myself, but then two realizations collided in my mind like atoms in a particle accelerator. One: I'd failed Sam. I didn't deserve a way around that. Two: Just because I'd been too afraid to stand up to Malcolm before didn't mean my legs didn't work now. It wasn't too late to burn this thing down.

"I *did* sign him up," I said, getting to my feet. "But I shouldn't have, in retrospect. As you and I have discussed, I've been having a lot of performance issues lately."

I risked a glance at Altan. He had his elbows on the table, his face propped against his clasped hands, so I couldn't read his expression. But his eyes: his eyes were sharp with either anger or fear or some marriage of them, a kind of terror that could touch off a brush fire. "Because I've been stealing Morpheum," I said.

There was quiet for five whole seconds, and then Diana gasped, "Holy fucking shit!" One of the toadies made a gargled noise; another threw a pencil on the table in resignation. Altan groaned and hung his head in his hands. Malcolm went pale.

"For personal reasons," I said loudly over the hullabaloo, "I was having trouble sleeping, so I stole some to see if it works, and I became addicted. I took too much and wasn't paying enough attention to my job. Nobody knew. And now a man is in a coma because of my negligence."

Another hush fell over the room as everyone turned to look at Dean, who leaned back in his chair almost too casually, like someone who'd had a lot of practice refusing to freak out in public. "How long?" was all he said.

"Pretty much since the beginning of the trial. I've been high at work for months," I lied, realizing I was actually kind of enjoying myself. The scene had a surreal, dreamlike quality, which might have been from adrenaline or from my mind warping to cope with the fact that I was committing career suicide at best and maybe also confessing to manslaughter at worst.

"So the whole trial is compromised?" Dean asked.

"Yup. You'll need to start over." And while they did, I thought, I'd report Morpheum's unusual side effects to the FDA, the NYT, the FBI, UCLA, UPS, KFC, and any other initialism that might be interested. The news that WellCorp was developing a mind-hacking drug would create a PR fiasco so mired in red tape that Morpheum would never see the light of day.

"OK," Dean said as if I'd just told him I'd eaten the last bagel. And then he turned to Malcolm and dropped the temperature of his voice from cool to downright frosty. "Son, as the office manager of Urban Campus, can you explain to me how the hell you let this happen?"

Everyone in the room inhaled all at once. Things were rapidly devolving into an episode of *The Jerry Springer Show*. "*Me?*" choked Malcolm. "Yes, I'm technically the office manager, but Diana is in charge of anything trial-related—"

"I see," Dean interrupted. "So Diana manages the trials, while you manage the office. And what do your duties entail exactly—making sure everyone has enough pencils and tissues?"

"We're probably due for more," I said. "Tissues, that is." The words were leaving my mouth before I was even sure what I was saying: "Malcolm used half a box just before this meeting when he masturbated in front of me in Diana's office."

If I'd thought my Morpheum confession had been a bombshell, it was nothing compared to the nuclear capabilities of this one. The air left the room. Even the overhead lights stopped buzzing for a moment. I'd never experienced such complete and exquisite silence.

"*What?*" whispered Dean. "Why?"

"To intimidate me, I guess." My voice was chirpy and informative, like a kindergartener reporting the school day's events. "He said he knew Sam's coma was my fault but that he'd protect me if I gave him a blow job. I didn't, hence the Kleenex."

Everyone toggled from looking at me to looking at Malcolm, who looked as though his own necktie were strangling him to death: his eyes were bugging grotesquely out of his head and his face had turned the color of merlot. "This isn't the first time this has happened to me," I babbled happily. "I was sexually assaulted in college, but I never told anyone and it fucked my head right up. So I figured it was better to immediately report what Malcolm did so he doesn't do it again."

The younger Jacobs turned to his father and laughed—*ha ha ha!*—like he was reading it out of a book. "Why should we even believe you?" he said.

"Because all you have to do is check the garbage can for the proof. You're going to want rubber gloves: I think we have some in the first aid kit in the kitchen. I can get them—"

"If you think this will save your job—" Malcolm growled.

"—I know it won't. I don't want it to." I said this so offhandedly that I even shrugged. "I don't want to work for a company that mandates blow jobs from its female employees."

"Ms. Brown, WellCorp *certainly* doesn't condone this kind of behavior," stammered Dean.

But I didn't let him finish. "Then I expect you to clean it up. And if I were you, I would seriously consider getting those gloves." I left my laptop on the table and started for the door.

"Where are you going?" Malcolm asked.

"To pack my stuff. I'm assuming I'm fired because I stole the pills?" When no one responded, I said, "I only need five minutes. You can call security to escort me out after that."

I made my way to my desk and threw my water bottle and some pens into my backpack. And then I sat there for the last time and waited for someone to fetch me, watching through the conference room window as all hell broke loose. Malcolm and his father were roaring at each other like warring grizzlies; some toady was heading toward the office, a pen held up like a magic wand, presumably to dig through the trashcan. At least three people were furiously punching into their cell phones, and Diana was applauding—actually applauding—like she was watching the most wonderful circus of her life.

Only Altan was still, his face still propped in his knuckles as he watched me through the glass. Security arrived to march me to the elevator; they held me by my elbows so I couldn't even wave goodbye.

THE EXIT

When I got back to my apartment, I kicked my boots off at the door, threw the keys on the counter, opened a beer, and dropped into the sofa. *Fuck WellCorp*, I thought. I'd been miserable there for too long, and that I could leave in such spectacular fashion—that I could sink Morpheum *and* Malcolm in one fell swoop—had me doped up on the greatest drug of all: revenge.

I was long overdue for a fresh start, and it was time to focus on my next steps. But first: relaxation! Propping my socked feet on the coffee table, I grabbed the remote. The TV was already tuned to HGTV: *hell* yeah. Frankly, I was tired—funny considering I'd spent most of the month asleep. Maybe Morpheum was more refreshing if you didn't spend all night trying to direct your dreams-slash-low-key seduce your coworker, but since my brain had been churning night and day for so long, I felt I was entitled to beer and a mindless *Property Cousins* marathon.

Which hit the spot for two episodes. And when the third one *also* ended with white people fawning over sconces (and not a single hardcore sex scene—how else was anyone supposed to make thirty minutes of tile placement interesting?), I started to realize the gravity of what I'd done. In ruining Morpheum, I was banished from experiencing the Technicolor magic of my own mind. Now I was left with caulking and rain. No Sasquatches or mermaids. Or Altan.

It was for the best, I tried to tell myself. After all, I'd committed myself to Pete (again) and was moving away from Morpheum toward a more meaningful future. But still I mourned what I'd lost, which was an intelligent, funny man who cared deeply about me and whose mind was the most beautiful place I'd ever been.

The adrenaline of my exit was wearing off, and the pain was setting in as surely as if I'd snapped a bone. My heart was broken: I imagined it spiky with shards of itself poking dangerously at my lungs, which explained why I couldn't breathe. My sorrow was soggy and cold, and I curled into bed to warm myself up. Naturally, I took a Morpheum and hoped I'd wake up a person who didn't love two men. But when the raw, cold afternoon turned into night, I opened my eyes to the sound of Pete clanging around the kitchen making dinner, and I still loved Altan.

"Hey," Pete said when I stumbled out of the bedroom, blinking against the overhead lights. "Sorry if I woke you." He didn't sound sorry, I thought, as I noticed he was still in his suit pants, the sleeves of his dress shirt rolled to his elbow. He was overdue for a haircut, probably hadn't had time since he'd been so busy with work. There was a pot of pasta boiling on the stove, which was strange because pasta wasn't known for being a loud dish to make. "You eaten?"

"Not hungry," I muttered, hoisting myself onto a barstool at our island and slumping my head in my hands. I had the distinct ache of waking up before the Morpheum had worn off—a sensation Altan called "blue brains." A fresh wave of regret washed over me to think of him.

"How was work?" asked Pete.

I didn't know where to begin explaining, so I didn't. "Fine."

Pete took the pot off the stove and dumped its contents into a colander in the sink. "Well, I had an interesting day," he said, answering a question I hadn't asked. "Billionaire X decided he doesn't want to go through with the divorce after all! Can you believe it? All that work!"

"That sucks."

He fished the pasta out with tongs to finish it in a pan with garlic and white wine. "Do you want to know why?"

I shrugged to be polite. I wasn't entirely in the mood to contemplate Billionaire X's palladium bathroom fixtures. All I wanted to do was sulk in my bedroom in the melodramatic, boneless way of teenagers. Why had I even come out here?

"He and his wife decided to make it work for the dog," said Pete, forking spaghetti onto two plates. "They couldn't agree on custody and didn't want to put her through a two-home situation. So they're staying together for the golden retriever. Isn't that nuts?"

"I told you I wasn't hungry," I muttered when he set a dish in front of me and hopped on the stool next to mine.

"So keep me company." He was trying to remain cheerful, though I could see his face starting to slide. He motioned to a bouquet of roses I hadn't noticed on the counter. "Did you see these? You kept going on about roses over the weekend. I thought you should have some."

I looked at them idly. "Nice, but not as good as the ones in Vancouver."

The color drained from Pete's face. I used to know all of his expressions, but now they were foreign to me, a different language. I couldn't tell if he was frightened or mad. "Can we talk?" he said.

"About what?" I put my head on the counter. The granite felt cool on my cheek.

"Anything. I feel like we haven't seen each other in forever."

"We just spent the whole weekend in Canada!" I griped. What more did he want?

"Yeah, but—" Pete paused, searching for the right words. "That wasn't exactly *quality* time."

"What do you mean?" I was slightly offended. "We went to the gardens; I took all those pictures. We decided I was going to go to therapy before we tried to have a baby . . ."

Pete's eyebrows met in a deep furrow. "We did?"

"*Yes!*" I was so sick of this game—whatever it was Pete was playing—where he acted mildly dubious anytime I spoke. "This is ridiculous," I said, charging toward the bedroom. I had problems to avoid, dreams to have, companies to undermine.

"Do you love me?"

I stopped like he'd speared me through the heart and pinned me to the wall. "Not at the moment," I answered. I didn't even turn around; I wouldn't have been able to bear the look on his face.

"But usually?" I heard him say.

What percentage of our love had I slept away with Altan? It was a small amount in the grand scheme of Pete's and my relationship, but I'd been a different person before Morpheum. That's what Pete couldn't understand; he was in love with a ghost. I turned. "Usually, I love the shit out of you," I said.

He looked lonely, sitting there by himself with his dinner. There was a time when we used to cook together, back when he made me happy. "Then why doesn't it feel that way?"

I went to our room and closed the door. It was dark now, since I hadn't bothered turning on the lights when I'd gotten up, but still I was able to lay hands on the Altoid tin next to my bed, recently refilled from Altan's sandwich bag, now nestled in my boot. I took one Morpheum, then another, then another, because fuck it. Fuck *everything*. I didn't want to deal with my life as it all came crumbling down.

THE WORST DREAM

The living room I found myself in when I woke in the dream was the largest I'd ever seen. Mentally, I calculated the square footage, admiring the spare accessories, the oversize lamps, the modern furniture crafted exclusively of right angles, and thought *Yep*: you could fit my whole apartment in here. The lights were off as if I'd broken in while no one was home, but the thick cream-colored draperies of the floor-to-ceiling windows had been pulled back to create a kind of interior twilight lit by the neon signs of Pike Place and the big Ferris wheel on Pier 52. Beyond, ferry boats schlepped between Seattle and Bainbridge Island. These stars of light were reflected in the polished marble floors.

Who lived here? I wondered. Must've been someone Altan knew, because I was not acquainted with anyone rich enough to own paintings. Not prints or posters but *actual paintings*. I felt the texture of the layered paints cut into my cheek when someone blitzed me out of the dark, crunching me against one of the canvases before I could even scream.

"I was wondering if I'd see you," growled a voice, as its owner pinned my arms behind my back. "You think that little stunt you pulled today was cute, but you fucked up, Nessie."

Holy. Fucking. Shit.

Malcolm had his full weight pressed against me so I couldn't fight him. He snaked his hand around my ass and then cupped me roughly between my thighs. "You didn't count on me figuring out what Morpheum does."

My mind went blank then, as cold and white as a full-blown blizzard.

He gripped the back of my shirt, reminding me eerily of the Sasquatch dream, and dragged me backward toward one of his conversation pits. I tried to Nightcrawl away, but the fear had me: I couldn't move. I couldn't even wake up, as Malcolm tossed me onto a sofa and then plunged his tongue into my mouth. There was a frantic clumsiness to this that reminded me of high school, and it occurred to me that maybe Malcolm thought of himself this way— a take-charge kind of guy instead a rape-charge kind of guy. Then again, he knew just how much I didn't want this. I bit down reflexively, and Malcolm sat up and punched me square in the face. It hurt as badly as it would have in real life, and the shock of it exploded into panic.

"Stop," I commanded, and slapped him, but he only laughed. "Ooh, Nessie. How'd you know I like it rough?"

He grabbed me by my wrists and threw me to the floor. When I hit I was already naked, as if by magic; the marble was so cold it took my breath away. *Wake up!* I told myself with that drowning despair I'd felt on Machu Picchu, like my mind was on the fritz. *Vanessa Brown, you wake the fuck up!*

Malcolm was laughing as he stood over me. "I have to thank you for your *performance* in sabotaging the Morpheum trial. You played your role perfectly. I've had more lucrative plans for that drug ever since we started developing it, but my dad wouldn't hear of them. He just wanted 'to help people.'" He said the last few words in a mocking, nasally tone. "Well, now he knows: people can't help themselves. Sam Stevens is proof."

I could barely process this: Malcolm's being here in my dream, much less his confessing to a conspiracy deeper than I could have imagined. "Screwing Sam," I clarified, "was about more than just screwing me?" My teeth were chattering from cold and rage.

Malcolm started unbuttoning his shirt. "Two birds. One stone. Sure, it was a complicated plot. But it got even juicier when I started taking the pills myself just to see what they could do. And who did I find night after night in my dreams? Nessie and Altan, holding hands and frolicking like it was summer camp. I figured it was easier to let you be my guinea pigs, so I just let you two run wild while I watched."

I stared at him in horror. All the times I'd been using the dreams to escape from Malcolm—he'd actually been there, spying on Altan and me. Had he been there when I told Altan about my abortion, when we'd made love? I wanted to throw up. The most meaningful experiences of my life had just been a TV show for my disgusting boss.

He laughed to watch me realize this, as he stepped out of his pants. "I was there the whole time—crowds, bushes, whatever. You two were too wrapped up in each other to notice."

"Even in the white room?" I blurted. There was nowhere to hide in the blankness.

"What white room?" Malcolm asked.

I shut my mouth then, knowing there was at least one place he didn't see. Malcolm looked at me uncertainly, worried he was missing something, but he recovered, reclaiming the upper hand. "Regardless, I saw you lusting over him. That look in your eyes—so thirsty," he growled. He was down to his briefs now, and he stood over me so as to place his crotch directly in my line of sight, per usual. Only right now I was too scared to roll my eyes about it. *Wake up!* "Well, Altan's not here, so you'll have to make do with me." He started to lower himself. "I promise, you won't mind."

I was frozen, staring up at him from the floor, when I saw a blur catch him around the waist and slam him into the window. The glass shattered spectacularly, catching the moonlight and glinting like snow as it fell. Before I could cope with what had even happened, Altan was kneeling next to me, having Nightcrawled back to the living room.

"Holy shit, holy shit," he said, pulling his flannel shirt off and draping it around my shoulders. I was curled in a ball, so it covered most of me. "I don't know what just happened. I fell asleep and showed up here, and Malcolm was undressing, and you looked terrified, so I just assumed—and then I pushed him out the window. And, oh god, Ness. Are you OK? Are you OK? Did he hurt you?"

I wrapped myself around Altan's neck like he was a life preserver, and I cried. Fully. Shamelessly. I sobbed my heart out. "Tell me I got here in time," he said frantically, worrying over me with his hands, rubbing my back, smoothing my hair. "Did I get here in time?"

I nodded, too broken to talk.

He took my face in his hands and looked into my eyes. "Why didn't you wake up, Ness?"

"I couldn't!" I choked. "I took three pills!"

He looked at me like I was crazy. "Why would you do that?"

"I don't know! Pete and I had a fight."

"Ness," he moaned, holding my face. His eyes bored into mine like he was trying to dig a hole in my skull through which I could escape. "What have you done?"

"I lost you. I fucked everything up."

"Don't say that." I looked up and was relieved to see he'd changed the setting of the dream to the white room. I was dressed in oversize prison-issue sweats dreamed up by someone who had obviously never designed women's clothing before. I didn't care. I leaned into Altan and cried harder.

He dipped his nose into my hair and whispered, "I'll be back."

"Where are you going?" I asked desperately. Now that I had him in my arms again I didn't want him to go.

"Somewhere, but I'll come right back."

"Don't leave me!" I said, gripping him with my nails, like that could keep him here. "What if Malcolm finds me?"

"Just hang on for five minutes."

"Altan! Don't!"

But he evaporated out of my grasp, and I panicked as the white room darkened, the brightness dimming and graying like a winter sky. "What's happening?" I shrieked. "Where's the light going?"

Altan returned then. He sat on the floor with me and motioned for me to put my head in his lap so he could stroke my hair. "There," he said, his voice smiling. "See? I'm here."

"Where's the light going?" I repeated. I felt miserable and weak, like I had food poisoning.

"Let's not worry about it," Altan said, using the tone you'd use for a tired child. "You're going to wake up soon. So let's just sit here until that happens, OK?"

We sat, Altan smoothing my hair like I was a dog. It was almost twilight in the room. "Altan?" I asked feebly. "Are you there?"

I was being blasted in the face with ice water.

When I opened my eyes, I was in the bottom of my bathtub. "Oh my god! You're alive!" choked Pete. He was crouched over me, soaking in his T-shirt and boxers; even his face was wet. "I thought you were gone!" he cried, wiping his eyes roughly with the back of his hand. "Goddammit, Ness! What did you do?" He twisted the shower knobs off with a little more force than necessary and reached into the tub to clutch me under my arms.

"What happened?" I murmured, limp in his embrace.

"Altan called. He said you'd been stealing pills from work and that he thought you might have overdosed. I don't know how he knew, but he told me to get you up. But I couldn't—not with shaking, not with screaming. So I threw you in the shower—"

"I'm OK, Worm," I said to reassure him.

"You are *not* OK."

For some reason I had the distinct feeling that I'd killed my marriage—not on purpose. But it felt like Pete was a ficus I hadn't watered in months. I thought of Diana, how she talked to her plants to keep their morale up. But I didn't have the energy to chat. I didn't even know what to think, much less what to say. My neglect knew no bounds.

I let Pete pull me up to standing, shivering in my T-shirt and underwear. He wrapped me in a towel and pulled me toward him. "I'm going to ask one last time. What's in the Altoid tin?"

"Sleeping pills from work," I said miserably into his shoulder.

He sighed. "Thank you for telling me. Now, what do we do? Do you need rehab? Do you need to be committed? Tell me what you need, and I'll get it for you."

"I just need time to get my shit together," I said.

Pete's body tensed against mine. "And you want me to— what?—wait here with a bucket of water in case you overdose again? How can you ask me to do that?"

I snapped. "None of this is your business!"

"You're my wife!" he roared, louder than I'd ever heard him get. "You *are* my business!"

He stalked out of the bathroom, leaving me in there, my clothes plastered to my skin. I peeled my T-shirt off and walked out naked, wrapped in the towel, to find Pete in dry clothes sitting on the bed. "Why are you taking these pills?" he asked without looking at me. "Tell me honestly. Help me understand."

Talk to the ficus, I thought, and I sat next to him on the bed so I wouldn't have to look into his face. "It started when you brought up having a baby," I said, "and I was having those nightmares and couldn't sleep. Having a baby sounded . . . like something I wanted to run away from. Like the death of all adventure. And I guess I wanted at least some adventure before that happened, and I thought it wouldn't hurt you . . . but I let it go too far. And now I don't know how to come back."

I leaned in to kiss him but pulled away and got into bed, rolling toward me so I could lie in his arms. "I'm going to stay up all night, Ness," he said, "to make sure you're OK."

"You don't have to do that—"

"Shut up," he said, and I flinched, even though I deserved his anger. Still, he held me in his arms in the half-light of his bedside lamp. We lay like that for a long, long time, and after a while, he said, "Ness, I love you."

"I know," I told him back. And that was the worst part, because I loved him too. I loved him so much and I'd still done this to him: made a mess of myself and our life. And I hated myself for doing that—but what I hated most was the fact that I couldn't do it anymore.

After a few hours, I felt his body go slack and his breathing slow. Soon he was twitching in his own dreams, but I kept myself awake— I sure as hell wasn't going to sleep the same hours as Malcolm. I lay in bed all night, just staring at the ceiling like the undead.

How do I even write this down? So much has happened I don't even know how to prioritize.

1. Ness quit work.
2. She confessed to taking the Morpheum.
3. In the dream tonight Malcolm tried to rape her, but she couldn't wake up because
4. She overdosed.

I don't like to think of myself as a hero or anything, but what would have happened if I hadn't been there?

And what do I do now? What if she puts herself in a coma? WHERE DID SHE EVEN GET SO MUCH MORPHEUM? I mean, she didn't take it from work, and she couldn't have found my stash in the kitchen—

Goddammit. She did.

Will have to go over there and straighten this out. I can't let her destroy herself like this.

THE
INTERVENTION

When I woke up in the late afternoon, Pete was at work. I almost couldn't believe he'd leave me alone after last night, but then I noticed my Altoid tin was gone. Joke was on him: I had more in my boots.

I didn't take any though, figuring I'd cool it for the moment after the overdose scare. It was stupid to take three: I'd stick to just one from now on. I'd take one tomorrow morning, when Pete and Malcolm were both at work and I could get a full eight hours by myself.

In the meantime, I needed something to take the edge off life. We were out of beer, but I was able to arrange for some to be delivered (god bless Seattle). I was in no mood for pants, so I was wearing nothing but Altan's (clean) Pike Place Market T-shirt and a pair of underwear; I'd put in a ten-dollar tip with my order so the delivery guy would have no right to complain. But when someone finally rapped on the door, it turned out to be Altan, holding two cups of coffee. His jaw dropped. I couldn't tell if he liked what he saw or if he was horrified by it. I don't think he was sure either, but eventually he rearranged his face in an approximation of his usual cheekiness. "Well, dreams *do* come true."

Every cell in my body wanted to fall into his arms, but I didn't. "You're not my beer."

"You don't look like you need beer. You look like shit."

Despite myself, I felt the corner of my mouth twitch up. It was the closest I'd come to a smile in days. "Well then you look like ten shits," I said, stepping aside so he could come in. He handed me the coffee, but I shook my head. "Not doing caffeine."

"That appears to be the only think you're not doing. Mind if I sit?"

I gestured to our sofa, where he sat on one end and I sat on the other. He put the extra coffee down in front of me like maybe he could trick me into wanting it. After all, when had I ever turned down an Americano? Turns out there's a first time for everything. I left it untouched.

We looked at each other in silence, and I couldn't remember a time when we'd been speechless. There had always been some witty remark to make, some obscure movie reference to recall, some joke to lob over the wall like a grenade. But no amount of frivolity could distract us from the fact that I was turning into a legitimate junkie. "Well, I'm glad you're alive," he said by way of conversation-starting.

"I've been catching up on my sleep," I said by way of deflecting. "How's work?"

He leaned back against the sofa with his coffee. "Everyone is shitting themselves. Papa Jacobs declared the trial inconclusive, and Diana and I spent the rest of yesterday arranging couriers to go pick up all the outstanding pills. We have to log every pill under a camera like a Las Vegas poker dealer so there can be no theft—which is just as well because after what happened to you with Malcolm, I don't think anyone should be taking this shit." Altan took a sip from his drink as if to punctuate the thought and went on. "New trial starts next month—"

"Wait," I interrupted. "The *new* trial?"

He nodded. "They're scrapping the current formula. I heard Malcolm saying something to Dean about marketing the new version to the government. They're going to weaponize it so that they can make enemy combatants feel something that isn't real— you know, like waterboarding, only more horrific."

Yes, this was terrifying, and I'd address it as soon as I got past a certain detail. "Malcolm is *still there?*"

Altan took another slug of his coffee. "He's taking two days administrative leave without pay next week, and then he's coming back. It's such bullshit," Altan said, reading my face. "I hated Malcolm before the Morpheum, but now I hate him in ways I did not know I was capable of. I could barely stand being in the office with him today. The good news is that they've stocked Urban Campus with dozens of Dean's flunkies, so we're rarely alone."

Altan put his coffee cup on the side table so he could scrub his hands down his face. "But I did have one meeting with him after you left. Malcolm knows I was taking the pills, and he's insisting I stay on at WellCorp to help him create the new formula, otherwise he'll charge me with corporate espionage and a bunch of other trumped-up charges. I don't mind going to jail if that's what happens, but considering only a handful of people in the world know how horrific this drug can be in the wrong hands, I don't feel like I can walk away."

I was trying to keep things light. "Besides, you have alimony to pay. Places to travel to."

He squinted up at the ceiling. "About that. June got remarried. Last week, apparently. She texted to tell me."

I didn't know what to say: was he happy? Sad? "How do you feel?"

"Free." He sighed. "I'm happy for her. For me. For us." He looked at me when he said the last part, and I didn't know if he meant *us* as in "him and his ex-wife" or *us* as in "him and his cerebral lover," me. Before I could come up with a comeback, a yawn crept through my nose. I hoped Altan wouldn't notice.

But, of course, he noticed. "OK, I'm going to ask you some questions. All you have to do is nod or shake your head. Just like Marrakesh. All right?"

I was too tired to argue, so I nodded.

"Are you still taking the pills?" he asked.

I sighed. Nod.

"Do you have a lot left?"

Nod.

"Because you stole them from my kitchen?"

Pause. Nod.

He wiped a hand over his mouth. "Do you love me? Don't overthink it. Just nod or shake."

My heart weighed nothing in that moment. It was like a passenger in one of those anti-gravity airplanes, suspended in mid-air. Why did people keep asking me if I loved them like my love was something worth having? I looked at him, and god help me, I nodded.

He stood, pulling me up with him. "Pack a bag. We're leaving."

"What?" I said again. I was so eloquent these days!

"Grab your toothbrush. Fuck it. We'll buy you a new one. Get your passport and your camera and we'll go."

"Where?"

"Wherever you want. Paris? Cambodia? I have contacts. We can teach English. We can be surf instructors."

"I can't surf."

"I'll teach you." Altan pulled me to his chest and wrapped his arms around me. He smelled good—normal—like laundry detergent and deodorant. He smelled like someone who functioned. "Malcolm can't get us if he can't find us. We can run. I love you. We'll keep each other safe."

My heart leapt at the prospect but then caught with a jerk, like a dog testing the strength of its leash. *I couldn't leave Pete.* Even if he hadn't had to save my life last night, we'd stood by each other for years. He was part of my history and mythology, and I had this Daisy Buchanan feeling that I couldn't walk away. Altan Gatsby and I had built our love on dreams and marshmallows: there was no proof that it would last in the real world. I stepped back. "I can't go with you," I said. "I love Pete."

Altan sneered, incredulous. "Then why are you fucking *me* in your dreams?"

I flinched against how callous he made it sound. "Oh, I don't know. Something about both eating and having cake?"

"Is that all I am to you? Look around, Ness! You need help."

"Don't tell me what I need," I fired back.

He didn't miss a beat. "Do you think you could use help?"

"Yes, but not from you."

"You're stubborn."

"You're judgmental."

"You're sleeping your life away."

"Yes, *my* life," I said, gesturing around my messy apartment. "This life I have with Pete. You and me: we don't know each other. We've dreamed together, but that's not the same as living together. We haven't taken care of each other when we're sick. We haven't been bored through a meal. We haven't talked about anything but Morpheum when we're awake."

"When's the last time you talked to Pete?" he spat. "I've been doing some math. You've spent about ninety percent of your recent waking and sleeping time with me. So where does that leave him?"

"You act like this is about the two of you, but the truth is you're the only two who are measuring. This isn't about *either* of you. This is about me and what *I* want."

"So what the fuck do you want?"

"I don't know!" I raged. "I want to be alone."

Altan stood there wide-eyed, gasping like a dying fish. He worked his mouth trying to find something to say, and when he couldn't, he reached into his jeans pocket and pulled out his Altoid tin. "This is all I have left," he said. He went to the kitchen and stood over the sink.

"Don't be like that," I scoffed. "We can still dream together."

"I don't want to," said Altan. "Not with you. Not like this. This is done." He dumped the pills and ran the garbage disposal, raising his voice over the noise. "If you want me, you can call me on the phone like a human. You can email me. You can send me a damn smoke signal, and I will run to you as fast as I can. But I can't just be waiting for you to fall asleep—especially when you might not wake up."

He switched off the disposal, then crossed the living room and ripped the door open to leave. The deliveryman was standing there with my beer in his hands. Altan turned to me, his brown eyes intense, angry, pleading, done. "How do you survive falling off a cliff?"

I thought of what he'd told me on Machu Picchu. "Don't hit bottom," I said to his back.

Ness and I are done with Morpheum dreaming together. I went over to her house last night, tried to convince her to come with me to get help, dumped out all my pills and told her I wouldn't dream with her anymore—and she was completely fine with it. She's in so deep I'm not sure anyone can pull her out.

I was up all last night. I keep telling myself it's Morpheum withdrawal, but I've lost enough sleep over women to know the truth: I'm too beat up over Ness. I love her, and she's ruining herself, and I don't know what to do.

THE TEST

The next morning, after Pete had gone to work, I realized I couldn't remember the last time I'd had my period. Definitely not since I started the Morpheum, which was over a month ago. Maybe delayed menses was a side effect no one had yet detected? *Fat chance*, I thought, thinking of when Pete and I made love in Vancouver.

I ordered a pregnancy test and answered the door in my underwear again, daring the deliveryman to judge me. In my bathroom, the answer was unmistakable. Two pink lines.

To which I thought, simply: *Whoa.*

The word gusted through my body like a blast of wind. *Whoa.* After everything I'd seen and done in my dreams, I was under the impression that my mind was officially un-blowable. But this was untrue, because I sat on the tile floor of my bathroom with a tiny person lodged in my abdomen, and I didn't feel the panic or tears or terror I'd thought I would. Instead I felt . . . *whoa*. And then *whoosh*, like everything was clean, like this development had puffed away the broken pieces of my life, leaving only things that were worthy of weight—like this baby, and my husband, and myself, and all the things I could do for this family of ours.

For the first time in weeks, I knew exactly which way to dig.

I stood and inspected myself in the mirror. *Ew.* My face was greasy; my hair was lank. The dark circles under my eyes had mysteriously gotten more profound despite all the sleep, and I'd lost even more weight—very bad for the baby. I made and ate an entire pot of pasta, and then I got in the shower, where I pumiced my feet, brushed my teeth, conditioned my hair, and generally spruced myself up. When I got out, I unearthed my blow-dryer for the finishing touch.

Four hours later, I came to on the bathroom floor, still holding my brush. It was mid-afternoon, and I'd fallen asleep without remembering, which was . . . disconcerting. *But fine!* I thought. Once I'd worked all the Morpheum out of my system, everything would be fine.

It was all reparable, even the apartment—which had gone to pot since I'd started the Deep Mope. I rushed around and tidied up, opened the windows, ran the vacuum cleaner. I even fluffed the sofa pillows, karate-chopping them in the middle like they do on HGTV.

My delivery bills were getting exorbitant, but I placed one last order—one of those meal kits that comes with all the ingredients, plus a bottle of wine for Pete and a case of La Croix for Baby and me. I put Cole Porter on the stereo and was bread-crumbing pork chops and being a clean, functioning human when Pete came home. "Hello, Worm!" I sang, scampering to the door with a glass of wine for him. I was wearing a dress and an apron, and he looked rightfully suspicious as he took his shoes off and accepted the drink.

"Hi," he said. "You look . . . awake."

"I am!" I said brightly. "Very awake."

"Really? You haven't had any pills today?"

"Nope!" I grinned and swanned into his arms. "Aren't you proud? I'm clean as a whistle!"

He smiled back tentatively. It wasn't the full-blown "I love you forever" smile yet, but he was warming up to it. "It's good to see you," he said, planting a kiss on my proffered lips. "I wasn't sure you'd bounce back."

"To be honest, I wasn't either, but it's all behind me now." I sailed back into the kitchen so I could finish making dinner. "How was your day?"

"It was good." Pete took a seat at the island with his wine. He still didn't seem convinced any of this was real, but who could blame him? I'd been a zombie for so long. "Did you really just quit the pills? Cold turkey?"

I snapped my fingers. "Like that!"

"What prompted this?"

"My love for *you*," I oozed, being obnoxiously sappy. "And other reasons."

"Such as?"

I looked at him across the island, pursing my lips to suppress my grin. For once I had a secret I didn't want to keep, but at the same time I wanted one more second to predict the face Pete would make when I told him. Would he yelp, or would he cry? There was only one way to find out. I walked over to his side of the island so I could hold both his hands. "I'm pregnant," I said. I thought my face would split open from smiling.

Pete stared at me, too stunned to move—which was disappointing because I hadn't even considered that could be one of his responses. "Did you hear me? I said I'm pregnant."

When he spoke, his voice was cold and dry and quiet, like the tundra—flat, and low on nourishment. "Whose is it?"

"What do you mean 'Whose is it?'" I giggled, releasing one hand to slap him playfully on the knee. "It's *yours,* silly!"

Pete pushed his chair back and stood almost violently, like something had bitten him. He crossed to the other side of the island so the granite was between us. "We haven't had sex in weeks," he said. "Not since before the Billionaire X case."

"You're forgetting about Vancouver," I cooed, twirling a pointed finger in his direction. "That afternoon we spent in bed after the gardens?"

"We never went to the gardens."

I dropped my hands on the counter, still disbelieving him. "Yes, we did. We drank the bourbon in the room—"

"No," said Pete, louder now. He paced back and forth through the living room, throwing his hands around. "None of that happened! After dinner on the first night—the night you told me about your assault—you went back to the hotel room and took some of your crazy pills. And then you slept. You kept sleeping the whole day after. I sat in an armchair next to you and watched TV." He turned to look at me and rubbed the back of his head furiously. "We didn't drink bourbon. We didn't see roses. We didn't have sex. You must have dreamed all that."

I was still smiling for some reason. "What?"

"We were supposed to have this nice weekend away and you slept the *entire* time! I didn't push it, because I didn't want you to feel guilty. You'd just told me about that night in college, and I figured it must have brought up some stuff you were just trying to process." Pete was panting now, his chest working up and down. "I didn't know you were *sleeping with some other guy!*"

When I was a child, my parents had taken me to the beach on Whidbey Island. It was foggy that day, and huge clouds had descended on the Sound. We could see the Coupeville ferry disappearing as it left for Port Townsend, fading into an opaque gray, obliterated. The sound of its horn was long and lonely. That's how my brain felt.

"I haven't been sleeping with anyone!" I swore. Had I? "I couldn't. I love *you*."

"*Then how are you pregnant?*" he roared.

I worked my mouth open and closed, then whispered, "I don't know."

He turned on his heel for the bedroom. When I followed, he had his duffel bag open on the bed and was blindly throwing clothes into it. He didn't even bother with his Dopp kit: he ran to the bathroom and threw his comb and toothbrush and deodorant right on top of his jeans. "What are you doing?" I squeaked.

"The baby," Pete said. He was breathing like he'd been jogging. "Is it Altan's?"

"No!" I stammered. "I— I don't think so."

"How can you not know?" A pair of sneakers went on top of the toothbrush. "When he called me the other night, I couldn't figure out how he knew you'd overdosed or that you were stealing pills. He even mentioned your assault! And I wondered how he could know so much about you: things I didn't even know, and I'm your *husband!*"

"Pete," I moaned. "It's not like that."

"And I asked! I asked and asked. All I wanted was to *know* you, Vanessa!" I winced as he used my full name. "I've always just wanted to *know* you. And you kept all these secrets."

"I want to have this baby with you," I told him.

He shook his head. "No, you don't. And that's OK. You didn't want to break my heart by telling me, so you did it this way instead. And the sad part is, I get why you did it. You were scared. You wanted an adventure. But did you get that with Altan? Did he take you to Paris? Did he show you the world?"

"No," I said. My voice, like my heart, was breaking. "He didn't." Not really.

"And you ended up with a baby anyway. Now we're ruined, and you didn't even get what you wanted. So what was it all for?"

He shouldered the bag and headed for the living room. I rushed him then, threw myself across the door so he couldn't pass. "You could take me back!" I said. "Like in *The Great Gatsby*. I could be Daisy, and you could be Tom, and you could take me back."

"Jesus, Ness. It doesn't work like that."

"Pete, don't go. I can figure this out. I just need time."

"You always need time. But there isn't any now. Please move."

"Pete," I choked. "Please."

He towered over me, looking at the ceiling. "I loved you, Ness. I loved you the best I could."

That was it: that's what killed me. I fell to the floor like I'd been shot, and Pete jerked the door open and slammed it behind him. The sound was a cannon blast through my ribcage.

THE PLEA

An hour later, I was still on the floor, contemplating just how bad this was. My husband—who knew, by trade, how to screw someone in a divorce—was leaving me, and I was pregnant and unemployed with no health insurance or assets. And I was maybe also a recovering pill junkie who was now prone to blacking out at inopportune times. But I was going to fix this, for the baby. I was going to get clean. I was going to start a new career as a travel photographer. I was going to go to Altan's and tell him I loved him and I'd changed my mind, and we'd go and see the world—the three of us. I had five thousand dollars, a plan, and a man with a studio apartment who loved me. It was going to be fine.

I changed out of the dress and put on jeans and a black top. Ankle boots, also black. I packed up my camera and a couple of changes of clothes in my backpack—all the essentials: my toothbrush, my wad of Doc Martens cash, my baggie full of Morpheum, my passport. Thus equipped for adventure, I set off for Altan's.

He buzzed me right in. I trudged up two flights of stairs to his apartment and adjusted my hair before rapping on his door. When he opened it, he was in his underwear again, but he didn't bother trying to hide this time. He just pressed his forehead against the jamb and exhaled a long breath out through his nose. "What do you want?"

Not exactly the homecoming I was planning, but it was OK. I felt relief flooding me, like I was whole again, reunited with the one person in the world who knew my mind. "You said if I wanted to see you, I'd have to come to you. Well, here I am."

"That's great," said Altan, flat as Kansas. "So glad you had to give my proposal some thought. Real flattering."

I shifted from foot to foot. "Can I come inside?"

He looked away. "I'm kind of busy right now."

"Please, Altan. It's important."

"Now really isn't a good time." He began to shut the door.

"I'm pregnant."

The door stopped moving. "What?"

"I'm pregnant," I repeated.

Altan's dark eyes were unreadable. I'd have given anything to be having this conversation on Morpheum. Finally he said, "Congratulations to you and Pete."

"It's not his."

"Then whose is it?"

Why was he asking me this? I took a deep breath. "That night after The Signature, when you came to get me and I slept here. Did we . . . I mean, did you . . .?"

His face turned purple. "What? Did I fuck you while you were unconscious? Are you seriously asking me this?" Altan said loudly enough for it to echo down the hall.

"Keep your voice down."

"Fuck you, Ness," he hissed. "I mean, listen to yourself. You've seen all I have: you've seen my mind, my memories. You've seen *everything.* And after all that, you're standing here accusing me of taking advantage of you?"

"Not accusing!" I said. "Just asking. I need help figuring out what happened, Altan. I need help."

"I know. And I tried to help you, and you threw it in my face."
The door was starting to close again.

"But the baby . . ." I said. I could feel desperation welling up on
a primal level. This wasn't a game about my whims anymore, my
twee little existential calamities, my willingness to fuck up my
perfectly fine life with wishes and dreams: this was survival. "I love
you," I said. "And you said you loved me."

"And you said you needed to be alone, and I completely agree."
He went to close the door again, but before it latched completely,
he shoved his face through one last time. "Are you sure you're even
pregnant? Or did you dream it all up?"

"Of course, I didn't dream—" But I cut myself off the exact
moment the door slammed shut.

Can't sleep. At all.

Ness showed up when Sarah was over. Said she was pregnant, that it was mine. I told her there was no way, since we'd never had sex in real life, and I kicked her out. But I've felt like shit ever since.

Had to send Sarah home, too, just to be alone with my head. That was five hours ago, and I'm still awake.

Really regretting that I threw all my Morpheum down Ness's sink. If I had some, I could sleep, and the dream could tell me what I want.

But who are we kidding? I already know.

THE ANSWER

The pregnancy tests were negative.

I'd ordered a set when I came home from Altan's at midnight (don't ask what the delivery charge was), and then I'd ordered another to make sure the first ones weren't defective (even more extortionate). And now all four of them lay before me on the bathroom floor like an especially judgmental Greek chorus: I was not even remotely with child. I'd dreamed the whole thing. Funny— I didn't even remember taking Morpheum yesterday, but apparently I had, and now I'd accidentally blown up my marriage for nothing, like a science project gone wrong.

Pete hadn't come home. He was probably holed up in a hotel downtown, and part of me wanted to call him up and gloat, "See? I *told* you I hadn't had sex with anyone!" But I'd already hurt him enough without waking him up at 3 a.m. to chat about how I hadn't accidentally fucked my coworker when we were high together, even though I'd thought it was totally plausible. This wasn't one of those misunderstandings you laugh about later over brunch. There was no coming back from this. The shock of that made me numb.

I lay down on the bathroom floor with my head on the tiles and stared at those tests for two hours trying to figure out how this had even happened. Why would I dream up being pregnant in the first place? No one comes to in the middle of a self-indulgent drug spiral with a sudden urge to procreate, so I wasn't completely sold that my subconscious wanted a baby. Rather, I had the feeling my subconscious wanted out of my marriage. I remembered watching Altan's memories, how his mind had been recording his entire life without his being totally aware of it. Had my brain been doing the same: keeping tabs on Pete, his suspicions, the timing of our sexual encounters? Had it conspired with my heart behind my back to concoct this pregnancy scare, knowing my lawyer husband would see through the flimsy alibi in a second? Was making Pete leave me what I really wanted? God, I hoped so. Because it was probably what I was getting—and definitely what I deserved.

Four negative pregnancy tests. Shit.

I wanted to send a photo of them to Pete, mostly to ease his mind and let him know that no offspring were harmed in the making of this bender. But it's hard to end a marriage via text. They don't have the GIFs for *I am worse than dog shit,* or *You don't deserve any of this,* or *Sorry I suck: here is a photo of things I have peed on.* There are some corners you just can't cut with emoji.

In the end I wrote: *You're wonderful, and I messed everything up. Leaving town for a week.* And I sent the photo of the tests with *P.S. Not pregnant. I'm sorry.*

He didn't text me back, probably because he was asleep—or maybe because he hated me.

And then—why not?—I sent the same photo/text combo to Altan, because I *also* didn't want him worrying about a potential fetus in the chemical wasteland I now called my body. And then I dumped my backpack out on the bed to keep from throwing myself on the comforter and crying until I dehydrated into a human raisin. Too tired to process emotions; I could just process commands. Count photography money. Check passport. Inventory the underwear. Refold everything and replace into backpack, except for the

Morpheum. That I stuffed in my trusty Doc Martens boot and threw it in the back of the closet. After having another *baby that never was* on my hands, I knew I would never take those pills willingly again. But it seemed irresponsible to toss them. And impossible. The Morpheum was part of my past, like WellCorp and my photography side hustle and the frat party and my marriage: it was all there in the annals of my life, and to toss any of it out like garbage felt cruel. Maybe this was why I had a hard time getting over things: I never threw anything anyway.

And I realized this with zero guilt—like it was a dream, like this was just me realizing truths passively as they sneaked into the sponge of my mind. There was nothing to apologize for but everything to be aware of. I was a mental hoarder. Next time I felt myself clinging to things, I would know this was just a habit of mine, and maybe I'd be inspired to break out of that cycle—like I was doing now as I checked for a third time to make sure I'd packed my passport. I had no job, no husband, no child, and nothing keeping me here. Instead of dreaming, I figured I'd get on a plane and try being happy with my eyes open. Vanessa Brown was finally going on tour.

It was five in the morning, and I was making a pot of coffee to energize me for the airport when I heard a soft knock at the door. Couldn't have been Pete; he would have let himself in. Briefly I was terrified to consider it could be Malcolm, but then I heard a soft voice call, "Ness? Are you awake?"

I put my eye to the door and pulled back. It was Altan, looking like ten shits, like he hadn't slept. He was running his hand through the long parts of his hair as if he was trying to yank his eyelids open via his scalp. "Ness. You're scaring me. Can you hear me? Tell me you haven't overdosed again."

"I haven't," I said through the door.

He smiled at no one—a small one, relieved. "Open the door."

"Are you going to yell at me?"

"No."

When I swung the door open, I saw Altan had an enormous backpack on the floor next to him. He picked it up and let himself in, like our intimacy transcended the etiquette of an invitation—which it did. "I can't sleep," he said.

"Me neither. I guess that's a first. Want a cup of coffee?"

He slung the backpack to the floor, and it landed next to mine with a thud that made the shoe rack jump. "You going somewhere?" he asked.

"Thought it was time I got my passport stamped."

"Funny. I had a similar idea," he said, and again I wondered if he could read my mind when we were awake, or if this was just destiny, the pieces falling into place. "Where are you off to?"

I shrugged. "Not sure yet."

"We could split an Uber to the airport?"

"OK."

I made him a mug of coffee and handed it to him across the island. He took a sip, nodded happily at the warmth, and then cleared his throat. "We could even share a plane somewhere. If you'd like some company."

I frowned. "So that's it then? You show up here after breaking my heart, after I broke your heart, and we just casually pretend it never happened?"

He rolled his eyes. "I was hoping we could just call it good, but if you're insisting on apologies . . ." He put his coffee down, then he turned to hold my hands—both of them, like we were about to say wedding vows. He looked soulfully into my eyes. "You first."

I laughed in surprise. "Wait, why am *I* apologizing? *You're* the one who turned me away when I showed up pregnant after you promised you'd be there for me."

"Well, *you're* the one who wouldn't leave your husband for me after we'd been having dream sex for weeks."

Jesus. We had some fucked-up history between us. "I'm not going to say sorry for that! You can't expect me to leave my husband without discussing it first. You have to *ask* what I want."

"Fine. What do you want?"

God, it was all so familiar, and for a moment I felt a pang for Pete. I didn't know what I wanted—not cosmically, anyway. I looked at Altan, the playfulness in his eyes, the hope on his lips, and then I took one step forward on my tiptoes and kissed him for the first time in real life. It was a soft kiss, tentative, like a bite of a new food. And when it was clear that I liked the taste, Altan caught me around the waist and pulled me into him. My breath hitched as I reached my arms around his neck and raked my hands through his hair—just as I'd done in the dreams, only this was so much better. His body was firmer. His smell was crisper. His touch was warm through my shirt as he moved his hands up my back to my neck, my jaw. And while there was a moment during our Morpheum trial when I had thought I knew Altan Young better than anyone else in the world, I suddenly realized there was so much more to learn.

I pulled back from him and looked into his eyes. "I want to go to Paris and take pictures," I said. "I want to eat a cheese board at one of those bistros where the tables face the street and photograph people going in and out of Notre Dame. I want you to come with me so we can figure out if we're lovers or lab partners." I let that sink in. When Altan didn't flinch, I went on. "We both have been through a ton of shit, and neither of us is in any shape to be making large life decisions right now. So I am promising you nothing except the chance to go to Paris and take pictures with me. Does that sound like something you would want, too?"

He looked up and to the left like he was considering, then said, "OK."

I smiled. "I make this big speech and that's all you got?"

"I am literally too tired to form sentences. But I'm good with everything you just said, and whatever else there is to talk about we can talk about later. Get your shit. I'm calling an Uber."

It took every ounce of energy I had to lock up the apartment and make it to the car. I didn't even say hi to the driver: once I'd slid into the backseat, I dozed off immediately. Ten minutes later, my phone buzzed in my pocket.

Where are you off to? asked Pete—presumably in response to the Dear John text I'd sent him earlier.

Paris.

Those three dots came and went a couple of times. *You're finally going to take pictures.*

I thought I was too tired to cry, but I was wrong. *I am,* I typed, dabbing my eyes with the cuffs of my hoodie. Altan had his head back against the headrest and was asleep with his mouth open, which was fine because I didn't want him to see. This moment belonged to Pete and me—and the Uber driver, apparently, because nothing's perfect.

I'm glad, said Pete. *It's weird. I'm so angry with you, but I want you to be happy. Is that weird?*

I don't know, I typed back. *I don't know what's weird. I'm obviously not the best at relationships.*

Yeah, no kidding.

I snorted a bit. The Uber driver flicked his eyes at me in the rearview mirror, and I tried not to notice.

My phone buzzed: *We'll talk about separating when you get back.*

A sob crawled out of my throat, and I covered my mouth so Altan wouldn't wake up. *I'm sorry, Worm,* I typed.

Better this way than with a kid in the mix. Thank you for that. Seriously.

I cried then, that silent, breathy cry of the broken. *Only you would thank me as we're breaking up.*

Fine. I'll be an ass when I draw up the papers. Bon voyage.

I knew he was joking because he sealed it with an emoji, but part of me wished he wasn't. Part of me wished he'd take me for everything I was worth, but Pete had seen enough people become monsters during a divorce, and maybe he didn't want to join them. Besides, I wasn't worth much. He was the one with the good job and the gym membership and the head full of hair. I was the unemployed addict with unresolved trauma and coffee-stained teeth. There was nothing of mine he needed.

By the time Altan and I got to the airport, I'd pulled myself together, but I was wrung out completely. There was no end to this fatigue. We were barely coherent enough to book tickets at the Delta counter for a flight that, miraculously, was leaving soon, and we cleared security and shuffled to the plane in near silence. The whole thing was beyond surreal: I was leaving my husband to detox in Paris with another man, with whom I'd never been on a real date. We'd never made love. We'd barely even spoken while awake during the past few weeks. Sure, I'd met his dead dog and he'd saved me from almost being dream-raped by our boss, but still: this was crazy and irresponsible and dangerous—but it was undoubtedly an adventure, which was what I'd always wanted.

When we found our seats on the plane, Altan took my hand across the armrest, and once I'd gotten over the real-life zap of his touch, I felt a buzzing between us, a contented warmth, like a purring kitten. I put my head on his shoulder and went out like a light. For the first time in what felt like forever, I didn't dream a thing.

MORPHEUM WILL RETURN IN

POISON DREAM

THE PERFECT DRUG SERIES
BOOK 2

STAY TUNED

http://www.kittycookbooks.com/newsletter
Instagram: @kittycookbooks
Facebook: @kittycookbooks

SLEEPING TOGETHER:
WAS IT GOOD FOR YOU?

If so, would you consider leaving a review?
You would have Kitty Cook's eternal gratitude!

https://www.amazon.com/kittycookbooks
https://www.goodreads.com/kittycookbooks

ACKNOWLEDGMENTS

This being my first novel, I was definitely on the pants-shitting side of the fence about publishing it, so I want to give a shout-out to everyone in my affectionately dubbed "Kitty Litter" for their love and support.

Special thanks to my brilliant copyeditor, Brian Colella, for cleaning up my prose and my designer/lifetime creative partner, Scott Howard, for creating a cover I am proud to have people judge this book by. Cheers to Molly Peacock, Catherine Adams, and Richard Goodman for teaching me how to write, and to my beta readers, reviewers, and friends both on social media and in real life for helping me believe I could. Every kind word and high five meant more to me than you'll ever know.

Thank you to my parents for being some of my earliest fans; even more props to my husband for being my best one. Finally, big ups to my children for inspiring me to prove that dreams come true. I love you for this, and everything.

ABOUT THE AUTHOR

Photo ©2018 by Nicole Pomeroy

Kitty Cook is a book chef based out of Seattle, specializing in salty heroines, spicy plotlines, and semisweet endings that hit the spot. With two energetic kids and a very patient husband, Kitty spends her free time exploring the Pacific Northwest in the sun and curled up with a book in the rain. Her writing has appeared in the *New York Times* and Salon.com under a different, less ridiculous name.

28582515R00190

Made in the USA
San Bernardino, CA
07 March 2019